'I wasn't thinking,' Jack groaned. His eyes were searching her face pathetically, looking for one small sign of forgiveness or compassion. 'All right, so I didn't look. I just opened the door and dropped a match inside. But I've paid for what I did then.' Tears welled in the corners of his eyes. 'I've lived with knowing that I killed that man for thirty-five years, and there are still nights when I wake up in a sweat from dreaming about it.'

'I wouldn't wonder,' Irene said. 'And what's to happen now?'

'The coroner's verdict was accidental death,' Jack said glumly. 'It's on record that the old man set fire to the place himself. There's no one can prove anything different. Not after all this time.'

Irene came forward and leaned her hands on the table. 'Maybe not in any court that could send you to prison for it. But there'll be another verdict now.' She picked up the newspaper Jack had dropped on the table and held it in front of him. 'This is all the proof Wrathdale needs. The mischief's done.'

Jack stared at the words that swam beyond the film of his tears. 'THE RIVALS'. He lowered his head to the table and let out a long, despairing moan . . .

HUGH MILLER

The Outsider

Based upon the TV series by Michael J. Bird

GRANADA
London Toronto Sydney New York

Published by Granada Publishing Limited in 1983

ISBN 0 586 05827 3

A Granada Paperback Original
Copyright © Michael J. Bird and Hugh Miller 1982

Granada Publishing Limited
Frogmore, St Albans, Herts AL2 2NF
and
36 Golden Square, London W1R 4AH
515 Madison Avenue, New York, NY 10022, USA
117 York Street, Sydney, NSW 2000, Australia
100 Skyway Avenue, Rexdale, Ontario, M9W 3A6, Canada
61 Beach Road, Auckland, New Zealand

Printed and bound in Great Britain by
Cox & Wyman Ltd, Reading
Set in Times

Chapter One

Ravensfell House stood in open ground near the heart of Wrathdale, two miles east of the tidy market town of Micklethorpe. The house was old and rambling, a forbidding place built to keep out the world. Time and neglect had done nothing to add charm. The gaunt frontage of sandstone ashlar had been pitted and flaked by the Northern climate; cracks and fissures like frown-lines surmounted the tall windows and the cavernous porchway.

It was past midnight. In the sitting room, wrapped in her dressing gown, Miss Banner sat in the shadows beyond the dim pool of light cast by the standard lamp. She was motionless, without expression, sitting upright in her chair with her hands turned down in her lap.

Dr Collett had come down the stairs and was standing in the sitting room doorway. Miss Banner didn't look at him. Her lustreless eyes remained on a point somewhere between the door and the Victorian armoire in the corner.

'I'm sorry,' the doctor said. 'There was nothing I could do. It was a heart attack.'

Miss Banner's head moved a fraction, the shadow of a nod. 'He said it was indigestion.' She appeared to be unmoved. 'Wouldn't eat when he came in. Went straight to bed.' She glanced coldly at the doctor for a second. She was sixty but the eyes were older. The deep lines at the sides of her mouth tightened. 'A while ago he cried out. When I went in to him he was unconscious.'

Collett shifted his feet, nodding sadly. 'Maybe if I'd seen him earlier . . .'

'I asked,' Miss Banner said dully. 'When he complained

5

about it, I suggested I might call you. But he wouldn't hear of it.' She glanced at the doctor again. 'I couldn't go against him.'

'No, I understand.' Collett crossed the room tentatively and stood by Miss Banner's chair. 'I know how stubborn your brother could be about some things.' He sighed. 'He was difficult at times, I imagine.'

Miss Banner looked up at him sharply. Her square jaw jutted a fraction. 'I dare say there are some who would say that.' She looked away again. 'Well, thank you, Dr Collett. I'll not keep you.'

The doctor appeared reluctant to accept the dismissal. 'Is there anyone nearby who could come in and stay with you tonight?'

'No one I'd want.'

Collett cleared his throat. 'My wife, perhaps. I'm sure that she'd . . .'

Miss Banner shook her head firmly. The light sparkled dimly on the bun of grey hair at the nape of her neck. 'Thank you, all the same. But she's not needed.'

'Well, if you're sure,' the doctor murmured. 'But of course I'll get the District Nurse to call in . . .'

'No, nor her neither.' Miss Banner was glaring at him, tight-mouthed. 'I'll do what has to be done.' Her expression made it clear that argument would be pointless.

'As you wish.' Collett leaned forward a little, wrinkling his eyes solicitously. 'Miss Banner, I really can't tell you how sorry . . .'

'Then there's really no point in trying, is there?' She stood up, tightening the cord of her dressing gown. 'I'll show you out, shall I?' She took a few steps away from the chair and stood waiting pointedly.

Startled by her abruptness, Dr Collett followed the tall, angular figure out into the hall. At the door Miss Banner thanked him again and watched as Collett got into his car and started the engine.

6

When he had gone, she closed the door and turned to face the staircase. The stillness of the house was total and for a moment Miss Banner was a part of it. Her eyes were fixed on the landing.

When she moved her step was firm and measured. She climbed the stairs slowly and crossed the landing to her brother's bedroom. She turned the door handle and pushed it inward, switching on the light before she entered.

At the foot of the bed she stood for a minute, staring at the counterpane and the bulge of the sheet turned up over the pillows. Then she went to the side of the bed and pulled down the sheet.

In death, her brother looked even more patriarchal than ever. The lean, grey-bearded, resolute face looked calm and assured, as if John Wesley Banner had found no surprises on the other side. His sister stared at him, her face as still as his own.

Then she glanced up at the framed quotation hanging on the wall above the bed.

THE JUST SHALL
LIVE BY FAITH.
Romans I.17

Miss Banner took down the frame and held it between her hands, studying it. She looked at her brother again.

Suddenly her mouth twisted open, exposing her parted teeth. A hiss of rage erupted in her throat. Livid, wild-eyed hatred contorted her face as she spun and hurled the frame into the fireplace, smashing the glass into a thousand glittering shards.

Chapter Two

Someone had observed that Sylvia Harper's movements always looked as if they had been choreographed. It was true that the symmetry of her face and figure were mirrored in her deportment; it was apparent even in the small things she did, like crossing a room or closing a door – or, as she was doing now, swaying gently to loud music from the radio and simultaneously pouring water into the coffee maker.

It was a time of day Sylvia found especially pleasant. Beginnings always pleased her, as long as she controlled them. She put down the kettle and hummed softly to the music, letting her eyes roam over the soothing, trendy solidity of her kitchen. Taking stock was pleasant, too.

The house had once been a row of three workmen's cottages on the outskirts of the village of Rawden. The original, heavy-stone exterior remained, with a few alterations, but the inside had been completely restyled. Sylvia had never had any doubts about how she wanted it done.

The combined talents of a fashionable architect and an expensive interior decorator had turned the place into a well-heeled townsperson's idea of what a house in the country should look like. The ground floor had been gutted and transformed into a spacious, open-plan living and kitchen area on two levels. There was piranha pine panelling, hessian, and strategically deployed natural stone; over the double glazing there were hand-printed fabrics that matched the fitted carpets. The furniture, throughout, was Habitat Rural.

Sylvia turned and looked across the living area. She

could see her reflection in the long mirror by the door to the hall. Her attire, like her surroundings, wasn't particularly rural. But the pyjama-style lounging suit looked good on her.

She shifted her weight slowly from one hip to the other and smiled at the effect. She was aware – and she was never less than glad of the fact – that she possessed one of the greatest natural advantages; she would age by the most gradual of stages and she would always be attractive. At thirty-five she looked years younger – her figure was trim and shapely and the skin of her oval, high-cheekboned face was taut and unlined.

Sylvia found it easy to like herself. She curled the fingers of one hand in her dark hair and smiled again, then she heard her husband coming through from the hall. She stepped back smartly to the worktop.

'Morning,' he called. Donald Harper was always cheerful in the morning. He dropped his briefcase on a chair and strode through to the kitchen, kissing Sylvia on the cheek and nuzzling her hair. 'You smell delicious,' he grunted.

Smiling, but modulating her voice to transmit a hint of bitterness, Sylvia murmured, '*Now* you notice.'

Donald straightened and frowned at the radio. 'Do we need to have that?'

Sylvia shrugged and switched it off. She pointed at the sheaf of mail in Donald's hand. 'Anything for me?'

He handed her two letters. 'The rest are bills.'

Sylvia slipped the letters into her pocket. 'Boiled eggs?' she asked airily.

Donald looked at his watch then shook his head. 'Haven't got time. Toast and coffee'll be fine.'

He went into the dining area and sat down at the table. His copy of *The Times* was lying alongside his plate. He picked it up and started scanning the front page.

'You could be late, for a change,' Sylvia suggested, bringing the cafetiere to the table.

9

'Not my style.' Donald said. He looked up from the paper. 'You know that.'

'True.' Sylvia poured his coffee. 'Mr Conscientious. What time did you finally give up on that report last night, for God's sake?' It was becoming harder to remember the nights when he came to bed while she was still awake.

'Not all that late. Finished it around two. Slept like a log.'

Sylvia moved round the table and poured coffee in her own cup. 'You always sleep like a log.'

Donald nodded brightly. 'Don't you?'

'Eventually,' Sylvia said. 'With a little help from my friends.'

A small frown creased Donald's brow, half concern, half reproach. 'Somadrin's not something you should make a habit of.'

Sylvia went back to the kitchen and slipped bread into the toaster. 'Heavens!' she cried, forcing gaiety into her voice. 'Don't knock the product. Somadrin's what keeps CorVol going, isn't it? That and the Pill.'

Something in the paper had caught Donald's attention. 'We do make other things,' he murmured absently.

'They're outside my experience,' Sylvia said. 'I'm just grateful for the two I know about.' She paused. 'Occasionally.'

She watched Donald as she waited for the toast. Her husband had style, she supposed. She knew other women thought that. He was forty-three, tall, good-looking rather than handsome, intelligent, healthy, and he always dressed well. All that, or some of it, probably did add up to style. Or perhaps it was the mysterious quality called Appeal. Lately, Sylvia believed that the thing she responded to most in Donald was his familiarity.

The toast popped up. Sylvia removed it, sliced it and put it in the rack. She filled an egg saucepan with water and put it on the stove.

10

'Another busy day, is it?' she asked.

He looked up from the paper and gazed vacantly at her. 'I'm sorry. What did you say?'

'I was asking about your day. Action-packed as usual, I suppose.'

Donald nodded, abandoning the paper. He only ever discussed business with Sylvia if she asked. He knew how boring the details of his work could be to other people. 'Pretty hectic,' he said. 'I've got to tie up the PR side of the Brussels conference, then I've got a couple of Japanese journalists coming up from London to have a look round. I suppose I'll be stuck with them for lunch.'

'Well,' Sylvia drawled, 'it's all go. You won't be late home, I hope.'

'Shouldn't think so. Why?'

Sylvia brought the toast rack to the table and sat down. She looked at Donald. 'It's Thursday,' she said.

'Is that significant?' The blank expression on his face was so familiar. It could amuse Sylvia or infuriate her, depending on her mood.

'Aren't you expecting someone?'

He remembered. 'Oh my God! Of course. Frank.' He shook his head. 'I'd completely forgotten.'

'Lucky I hadn't, isn't it?'

'Yes,' Donald said, 'very lucky. And unusual.'

For an instant Sylvia's eyes flashed defensively, then she said, 'Well, we don't have that many visitors.' She reminded herself sharply that Donald couldn't have been implying anything special. He had simply pointed out a fact; she had a poor memory.

'You'll like Frank,' Donald said.

'Will I?' She said it offhandedly, hoping she'd introduced the right note of semi-indifference. 'What time is he arriving?'

Donald sipped his coffee and shrugged. 'No idea.' He had told Sylvia that Frank Scully would be dropping in on his way to Scotland, where he was going to write a novel. 'He simply said he's driving up. So he'll arrive when he gets here, I suppose.'

Sylvia frowned delicately. 'That's a bit vague, isn't it?'

'Frank's like that. A bit vague.'

'I've never found that a particularly endearing quality,' Sylvia said coldly. 'I wouldn't have thought you did, either.' She was setting up her attitude carefully – a hint of misgiving about their expected guest, a measure of hostility. 'How long have you known him?'

'A long time. He's one of my oldest friends – I told you already.'

'Did you? I was probably half asleep. It can't have registered.'

'We worked together. On the *Express*.' Donald smiled faintly at the reminiscence. 'It was Frank who persuaded me to apply for the job with Freedman Chemicals.'

'Oh.' Sylvia pouted slightly, a characteristic prelude to sarcasm. 'And he's your friend, you say.'

'Oh, come on.' Donald stared at her. 'It was the best thing I ever did. I wouldn't have got where I am today if I'd stayed in newspapers.'

'I must make a point of thanking him.'

'Yes,' Donald snapped. 'Perhaps you should.'

Sylvia realized she had overshot. 'Sorry,' she said, smiling apologetically. 'I was just exercising my tongue.'

'It doesn't need it.'

'All done,' Sylvia said softly. She reached out a hand and closed it over Donald's. 'Promise.'

Donald frowned for a moment, then he smiled back at her.

'I'm surprised you didn't invite Frank to our wedding.' Sylvia's tone was neutral now, chatty.

'I would have,' Donald said, 'but we lost touch when I went to the States. And when I cam back . . .'

'You found me waiting.'

12

'Well you were more available, anyway. Frank wasn't around any more. He'd taken a job in Spain editing an English-language newspaper for tourists, he now tells me. I didn't know that then. If I had, I'd have called him and got him to be best man.'

'He knows you're married though, does he?'

'Yes. I mentioned it in passing.'

'Charming!'

Donald drained his coffee cup and sat back, smiling at Sylvia. He had only run into Frank briefly the previous week. Frank had been coming out of the Hilton as Donald was going in to attend a press conference. It had been their first meeting in four years. They had one drink together and made swift arrangements for Frank's visit.

'There wasn't time to go into detail,' Donald said.

Sylvia's fingers drummed the table softly. 'How long's he staying?'

'He's just passing through.'

'Just overnight, then.' Again, Sylvia hoped she sounded moderately indifferent.

'I don't know. He might stop for the weekend. I don't suppose he'll be in any rush.' Donald looked at his watch and immediately pushed back his chair. 'I've got to go.'

He crossed to the living area to get his briefcase and Sylvia went back to the kitchen. The pan on the stove was boiling now and she took an egg from the refrigerator and lowered it gently into the water.

On his way to the back door Donald paused and pecked Sylvia lightly on the cheek. 'I'll see you later,' he said.

'What'll I do if Frank arrives before you get back?'

Donald paused in the doorway. 'Keep him amused,' he said. 'But go easy on the booze. He shouldn't take too much.'

'Oh, my God,' Sylvia groaned.

'We all have our problems,' Donald intoned solemnly as he stepped outside and closed the door.

Sylvia switched on the radio again and stood staring down at the frothing water in the saucepan. She began humming to the tune that was blaring from the speaker. A faint smile moved her lips. Her thoughts were moving ahead. Cautiously.

Chapter Three

The ground floor of the old building on Micklethorpe High Street was a combined shop and printing works. The shop window was filled with examples of printing; the name of the firm, S. R. Neave & Son, was stencilled on the glass. A door beside the shop led to the offices of *The Micklethorpe Messenger* on the floor above.

It was almost 9 A.M. Just behind the side entrance to the printing works, Reuben Flaxman was putting on his overalls. He was close to retirement age, a leathery, compact, dour-faced man with the slow, deliberate movements of someone who knew precisely the pace of his day. As he was methodically doing up the metal buttons, the door opened and Tom Holliday came in. He was a decade younger than Reuben, but he tended to move at the same careful pace.

'Now then, Reuben,' Holliday murmured.

'Now,' Reuben grunted, without looking round.

Tom Holliday came and stood in front of Reuben. 'Have you heard?'

Reuben nodded. 'I've heard.'

Tom looked disappointed. He took off his jacket and hung it on a hook by the door, then he picked up his overalls and began putting them on. 'From what I hear, it was a heart attack,' he said. 'Folk seem surprised. But not me.' He paused for effect, but Reuben was still concentrating on his buttons. 'I saw the mark on him on Tuesday.' Tom sighed. 'He'll be missed, will John Wesley.'

'If you say so,' Reuben murmured. He finished his buttoning and moved across to one of the ancient printing presses.

Tom followed him. 'So what's going to happen to *The Messenger*, then?'

'With any luck,' Reuben said, 'we'll be rid of it.'

The door leading from the shop opened and the proprietor, Fiona Neave, came into the works. She was carrying her handbag and an artist's portfolio case. She was dressed in a plain dark suit that did nothing to disguise her figure; similarly, her straight, businesslike hairstyle couldn't detract from her stunningly attractive face.

She walked briskly towards her office, greeting the two men as she went. Tom Holliday moved across in front of the linotype machine and intercepted her.

'Have you heard about John Wesley?' he said.

Fiona watched the overdone sorrow developing on Tom's face. 'Heard what?'

'He's dead.'

The impact on Fiona was visible. Her eyes widened and for a moment she was speechless, staring at Tom with her mouth half open. 'No,' she said finally, 'No, I don't believe it!'

Tom nodded sadly. 'It's true.'

Fiona glanced across at Reuben. He was nodding too.

'When did it happen?'

'Early this morning,' Tom told her. 'Heart attack. I was saying to Reuben, I could see the mark on him on Tuesday.'

'That's nonsense, Tom,' Fiona said sharply. 'He was in the office yesterday. He looked well enough then.'

'It was there just the same,' Tom muttered. 'For those who could recognize it.'

Fiona had turned pale. 'Poor John Wesley,' she breathed. 'But then, I suppose he wouldn't have thought of it like that.' She shook her head slowly. 'Still, it's a great shame. I'll miss him. We all will.'

Tom Holliday was still standing between Fiona and her office door. 'What about *The Messenger*?' he asked.

Fiona thought about it. 'Good question. It belongs to Miss Banner now, I suppose.'

'Most likely she'll sell it,' Reuben Flaxman said.

'Maybe. But not before next Tuesday.' Fiona's blue eyes went dreamy for a moment. 'I won't bother her now but tomorrow I'll give her a ring.'

Reuben sniffed. 'She's not answering. And I doubt it'll be different tomorrow.'

'Then I'll drive out to the house.'

'I'd leave it,' Reuben said. His voice was heavily paternal. 'She'll be in touch when she's got something to say. And she will have,' he added, smiling humourlessly. 'In her own time.'

Fiona turned and looked at Reuben, studying his expression. Then she shrugged. 'Well, just so long as she doesn't leave it too late.'

She moved past Tom and went into her office, closing the door behind her. She crossed to the desk and put down her bag and the portfolio. For a few seconds she remained by the desk, looking round the simple, pleasantly furnished room, running her gaze past the powerful binoculars on the side table and the framed bird photographs on the walls without really seeing them. Fiona was thinking. Speculating.

Her wide, sensual mouth tightened suddenly. She reached across the desk and snatched up the telephone receiver. She dialled a number and waited.

'Lewis?' Fiona spoke as if somebody might be eavesdropping at the other end. 'Could you meet me somewhere this morning – up by the old lead mine, say? There's something I'd like your opinion on. And it's reasonably urgent, I think.' She listened, then nodded at the mouthpiece. 'Fine. I'll see you there.'

The moorland of Wrathdale rose to a dozen small summits on the north, east and south, like a shallow bowl with

17

irregular sides. At every season stillness was implicit in the landscape; it looked, from a distance, as if the territory had been left deserted, even by the wind. But real stillness hardly ever touched the region. Continually, the air rang with the cries of lapwings, curlews, gulls, plovers – and in season, the red grouse.

On a wooded rise five miles north of Micklethorpe, the Wrathdale Mine had operated for thirty years until 1947, when the lead seam ran out. The mine buildings and the once-busy approach track had fallen into gradual disuse. Birds, small animals and the creeping flora of the district had taken over, colonizing and enshrouding the dead markers of commerce. People rarely went there any more.

At five past ten a Range Rover came over the brow of the hill and down the road towards the drystone wall where Fiona Neave was leaning with her binoculars, watching a sparrowhawk on a tree fifty yards away.

Fiona lowered the glasses and watched the car approach. As it drew close the driver waved to her, then turned and drove along the track that led up to the cluster of mine buildings. As the vehicle reached the top and disappeared behind one of the buildings, Fiona crossed the road and dropped the binoculars into the offside seat of her MG Sports. She looked around her for a moment, then started walking towards the mine.

The Range Rover was parked close by one of the buildings, three yards off the track. As Fiona approached it the driver opened the door for her.

She paused with one foot on the step and smiled. 'Good morning,' she said, then climbed in alongside Lewis Frederick Haddon, The Right Honourable The Lord Wrathdale. She closed the door firmly and turned to him.

'Morning,' he said, returning her smile. He reached across and took Fiona in his arms. They kissed long and lingeringly, then Lewis sat back. 'Sorry I'm late,' he said.

'That's all right.'

As always, Fiona felt herself momentarily daunted by the man. It was something that went beyond his appearance – he was handsome and square-featured, a very youthful forty-two-year-old – and it even transcended his athletic build. Lewis, as Fiona had explained it to herself more than once, was quite simply gifted with presence.

'What's the big emergency?' he asked her.

'Well . . .' Fiona looked out of the window for a moment, still gathering her composure. 'It's not exactly an emergency, but it's something I'll have to act on smartly – if I'm going to do anything at all.' She explained about John Wesley Banner having died that morning. 'It means the paper belongs to his sister now. And I think I'd like to have it.'

'Do you think she'll sell?'

'Probably,' Fiona said. 'She doesn't have any experience of running a newspaper. She certainly couldn't step into John Wesley's shoes.'

Lewis nodded. 'And you really think *The Micklethorpe Messenger* would be worth having?'

'It's a very profitable little business.'

'Really.' Lewis sounded sceptical. 'Have you seen the figures?'

'No. But I'm getting seven hundred a week for printing it,' Fiona said. 'And Banner told me once that he'd never run at a loss. My guess is *The Messenger*'s showing a clear profit of around three hundred a week.'

Lewis put his elbows on the steering wheel and smiled. 'Impressive,' he said quietly.

Fiona wrinkled her nose at him. 'All right, maybe it's nothing in your world of high finance. But I'd settle for it. To start with, anyway.'

'You think there's scope for expansion?'

'The circulation figure hasn't changed for God knows how long,' Fiona said. 'Brighten the paper up a bit and I reckon it would double in two years. And that means higher advertising rates.'

Lewis was nodding. 'You'd have to bring in an editor, of course.'

'Of course. And that's not all.' She enumerated on her fingers. 'I'd need an editor, a reporter, a trainee and someone to sell space and look after the distribution.'

'That would eat into your profits,' Lewis said.

'There'd still be enough left over for me.'

Lewis looked at her, reading the determination on her face. 'How much do you think Miss Banner will want for the paper?'

'I've no idea. A fair bit, probably. But if you agree with me it's a good idea to buy it, I'll talk to Alec Thurston at the bank. I'm sure he'd give me a loan.'

'That won't be necessary.' Lewis leaned closer to Fiona. 'If Miss Banner will let it go at the right price,' he said confidentially, 'I'll lend you the money.'

'You?'

'Why not?' Lewis made a tight, businessman's smile. 'But on one condition. That you form a limited company and let me have a small shareholding. Say ten percent. And you must make me a director.'

'That's important?'

Lewis nodded. 'It wouldn't be a bad idea for me to be seen to be involved with the local newspaper. It might be very useful, in fact.' He put his arms forward slowly and folded them around Fiona, drawing her close. 'Think of an obvious advantage,' he said softly. 'If we were both directors, we could keep having board meetings.'

'I'd like that,' Fiona murmured.

They kissed, and for a moment it seemed as if Lewis would abandon himself to her closeness, letting business drift aside. But he sat back suddenly, straightening his jacket.

'Of course,' he said, 'this won't exactly put me in the same league as Rupert Murdoch, but it's a start. When will you sound Miss Banner out?'

'Well,' Fiona sighed, 'Reuben thinks I ought to wait for her to get in touch with me. He's probably right. But meanwhile nothing's being done about getting the paper out next week. So she'd better do it soon. I'll let you know what the situation is on Sunday.'

Lewis shifted in his seat. 'Yes, well . . .' He looked straight at Fiona, frowning. 'I wanted to talk to you about Sunday.'

She sat upright suddenly, glaring at him. 'My God! Not again!'

'I tried,' Lewis said placatingly, touching her arm. 'But there was nothing I could do about it. It's business.'

Fiona's cheeks were reddening. She was searching his face desperately. 'You bastard!'

'Fiona. Honestly. I tried.' His eyes were wary, trying to avoid the scathing intensity of her stare. 'I'll make it up to you. I promise.'

'How? By increasing the loan?'

'That's not fair!'

'Oh, I'm sorry,' Fiona said coldly. 'We must be fair, mustn't we?'

'I know how you feel . . .'

'Do you?'

Lewis closed his fingers around her arm. 'Next week. I promise.'

'Go to hell!' Fiona spat at him. She turned and twisted the door handle, kicking the door open and jumping out. She landed awkwardly and began running, digging her heels into the dirt track, heading down to where her own car was parked.

Lewis scrambled out and galloped after her. 'Fiona!' he yelled, hearing his voice carry across the hillside. She kept on running. 'Fiona!'

Dust flew up behind them as they ran down the path and out on to the main road. Breathless, Lewis drew level with Fiona as she reached her car. He grabbed her arm.

'Be reasonable,' he groaned.

'Again?' The sprinting hadn't diminished her anger.

'I know what it meant to you,' Lewis panted. 'It was just as important to me.'

'Obviously.'

Fiona's smokescreen of tough independence always thinned when Lewis was around. Now it had vanished and she was looking wounded, vulnerable. She shook her arm free and opened the car door. Reflexively, Lewis tried to put his arms around her.

'Fiona, I've said I'm sorry . . .'

She wrenched herself away from him. 'Yes, you have. But there's a limit.'

They both turned suddenly at the sound of another car. It was a battered Marina, coming down the road towards them. As it drew level with them it slowed. The driver, an inquisitive-eyed man in a suit that looked roughly the same vintage as his car, stared hard at them both before he accelerated on down the road.

Lewis stared after the car. Fiona shot him an anxious glance.

'He's not local,' Lewis grunted. 'Just someone passing through.' He turned to Fiona. 'I'll call you tonight. OK?'

Fiona looked at him for a minute, then sighed and nodded. 'I suppose so,' she said, and looked down the road again at the distant, dwindling plume of the Marina's exhaust.

Chapter Four

Sylvia Harper had bathed after breakfast and changed into a light summer dress. After attending to her make-up she sat in the dining area for a while going through the morning paper. At ten-thirty she went into the garden.

She had already gathered an armful of flowers when she heard the car draw into the front driveway and stop. Sylvia touched her hair and began walking back to the house. She didn't hurry. Before she was halfway across the lawn she could hear the doorbell ringing. She stopped, listening. Footsteps were going around the side of the house towards the kitchen door. Sylvia headed for the door leading to the dining area.

'Anyone at home?' the man's voice called.

The sound of it put a tight smile across Sylvia's face. She kept walking slowly, measuring her steps, hearing the footsteps in the kitchen now. As she entered the house the man was standing in the kitchen doorway with his back to her. Sylvia put down the flowers.

'Hello, Frank,' she said calmly.

The man spun, staring at her, frowning.

'Remember me?'

He went on staring.

'This *is* nice, isn't it?' Sylvia said, coming across the room and standing in front of him. 'A double reunion.'

'I had no idea,' Frank Scully said. The bewilderment showed on his face and in the way he was standing, one hand awkwardly half out of his pocket, the other fingering the lapel of his shabby jacket.

Sylvia smiled. 'So I understand. Surprise, surprise, eh?'

'Donald told me he was married but it never occurred to me . . .'

'That she was one of your cast-offs?' Sylvia said lightly. 'Small world.'

Frank drew his fingers through his thick hair and stared at her. 'He told you I was coming?'

Sylvia nodded. 'Of course.'

'And you didn't say anything?'

'Hardly.'

His eyes narrowed a fraction. 'Why?'

Sylvia rolled her eyes. 'What would I have said? "I'm sorry darling, but you'll just have to call him and cancel the invitation. Otherwise it could be rather awkward. You see Frank Scully and I used to be lovers." Something like that?'

Frank moved to the window and looked out at the garden. 'Less specific, perhaps. Just that we never got on, maybe . . .'

'We haven't met,' Sylvia said.

He turned and faced her. 'Oh, great!' His face was pained. 'Why didn't you tell him at the beginning? I don't imagine he thought you were a virgin.'

Sylvia laughed. 'He knew better.'

'Then why?' Frank sighed.

'I never provide references.'

Frank watched as Sylvia went to a cupboard and took out a vase. She set it on the dining table and started arranging the flowers in it. She looked as if she was enjoying herself.

'You could still have got round this,' Frank insisted. 'You could have given some other excuse. You were always very inventive.'

Sylvia paused with one long-stemmed bloom in her hand. 'To tell the truth, I had an excuse. Right on the tip of my tongue.'

'So why didn't you use it?'

'Curiosity.' She looked at Frank, openly assessing him. 'You haven't changed. Do sit down.'

Frank shook his head. 'No thanks.' He turned towards the door. 'I'd better be on my way.'

In the space of a moment Sylvia managed to look deeply hurt. 'What do I say?'

'Nothing,' Frank said. 'I wasn't here. I'll call Donald later and tell him I had to change my plans.'

'He'll be very disappointed.' Sylvia picked up the vase and took it to the sitting area, where she set it down on a table. 'So you went to Spain when you ran out on me,' she called to Frank.

He came to the doorway and stood watching her. 'I didn't run out.'

'Didn't you?' She looked up. 'Not even a note pinned to the mantelpiece.'

'Well . . .' He dug his hands in his pockets and studied the ceiling for a moment. 'I didn't run out on you in particular. Just things in general. It was all getting a bit too much.'

'So you quit.' Sylvia paused. 'Again. That's the story of your life, Frank.' She stood back from the flowers, judging the effect. 'How long have you been back in England?'

'A couple of years.'

'Doing what?'

'This and that,' he said.

'Of course. Silly question. You like to keep moving, don't you?'

There was no contrivance in Frank Scully's nature. Sylvia had known that almost from the time she met him. Even his face, 'lived-in and interesting' as she had once described it, broadcast the fact that Frank was a man without guile. But he had a way of letting himself act on wayward impulses so that there was no discernible logic to his life, and that made him something of a mystery – perhaps even to himself. To Sylvia, it also made him undeniably fascinating.

She crossed to the drinks cabinet and started pouring two

25

large whiskies. 'And now you're planning to write a book, I'm told.'

'That's the idea.'

'Well, you might get the first four chapters done, I suppose.' Sylvia turned with the glasses and held one out towards Frank. 'Drink?'

He shook his head. 'It's a bit early for me.'

She came across, still holding the glass, a coaxing little smile on her lips. 'For auld lang syne,' she said. 'A cup of kindness.'

Frank was regarding her coldly. 'Are you enjoying this?'

'Of course,' she said in a little-girl voice. 'Don't you want to play?'

Frank took the glass from her.

Sylvia smiled and raised hers in salute. 'Lest auld acquaintance.'

They drank, both aware of the unique tension between them. Old familiarities shifted disturbingly within the framework of new circumstances.

They looked at each other over their glasses for a moment, then Frank said, 'How long have you and Donald been married?'

'Seems like ages,' Sylvia murmured.

Frank looked at his drink. 'Where did you meet?'

'I don't remember. At a party, I think. It was love at first sight.' She smiled lopsidedly. 'Well that's Donald's story, anyway.'

'Are you happy?'

Sylvia tasted her drink again. 'Ecstatically.' Her voice was cold, almost bitter. She gave Frank a challenging look. 'Why? Would it matter to you?'

'Yes,' he said, 'I think so.'

'That's right,' Sylvia said, mock-approvingly. 'Don't commit yourself. That would be out of character.' She gulped back some more scotch. 'Now tell me, are you bedding on a permanent basis these days? Or just when the opportunity arises?'

Frank sighed, shaking his head. 'I'm sorry, but this is all too bright and brittle for a simple country lad.'

Sudden anger flared on Sylvia's face. 'It's owing me!'

Frank put down his glass. 'Why not slap my face and be done with it?'

'I don't like violence.'

'Oh?' Frank raised an eyebrow. 'And what's this, then?'

'Surgery.'

He studied the naked, raw hurt in her, keeping his own expression calm. 'Well, if that's what you want . . .' He shrugged. 'And you're right, of course. I've got it coming. So go ahead. Next incision.'

Sylvia turned away from him, crossing to the window and staring out.

Frank watched her for a minute. She was motionless, her shoulders drooping. 'What?' he said. 'All done?'

Sylvia nodded. Without turning she said, 'No point if you're going to grin and bear it. Besides, it's not nearly so much fun as I thought it would be.'

'Right then.' Frank picked up his glass and swallowed the whisky that was left. He put the glass back on the table. 'Thanks for the drink.'

He went to the back door and Sylvia swung round.

'Running away again?'

Frank paused by the door. 'Beating a tactful retreat, I'd call it.'

'Why? There's no need.' She was looking at him frankly, letting him see into her isolation. 'The bloodletting's over. And I'm certainly not going to let on to Donald, for God's sake.' She smiled a little. 'And he really will be extremely disappointed.

'Maybe.' Frank shuffled his feet indecisively. 'But what would it prove? That we can both keep a secret?'

27

'Look on it as a challenge,' Sylvia said. She held Frank's gaze for a second then crossed and picked up his empty glass. 'Another one?' she asked.

Donald Harper braked his Volvo at the front of Ravensfell House. He got out and crossed the drive towards the door. Halfway across he paused and looked along the length of the house to the overgrown gardens at the side. Someone was standing there. It looked like Miss Banner.

Donald walked slowly towards the garden. It definitely was Miss Banner. She was standing with her back to him, close to some beehives. Donald could hear the buzzing. He took a few steps closer then stopped. Bees were flying all around Miss Banner; some were crawling on her clothes and hair. Donald stood there, horrified, not knowing what to do, not sure if he *should* do anything.

Quietly and still with her back to him, Miss Banner said, 'It's all right, Mr Harper. They'll not harm you.' She turned slowly to face him.

Donald felt his heart thud against his ribs. The bees were crawling all over the woman's face. 'Miss Banner . . .' his voice was husky, cautious. 'Are you all right?'

'Why shouldn't I be? They know me.'

She started to move towards Donald. As if it were a signal, the bees left her in clumps and flew off to join the others hovering around the hives.

'I was telling them of my brother's death,' Miss Banner said. 'They'll not leave now.'

Donald was staring at her, fascinated. 'And if you hadn't talked to them?'

'They were his bees,' Miss Banner said patiently, as if she were explaining something very obvious to a child. 'They would have no call to stay without knowing they'd passed to me.'

Side by side, they began walking back slowly towards the house.

'I've not heard of that before,' Donald admitted.

'Haven't you.' It was said with finality. The matter had been disposed of. 'What can I do for you, Mr Harper?'

'I came to pay my respects.'

Miss Banner stopped walking and turned to Donald. 'Did you?' She looked at him with steady-eyed candour, silently weighing the truth of his remark. Then she nodded. 'Good of you.'

'Your brother was very highly thought of by everyone at CorVol,' Donald told her.

She was reading his face again. 'Why?'

Flustered, Donald scoured his mind for an answer. 'He – he was a good man,' he stammered. 'A leading figure in the community. Very good at his job. A prominent member of the church . . .'

'Chapel,' Miss Banner said.

'Of course, I'm sorry. Chapel.'

Miss Banner's face was as impassive as ice. 'And what did *you* think of him?'

Donald swallowed. 'I liked him very much. I didn't know him all that well, of course. Just from the newspaper. But we seemed to hit it off.'

Miss Banner started walking again and Donald fell into step beside her.

'Did you ever hear my brother preach?'

Donald nodded. 'Yes, as a matter of fact I did once.'

'And did he turn you away from sin?'

Donald glanced sideways at her, floundering again. 'He was extremely . . . eloquent.'

'Oh,' Miss Banner said dryly. 'Is that the word for it?'

They reached the front door and stood facing each other. Donald cleared his throat and explained to Miss Banner that the company would like to be represented at John Wesley's funeral. 'Unless, of course, you want to keep it private.'

'There's nothing private about a cemetery,' she told him.

29

'Except the grave. It's ten o'clock Monday morning.'

Donald thanked her, then bracing himself for a chilly rejection, he said, 'Is there anything you need, Miss Banner? Anything I can do for you?'

The woman thought for a moment. 'Yes,' she said. 'Perhaps.'

Donald was surprised, but he tried not to show it. 'Well, if I can . . .'

'My brother told me you were once in the same line of work as him.'

'A journalist,' Donald nodded. 'Yes, I was at one time.'

Some pigeons flew over. Miss Banner watched them until they were out of sight. Donald had heard she was good with a shotgun.

She looked at him again. 'I need someone for *The Messenger*. To tide over.'

Donald was interested immediately. He had already speculated about what she might do with the paper. 'You're going to keep it on, then, are you? I mean, you're taking control of it?'

Miss Banner nodded once. 'For now, anyway. And there's next week's issue to be got out.'

'Yes, of course,' Donald said sympathetically. 'Your brother would've wanted that.'

'Would he, Mr Harper?' Miss Banner's eyes had hardened. 'Perhaps. But my brother's got nothing to do with it.' She folded her hands in front of her. 'I'm telling you what I want. So, can you do it?'

The shock to Donald was considerable. 'Me, Miss Banner?' The idea struck him as ludicrous. 'Well, that's very flattering and I'd like to help. But I'm afraid it's just not possible. My job's pretty demanding and the newspaper – well, it's not something you can do in your spare time. And I don't have much of that.' Despite the truth of everything he'd told her, Donald was sure his excuse

30

sounded inadequate. 'I'm very sorry,' he said lamely. 'Isn't there anyone else locally?'

Miss Banner didn't look disappointed. 'No one that has the ability,' she said. 'Or that I'd trust.'

Donald shook his head. 'I don't know what to suggest, then.' There was a small silence which he felt obliged to fill. 'You do understand my position, I hope.'

The old woman nodded slowly. 'You said your piece,' she said. 'It makes sense. And as your time's so filled I'll not ask you into the house to waste it in further conversation. Thank you for calling.'

Flustered again, Donald smiled weakly and started to move off, muttering his farewell. Then an idea hit him. He turned to Miss Banner, who hadn't moved.

'I've just had a thought.'

She looked at him, waiting.

'I've got a friend coming up today from London. He's a journalist. A very good one. And he's got a great deal of editorial experience.'

Miss Banner looked neither impressed nor disappointed by what he had said. She was still waiting.

'He's in between jobs at the moment,' Donald went on. 'Taken some time off. I don't know if he'd be willing to help. But he might. I'll ask him, shall I?'

'Tell him to come tomorrow,' Miss Banner said curtly.

Donald started to put up a warning finger, then decided not to. 'I can't promise anything. He may not be interested. How long would it be for?'

'Just for now.'

Donald nodded and started moving towards his car again. 'Well, I'll see what he says.'

'Tomorrow at nine, tell him.'

Donald smiled and got into the car. Impassively, Miss Banner stood by the front door and watched him drive off.

Chapter Five

Dinner that evening was a pleasure for Donald Harper. For his guest it was something less, and for Sylvia it appeared to be an event that provided the ideal atmosphere for advanced nerve games. By the time they had finished the main course, Frank Scully had decided that he was the only one not enjoying himself.

It wasn't that Sylvia had done anything too provocative. Quite the contrary. She had behaved like the exemplary little woman, but she had done it in such a way that Frank knew – was being *told* – that it was all a splendid game, an immaculate charade in which he had no choice but to take part.

Several times Frank had told himself he shouldn't have stayed. He should have jumped right back in his Marina and hit the road north. Now, watching Donald, watching that poor, happy, deluded friend of his, Frank promised himself he would stay there no longer than he had to. He glanced momentarily at Sylvia and felt a tiny lurch in his stomach. He would *definitely* curtail this visit.

Donald was nibbling sliced apple from his plate and telling Frank about Miss Banner.

'There she was,' he said, 'covered in bees, with no protection mind you, and chatting them up, so she said.' He shook his head, smiling at the recollection. 'She's an incredible character. And in the two and a half years we've been here, I don't think she can have left the house more than a dozen times. If that. It's quite an event when Miss Banner's seen in town.'

'Personally, I think she's a little crazy,' Sylvia said. 'Still, that's hardly surprising with a brother like John Wesley.'

Frank had been making every effort to avoid engaging Sylvia directly in conversation. Now he looked questioningly at Donald, preferring him to explain.

'Staunch Methodist from way back,' Donald said. 'Brother John preached the word. He was particularly strong on hellfire and damnation. But . . .' He shrugged and popped a piece of apple into his mouth. 'They love that kind of thing round here. In Wrathdale they only acknowledge two masters – God and the lord of the manor.'

'Still?' Frank said.

Donald nodded. 'Still. But I suppose if you've lived all your life in a place where one family owns most of the land and their motto says they hold it for God, you don't argue about who's boss, do you? Not if you want butter on your bread. Or bread, for that matter.'

Frank looked doubtful. 'There's CorVol.'

'Recently,' Donald said. 'And not just butter. Jam, too. But I'm not sure we'll really make our presence felt until the day we pull out.'

'Is that on the cards?' Frank asked him.

It immediately became clear, from the way Donald's neck turned pink and from the guarded way he glanced at Sylvia, that he believed he might have said too much.

He looked at Frank. 'No, I don't think so. But it's an uncertain world. You never know.'

Sylvia turned to Frank, smiling warmly and offering him the cheese board.

'No thanks,' he said. 'I really couldn't. That was an excellent meal.'

'It certainly hasn't done you any harm,' Donald observed. 'You're looking a lot more relaxed now.'

It had to be nervous exhaustion, Frank thought.

Sylvia put her head on one side and beamed. 'He's starting to feel more at home.'

Donald grinned. 'Well, that's what we want, isn't it?'

'Of course,' Sylvia said. Her eyes slid to Frank. 'One of the family.'

Frank snatched up his glass and swallowed the remainder of his wine.

The small tension was defused by Donald. He threw his napkin on the table and suggested they go through to the living area and make themselves comfortable.

Frank began to feel easier as Sylvia busied herself in the kitchen making coffee and Donald poured the brandies. It was a breathing space that gave Frank some time to evaluate his position more calmly.

Laid out plain, the situation had the makings of a good fictional episode – former lovers pretending to be new acquaintances to save the feelings of the unsuspecting husband. A writer, Frank knew, should count it a plus to be involved in something like that. Except that it wasn't like that. The true scenario was darker; one former lover was taking perverse pleasure in hoodwinking her husband, while the other former lover – helplessly providing her with a bonus – stood by and squirmed.

Pretending to inspect the album sleeves on the shelf above the hi-fi, Frank watched Donald clipping the end from his cigar and lighting it. The nub of all this, he thought, the most painful component of the small tragedy, was that he didn't dislike the husband. This was good old Donald, the pal from the past who had unwittingly got involved in one of those random ironies that could tear holes in a person's life.

'Here we go, then.' Donald handed Frank a large brandy. 'Cheers.'

Frank sipped and as he did so he knew that Donald was working up to something. There was a forewarning he recognized from the past; Donald had his head tilted and he was frowning and puffing too deeply on the cigar. People signalled their intent a lot more clearly than they ever realized.

'Tell me something, Frank.' Donald sent a puff of blue smoke towards the ceiling. 'Are you in any great rush to get to Scotland?'

'Well, the sooner I start on the book the better.'

'You haven't got a deadline, have you?'

Frank grinned at him. 'I haven't even got a contract.'

'So a few days wouldn't make much difference then, would it?'

Now an element of farce was entering the scenario, Frank thought. He was anxious, above all else, to get away from there, and here was Donald about to pressure him into staying a while longer.

'Would it?' Donald prompted.

'No,' Frank said reluctantly. 'I suppose not. But why are you asking?'

Donald puffed again. 'Well, our Miss Banner's got a problem. With her brother dying so suddenly she urgently needs someone to see next week's *Messenger* to bed.' Donald sighed. 'She asked me if I could do it, but of course that's impossible.'

Frank was ahead of him. He shook his head firmly. 'That goes for me too. I certainly can't.' He crossed the room and dropped into an armchair.

Donald followed him and perched on an arm of the settee. 'But you could. It would be no problem at all for someone with your experience. The big question is, will you. You'd be doing her a big favour. And me too, in a way.'

Frank shook his head again. 'I'm sorry, Donald. It's not on.'

'But there's nothing to it.' Donald was clearly going to push the matter. That was another old trait Frank recalled; the Harper ability to pursue straight lines despite the obstacles. 'It's mostly adverts. And knowing how John Wesley worked, my guess is that a good bit of the rest of the material is already set up. Or ready for setting. None of it's red-hot news. And Banner's made you a gift of your lead story.'

'Why me?' Frank sighed.

'Because there isn't anyone else. At least no one who's available immediately.'

'Don't they have a chief sub?'

Donald laughed. 'You must be joking. There's no staff. John Wesley was everything – editor, chief sub, reporter, the lot. He even took most of the pictures.'

Frank sniffed. 'Did he print it as well, by any chance?'

'No,' Donald said, 'that's contracted out.'

'Look,' Frank gestured with his glass, almost slopping the brandy. 'Couldn't the printers handle just one issue on their own?'

'They're jobbing printers, Frank. Not journalists.'

'What about Miss Banner herself?' Frank could be persistent, too. 'If the paper's been in her family as long as you say it has, she must know something about how it works.'

Donald shook his head. 'She was John Wesley's house-keeper. You could probably count the number of times she's been in that office on one hand.'

Frank made a little scowl of disbelief. 'Are you telling me that one man covered everything?'

'Well no,' Donald said, 'not entirely. There are a few part-time correspondents around the district who regularly send in stories. You know, penny-a-line stuff. And then there's the wedding and funeral forms people fill in. Just needs some editing and marking up.'

'Maybe,' Frank said flatly. 'But not by me.'

Donald sipped at his brandy and then drew thoughtfully on his cigar. Frank waited for the emotional side of the argument.

'Pity,' Donald said at last. 'I don't like to see any newspaper losing an entire issue.'

Frank felt that some mild scoffing was in order. 'It

36

happens all the time these days,' he said.

Donald came back without hesitating. 'Not in Wrathdale.' He changed tack suddenly, leaning forward and imploring Frank with his eyes. 'Come on. What have you got to lose?'

The question turned itself around in Frank's head. What did Donald stand to lose if his guest stayed there any longer than he need to?

'Your time's your own,' Donald went on. 'And, as I said, you'd be doing me a favour, too.'

'How come?'

'Well, strange as it may seem, *The Messenger* is quite important to CorVol. It gets the company's message over locally. And it doesn't hurt to have it on our side. If Miss Banner's going to hold on to the paper, it could be to our advantage if she owed me a favour.' He smiled. 'Which it would, if my good friend Frank Scully helps her out now.'

'Looking for a seat on the board, are you?'

'No,' Donald said. 'Just doing my job.'

To begin with, there had been no dilemma. Frank wanted out, whatever the inducements to stay. But the attractiveness of Donald's request was gaining rapidly on Frank's caution. The notion held his imagination; an opportunity to take a small paper in hand, to run it, to produce even one issue that had his stamp on it. Frank weighed that happy thought with the image of Sylvia, revelling in her deceit – *their* deceit – scheming, conniving, and most disturbing of all, becoming more attractive to him by the hour.

Frank looked squarely at Donald. 'What's in it for me?' He watched the small, twitching smile of triumph on Donald's face.

'You mercenary sod!' Donald pulled on the cigar, blowing out the smoke flamboyantly now, a winner on the home stretch. 'She'd pay you, of course. Not much, I wouldn't think. But something.' He watched Frank's face carefully. 'Besides all that, think of the satisfaction you'd get out of the job. That's worth more than money, I'm told. It's a challenge, Frank. A challenge.'

Frank frowned and took a drink from his glass.

'You'd stay with us, of course,' Donald said.

Frank's head snapped up. 'No,' he said adamantly. 'I couldn't possibly do that.' It was as if Donald were deliberately inviting grief. 'I'd have to find an hotel.'

'Don't be so bloody silly. We'd love to have you.'

Sylvia came through from the kitchen, carrying a tray with the coffee things. She smiled at them both.

'Sorry to have been so long, but the percolator wouldn't perk.'

She set down the tray on a low table and Donald crossed to help her set out the cups.

'There's a chance that Frank may stay on for a while,' he told Sylvia brightly. 'And I was just saying that we'd be only too happy to put him up. He's talking about booking into an hotel.'

Sylvia began pouring the coffee. 'You mustn't do that,' she told Frank chidingly. 'That wouldn't be any fun at all.'

Frank was pulling himself back to what he hoped was a sense of proportion. 'I don't think it's going to happen,' he said gruffly. 'My staying on, I mean.'

Sylvia looked up at him. 'No. Well, I agree with you.'

Donald glared at her indignantly. 'What do you know about it?'

Sylvia picked up a cup and took it carefully across to Frank. 'I was listening,' she murmured. 'To hell with challenges, eh, Frank? Who needs them?'

Frank blinked at her, frowning, then he glanced cautiously at Donald.

Sylvia handed over the cup and paused there for a moment, bending down over Frank, holding his eyes with her own. 'You mustn't let Donald talk you into anything you can't handle,' she said.

Sylvia decided to turn in just before midnight. The two men followed a few minutes later. On the landing, Donald put his hand on Frank's shoulder.

'Think about it,' he said. 'Sleep on it. Talk it over with Miss Banner in the morning. That won't commit you to anything.'

Frank sighed. 'All right. I'll talk to her.'

Donald smiled his thanks.

'I'm not saying I'll do it,' Frank warned him. 'Just that I'll go and see her.'

'Well, you won't be there long. She's not a great conversationalist.'

The bedroom door behind Donald opened. Sylvia was standing in the doorway, holding a pillow at her side. She was wearing a flimsy, revealing nightdress; the light from the bedroom silhouetted her figure clearly. She was feigning surprise and embarrassment – expertly, Frank thought, but feigning nevertheless. She made no immediate move to cover herself.

'Oh, I'm sorry,' she blustered, 'I thought you were still downstairs . . .' She turned and went back into the room.

Donald winked at Frank. 'I'm a lucky man, eh?'

'Very,' Frank said, keeping his face expressionless. 'Goodnight.'

He watched Donald go into the bedroom and close the door, then he turned to enter his own room. There was a click behind him. Frank glanced over his shoulder. Sylvia had come out of the bedroom again. She was still carrying the pillow, but now she was wearing a negligee over the nightdress. She walked right up to Frank and stood close to him.

'If I remember rightly,' she said softly, 'you're a two-

39

pillow man.' She handed him the pillow. 'I wouldn't want you to be uncomfortable.' She stood back, allowing Frank another look at her. 'Goodnight,' she whispered. 'Sleep well.' She turned and walked slowly back to her bedroom, closing the door softly.

Frank stood where he was for a minute, looking at the closed door. The cheap calculation of it angered him. So did the cold-blooded disregard for Donald. For one sharp moment he felt like knocking on that door, hauling Donald out and levelling with him. But it passed. Frank realized that would be crazy, destructive.

He went back to his bedroom door and turned the handle. Pausing for a second, he closed his eyes tightly. He could still see the backlit image of Sylvia, burning bright and firm at the centre of his mind.

By midnight Miss Banner had removed all her brother's clothes, hats, shoes and other possessions from the wardrobe and drawers in his room. She heaped them on the middle of the bed and when she was finished she stood back, panting slightly from the effort, staring at the silent mound.

She turned after a minute and went to the chest by the door. Standing on it was a framed group photograph. Miss Banner stared at it coldly for a moment, then picked up John Wesley's hairbrushes and added them to the pile on the bed.

With an effort that left her almost exhausted, she carried her brother's belongings downstairs and out to a clearing in the garden. A bonfire had already been prepared from wood and refuse. She threw her bundle on to it.

From her pocket she took a box of kitchen matches and lit one. When she touched it to the dry twigs at the base of the mound the flame spread instantly, creeping and crackling around the perimeter and up along the sides.

Miss Banner stood back and watched. The flames put

40

dancing flickers on her face as they roared softly upwards, consuming everything. She stood there for a long time, never taking her eyes from the fire. She remained even when the spindly stucture had collapsed inward, throwing sparks high in the air and making a crackling, glimmering circle on the ground. Finally, when the last flame had died and there was scarcely anything left but smouldering ashes, Miss Banner turned and went back to the house.

Later, she took a mug of cocoa with her to the sitting room. She sat down at the table. In front of her was the framed picture from John Wesley's room. Beside it was a pair of scissors.

Miss Banner dismantled the frame and removed the picture. She sat staring at it again for a few minutes. It was an outdoor photograph, taken at a garden fête. Miss Banner looked at each face in turn, over and over.

She picked up the scissors and poised them for a moment, blades parted. Carefully she cut off the end of the print, isolating the photograph of her brother from the others in the group. She then cut John Wesley's picture into small slivers, letting them fall on the table.

She sat back when she had finished and slowly laid the scissors aside. She looked at the fragments; in one abrupt, savage moment she swept them off the table, as if she were ridding herself of something unclean.

Miss Banner drank some of her cocoa, then picked up the remainder of the photograph. Three faces, all smiling; Lord Wrathdale, Fiona Neave and Reuben Flaxman. Miss Banner stared fixedly at them, her mouth tightening.

Chapter Six

At mid-morning, Frank Scully entered Neave's printing works through the door that led off the stairway from the *Messenger* offices above. The two men who were working at the presses didn't notice him come in. He stood in the doorway and surveyed the place, then crossed and began examining the old linotype machine. It was a virtual antique, but it still appeared to be operational.

Frank spotted a copy of the previous week's *Messenger* on a table. He crossed and picked it up, leafing through it.

Reuben Flaxman glanced up from the machine he was attending and saw Frank. He looked surprised, then indignant. He came across and stood in front of Frank, hands on hips, scowling.

Frank lowered the paper and nodded. 'Morning,' he said brightly.

Reuben nodded curtly.

'You're Reuben, aren't you?'

The older man's scowl deepened. 'Was there something you wanted?'

Frank held up the paper. 'What's the print run?'

Reuben opened his mouth then closed it again. He eyed Frank full length from the feet up, saying nothing.

Frank put the question another way. 'How many copies do you print each week?'

'About five thousand,' Reuben said reluctantly.

'Always eight pages?'

'Mostly,'

'And you put it to bed on Tuesday around six. Right?'

The office door opened and Fiona Neave came into the works, head down, preoccupied. 'Reuben,' she called, 'can I

42

have a look at one of the posters we . . .' She glanced up and saw Frank. A flick of the eyes and she caught Reuben's truculent expression. She crossed to where they were standing.

'Man here wants to know all about *The Messenger*,' Reuben said. 'Maybe you can help him.'

Frank recognized Fiona at once. She was the woman he had seen grappling with the athletic-looking type near the old mine. He could tell that she remembered him too, though she was having difficulty placing him.

'I'm Mrs Neave,' Fiona said tentatively.

'Frank Scully.'

The tip of Fiona's tongue appeared for an instant, moistening her lips. 'You're not from around here, are you, Mr Scully?'

'I am today,' Frank said pleasantly.

Fiona glanced at Reuben, who still looked suspicious. 'I see,' she said. As she returned her attention to Frank her eyes widened momentarily. She had made the connection. The man in the battered Marina. 'Shall we go into my office?'

She led the way. When they were in the office she closed the door and made a quick appraisal of the stranger. Frank was standing looking round the office, relaxed, waiting. He didn't look like a potential buyer for *The Messenger*, but appearances counted for practically nothing these days.

'So you're interested in *The Messenger*, are you, Mr Scully?' Fiona moved behind the desk. Its solidity was comforting, a barrier between herself and something unpredictable.

'Moderately,' Frank said. As Fiona stood waiting for him to say more, he started drifting round the office, looking at the photographs.

'In what way are you interested, exactly?'

'Professionally,' Frank said.

Fiona was becoming annoyed, but she was still wary.

43

'You're in the newspaper business, are you?'

'From time to time.' Frank paused in front of the table where Fiona's binoculars were lying. He leaned forward, peering at a photograph of a pair of nesting Merlins. In a tone of genuine admiration he said, 'That's nice. Very nice indeed. Not an easy shot to get, I wouldn't think.'

'No,' Fiona said stiffly. 'Extremely difficult.'

Frank glanced at her. 'Did you take it?'

'Yes.'

Frank smiled. 'Congratulations.'

'Thank you.' Fiona was staring at him, waiting to be enlightened.

Frank picked up the binoculars, hefting them, turning the focusing ring. 'It's an interesting hobby, bird watching. And good for you, they tell me. Gets you out into the fresh air.' He put down the glasses.

Fiona spread her fingers on the desk top. 'You said you're in the newspaper business from time to time. What does that mean?'

Frank looked at her. 'Journalists tend to move around a bit.'

Relief spread on Fiona's face like the kiss of sunlight. 'Oh! You're a journalist! Forgive me.' She shook her head. 'I thought for a moment you might . . .' She checked herself. 'Which paper are you with?'

'I'm not at the moment,' Frank said. He came towards the desk. 'That's why I'm here.'

Now that she presumed she was in the picture, Fiona became brisk. 'I see. Well, I'm sorry, Mr Scully, but I'm afraid it's been a wasted journey for you. There isn't a vacancy on *The Messenger*.'

Frank hammed surprise. 'Really? I thought there was.'

Fiona shook her head. 'Later, possibly.' She faced him squarely, altering her stance and emanating courteous rejection. 'To be honest with you, what I'll be looking for then is a local man. Someone from the Dales, ideally – from

44

this part of the country, anyway.'

Frank looked puzzled now. 'What *you'll* be looking for?' he said. '*The Messenger* belongs to you then, does it?'

Fiona's eyes wavered. 'The ownership is in a state of flux at the moment. I'm talking about the future.'

'Oh.' Something like sly understanding dawned. Frank winked at Fiona. 'Right. Got you.' He turned as if to make for the door, then stopped and jerked his thumb towards the ceiling. 'Before you take anyone on, you'll need to get that office cleaned up a bit. It's in a hell of a state.'

'The office?' Fiona glared at him. 'How did you get in there?'

'I've got a key,' Frank said, smiling at her.

The door opened and Tom Holliday looked into the office. 'Can you spare Lord Wrathdale a minute?' he asked Fiona.

Fiona nodded, tight-lipped.

'I'm sorry to burst in like this, Mrs Neave,' Lewis said, striding in past Tom. 'My wife insisted I have a word personally with you about the tickets you're printing for the . . .' He caught sight of Frank and broke off. 'Oh. I beg your pardon.'

'It's no problem,' Frank said. 'Goodbye, Mrs Neave.' He crossed to the door, watching Lewis trying to identify him.

'Haven't we met?' Lewis asked.

Frank smiled. 'Only in passing.' He went out, closing the door.

Lewis looked silently at Fiona for a moment. Then he remembered. 'The man in the car!' he breathed. 'What the devil did he want?'

Fiona said nothing. She remained by her desk, staring at the door, wondering.

Chapter Seven

John Wesley Banner was buried on Monday morning. It was a dull, overcast day, a sombre backdrop to the proceedings in the old cemetery a mile outside of Micklethorpe. Throughout the committal Miss Banner stood alone at one side of the grave, listening to the droning of the Methodist minister, never once looking at the mourners gathered opposite.

When the ceremony was over, she shook hands with the minister and then stepped abruptly away from the grave, ignoring the few people who were hovering, waiting to speak to her. She crossed the grass to the main path then began walking towards the gate.

'Miss Banner . . .'

She stopped and turned. A man had followed her from the graveside. He was thin-faced, about thirty; he looked deeply apologetic as he approached.

'I'm David Liddle,' he said. 'Lord Wrathdale's estates manager.'

Miss Banner nodded. 'I know,' she said flatly.

'His Lordship is very sorry he wasn't able to be here himself today. He was deeply upset by your brother's death.'

'Yes,' Miss Banner said, 'he told me he was, in the note he sent. Kind of him.'

Liddle was looking at the row of vehicles beyond the gate. 'Which is your car?' he asked.

'I didn't come by car.'

Liddle looked surprised. 'Oh. Well, in that case I'd be delighted to give you a lift.'

Miss Banner shook her head. 'No thank you. I'd rather

walk.' She started to move away.

'I was wondering . . .' Liddle said hesitantly.

She stopped and faced him again. 'Yes?'

'I wondered perhaps if some time soon I could have a word with you about *The Messenger*.'

'What's to be said about it?' Miss Banner asked bleakly. 'To me, anyway? I just own it. If anything's bothering you, you'd best have a word with the editor.' She turned and walked away.

Liddle remained where he was, staring after her, looking confused.

Twenty minutes later, Fiona Neave, Reuben Flaxman and Tom Holliday arrived at the printing works in Micklethorpe. They were still in the clothes they had worn to John Wesley's funeral. While the two men stood by their machines putting on their overalls, Fiona made for her office. She was halfway there when Frank Scully came in from the door to the shop. He was in his shirtsleeves, carrying a large sheaf of paper.

'Ah,' he said, 'you're in at last, are you?'

Reuben and Tom froze. Fiona, bewildered and suddenly furious, spun on Frank, but before she had opened her mouth he drew a bunch of keys from his pocket and dangled them in front of her.

'I told you. I've got a key.'

'How long have you been here?' Fiona snapped.

'All weekend, on and off.' Frank turned and handed his sheaf of paper to Reuben. 'Here's your page-one lead,' he said. 'I've marked it up.' He watched Reuben glare at the typed sheets. 'There'll be more copy coming down later.' He started to move off, then swung back to Reuben. 'By the way, I've killed that piece about the cattle market you'd set. It's five hundred words about nothing. I hope that's not going to offend anyone.'

Reuben was scarlet with anger. 'I don't know about that!' he blustered. 'What's going on here?'

'We're producing a newspaper, Mr Flaxman,' Frank said calmly. 'I'm the acting editor.' He took a letter from the breast pocket of his shirt and handed it to Fiona. 'This is for you. From Miss Banner. It's all in there. I'm only temporary – just for now, she says.' He paused, then added, '*She's* looking for someone local, too.'

Frank went upstairs, leaving Fiona, Reuben and Tom to stare at each other.

Before nine o'clock on Thursday night, that week's edition of *The Micklethorpe Messenger* was printed and bundled, ready for distribution.

It hadn't been the easiest week of Frank Scully's life; on balance, however, he decided it had been challenging, enlightening and every bit as exhilarating as he had expected. He had interviewed people, taken photographs, typed the stories and marked up copy. He had coaxed, cajoled and occasionally bullied Reuben and Tom into setting the type the way he wanted it and pulling proofs when he needed them; he'd also talked them into abandoning some of the more archaic procedures they adopted with the layout. Fiona had co-operated, too – though sullenly.

Every evening that week Frank had returned late to the Harpers' house. The charade, which Sylvia continued to maintain and enjoy, had become second nature to Frank, and most of the time he was too tired to be troubled by guilt or temptation. In the mornings, he made sure always to be out of the house before Donald left for the office.

By Thursday night Frank was feeling measurably satisfied with himself. At three minutes to nine he stood in the printing works with the stringed bundles of papers at his feet, puffing thoughtfully on a cigarette and looking at a copy of his handiwork. On the front page, over a picture of the deceased owner, there was the headline WRATHDALE MOURNS DEATH OF JOHN WESLEY BANNER. At the bottom right hand corner there was one of Frank's photographs, a two-car pile-up he had travelled to High Kershaw to report. The page layout was symmetrical, neat, uncluttered. Frank was guardedly pleased with it.

Fiona came out of her office while he was still looking at the paper. She was ready to leave. She paused by a stack of *Messengers* on a table by her door and picked one up. Frank watched her approach him, reading the paper. As she drew level, she looked up.

'Nice job,' she said.

'Thank you.'

'So what now?'

Frank shrugged. 'Who knows. A drink wouldn't be a bad idea.' He looked at her questioningly. As the week had worn on, they had grown accustomed to confronting each other eye to eye. 'Care to join me?'

'Sorry,' Fiona said. 'I can't.'

'Better offer?'

Fiona folded her newspaper and turned away. 'Things to be done,' she said.

'Pity,' Frank said. 'Some other time, perhaps.'

'Maybe.'

Frank watched her go. As he turned he saw Reuben and Tom come across with the last of the stringed bundles of their paper. They dumped them beside the others.

'All done, then,' Reuben said. His hostility towards Frank had cooled over the past few days, but his approach was still less than cordial. He pointed to the bundles. 'That lot goes out to the villages. Hunderston, High Kershaw, Rawden, Staitholme, the lot. They're all labelled.'

Frank nodded. 'How are they delivered?'

'Not by us.' Reuben smiled tightly. 'We're finished.' He paused, savouring the moment. 'John Wesley took 'em round himself. As long as I can remember. The shops stayed open for him. He kept in touch with a lot of folk that way. So you'll be doing it this week, I reckon.' Reuben looked deeply pleased at the idea.

'How?' Frank asked.

'In your car,' Tom said. 'Same way John Wesley did.'

Frank was dismayed. 'But I don't know my way round here.'

'Then you'd best get started if you want to get home before daylight,' Reuben told him. 'There's a good few villages to call at.' He moved away, with Tom following. 'Goodnight.'

Frank stood among the bundles, feeling his self-satisfaction crumble. He could hear the men murmuring over by the door as they took off their overalls. Tom was chuckling softly. It was a moment of enormous satisfaction for them, Frank realized. They were convinced they had beaten him. The smart interloper had been put squarely in his place – and right at the moment when he thought he'd overcome all the obstacles.

'Damn . . .'

Frank looked down at the papers again. The old law, the one that had always driven him, insisted that he start, continue, then finish. To break the law was to open an inroad for depression, however small the job on hand. His serious drinking had begun a few years ago because he had started, continued, then abandoned a couple of jobs. There was no point in Frank telling himself it was superstition; he knew better than that. His self-esteem, never better than flimsy, could only be held if he stuck strictly to that one solid principle.

He sighed and looked at his watch. There was time, he decided. And there were plenty of signposts around Wrathdale. The only other necessary ingredient was purpose. He had that, he supposed – if only because personal failure, of any kind, was rather too much to live with these days.

It was after two o'clock when he finished. The old Marina might never be the same, nor might a couple of small, nagging muscles at the base of Frank's spine, but he had delivered every bundle of newspapers and the accomplishment was like a beatification.

In the Harpers' silent kitchen he permitted himself one small scotch before going to bed. Climbing the stairs a few minutes later, he heard the small, soft sounds of sleep coming from his hosts' bedroom. Frank was grateful they hadn't waited up for him. He had no energy left for conversation or pretence.

As his head touched the pillow he left the weariness close in on him. He sank rapidly towards sleep, holding an image of Reuben Flaxman's face, watching its triumphant smile dying.

The next day Frank went to Ravensfell house. He took a copy of *The Messenger* with him. For ten minutes he sat in silence on an uncomfortable couch opposite Miss Banner's table, watching the old woman read the paper. When she had finished, she folded it and looked up.

'I'm satisfied,' she said. Her words were the only clue. 'Not that you had a lot to do,' she added.

Frank was on the point of giving her a summary of just what he had been through when her next question stopped him.

'Will you be staying on?' Miss Banner asked.

It was the last thing Frank had expected to hear. 'You said just one issue,' he reminded her.

'Till I get someone,' Miss Banner said, as if he hadn't spoken. 'From *The Echo*, perhaps.'

'Have you advertised?'

'I'm asking.'

Now Frank did run a summary of all he had done; he ran it in his head, remembering the effort of humping the bundles of *The Messenger* around Wrathdale, picturing the recalcitrant, grudging behaviour of the printers. It had given him a lift, certainly, but all along he had been regarding the challenge as a one-off proposition.

'That could take a while,' he said. 'I've other things to do.'

Miss Banner nodded. 'So you said.' There was something in her tone that could trigger guilt, even when Frank had nothing to feel guilty about.

He sighed. 'How long?'

'Two, three weeks more. A month, maybe. I'll not take on just anyone, you understand.'

'I couldn't stay longer than a month.' Frank scarcely believed he had said it. A month, an entire *month* of putting up with Reuben and Tom and the permanently prissy, disapproving Fiona Neave. Four more exhausting, exasperating journeys around Wrathdale in the dark, carting newspapers to every far-flung settlement . . .

'A month, then,' Miss Banner said.

A little reminder flashed in Frank's head. 'We haven't talked about money.'

Miss Banner nodded. 'How much would you need?'

'Well, I'll have expenses. I've got to find somewhere to stay, for instance.'

That appeared to surprise Miss Banner slightly. 'Are you not comfortable where you are?'

'It's an imposition.'

'Oh, yes. Well, that's up to you, of course.'

Frank clasped his hands, wondering if he was really in a bargaining position. 'So what shall we say?'

'I'll think about it,' Miss Banner told him. 'Come and see me on Monday, we'll decide on it then.' She paused. 'And I'll give you something for next week's paper, too.'

'A news item?' Frank smiled.

'A little something to maybe stir a few memories of the old days,' the old woman said coldly. 'You're free to use it.' She stood up. 'Monday, then.'

At six that evening Frank left the offices of *The Messenger* and drove slowly back to the Harpers' house. Throughout the day he had moved between two points of view; either he had been coerced effortlessly by an old woman with more strength of character than he had ever come across, or he had been granted the opportunity to put a real mark on the future policy and presentation of a newspaper. It had been interesting to test the sensations thrown up by both possibilities – feeling put-upon one minute, privileged the next.

Either way, Frank now believed he had been less than prudent to take on the extension. The effort of it aside, there had been something unnerving in the way Fiona Neave had looked at him when he announced he was staying. That, plus the renewed promise of acrimonious resistance from Reuben and Tom, led Frank to predict he was in for a rougher time than he'd already had.

As he got out of the car in the Harpers' drive he heard music. It was familiar, a romantic ballad·he had been fond of a few years before. As he went in through the back door the music swelled. Sylvia turned from the drinks trolley, a glass in each hand.

'I heard your car,' she said, offering him a drink.

Frank had never seen her look more attractive. Her dress was light and cool-looking, a silky creation that emphasized the lines of her body and whispered with every small movement. She had taken a lot of trouble with her make-up and her hair, too. As he took the glass from her, he wondered momentarily if she might be going somewhere.

'I didn't realize you would be out all day,' Sylvia said. 'Avoiding me again, were you?'

'I'd things to do,' Frank said.

'I thought you'd finished. Going by what they were saying in the village this morning, you did a very good job.'

Frank made a modest shrug, crossing to the hi-fi. 'There was nothing to it.' He picked up the sleeve of the album that was playing on the turntable.

'Used to be one of your favourites,' Sylvia murmured softly.

'A long time ago.'

Not that long. Not long enough to forget.' Sylvia set down her glass on the trolley and crossed to Frank. 'So how shall we celebrate your triumph?'

Frank put down the record sleeve. 'I thought I'd take you both to dinner.'

Sylvia moved closer. He could smell her perfume, light, flowery. 'Nice idea,' she said. 'But Donald's in Brussels.'

Frank looked at her, genuinely startled. He was aware instantly of the tableau; the house set apart from the village, only the two of them in it . . .

'Some crisis or other with the conference arrangements,' Sylvia said lightly, keeping her eyes on Frank's. 'He flew out this afternoon – company jet and all that jazz.' She moved closer still. 'He won't be back until some time tomorrow. We're on our own.' She reached up and put her arms around Frank's neck. 'Isn't that nice?'

He made to ease himself away from her embrace, but Sylvia tightened her grip and smiled up into his face.

'Don't be a fool, Frank. It's what you want. What we both want.' Her eyes hardened fleetingly. 'It's why you stayed.'

What she said was partly true, Frank thought. He felt himself respond to her. It was *largely* true, if the facts were faced squarely. He had been aware of offering less resistance to events that he could, of concocting a self-righteous mental stance while he followed the current. He could even believe, now, that he had overstated to himself the desire to work on *The Messenger*; he had wanted that, but he had wanted more.

Sylvia moved against him and he felt his hands close around her slim, smooth waist. It had been a long time but the familiarity was there – her response to his touch, his own anticipation.

'Frank . . .'

He drew Sylvia to him, feeling the length of her body

against his own. There was nothing in his mind, nothing beyond the urgency of that moment. As Sylvia groaned he put his open mouth over hers and kissed her hungrily.

At approximately the time Frank Scully and Sylvia Harper were moving together across the darkness of Frank's bedroom, Miss Banner was settling into her chair in the sitting room at Ravensfell House. Her expression was fixed, almost grim.

She reached out and drew an embroidery frame towards her, then removed the protective linen cover from the fresh sampler underneath. She gazed for a moment at the text stencilled on the fabric.

> BURNING FOR BURNING,
> WOUND FOR WOUND,
> STRIPE FOR STRIPE.
> Exodus 21.25

With scrupulous care, Miss Banner took up her embroidery needle and made the first stitch in the first letter of the first word.

Chapter Eight

Lord Wrathdale's Land Rover was parked by the side door of Aynsgill Lodge, a large house standing in the grounds of Aynsgill Castle, the Wrathdale family's ancestral home. Nowadays the castle was open at certain times to the public, but it was not lived in. The lodge was Lord and Lady Wrathdale's home, and Lewis conducted his business from there. Fixed to the side door was a board, discreetly lettered:

WRATHDALE ESTATES LIMITED.
AYNSGILL DEVELOPMENT LIMITED.
AYNSGILL CASTLE TRUST.

Lewis was at the desk in his spacious, comfortably-furnished office. David Liddle was beside the desk, holding a slim attaché-case. After carefully reading a two-page typed letter, Lewis signed it and handed it to Liddle.

'Thank you.' Liddle put the letter in his case and took out a thin sheaf of papers. 'This arrived this morning. It's the report you asked for on *The Messenger*.'

'Ah, good.' Lewis took the papers and started glancing through them.

'Until the other day,' Liddle said thoughtfully, 'I'd no idea you were interested in buying the local newspaper, sir.'

Lewis looked up at him. 'You don't understand. I'm not. Not my line of country. But I might well go in with someone who *is* interested.' He looked at the papers again. 'Just for the fun of it, more than anything. But not if it's all going to be uphill.' He held up the report to Liddle. 'How does it look to you?'

Liddle put on his analytical face, which made his features look even narrower. 'If the price was right, I'd say that on those figures it was a pretty good investment. And there seems to be plenty of scope for expansion.'

Lewis nodded. 'As far as I understand it, that's that idea. But first things first. Any news from that fellow Hennessey?'

'I understand he's written off,' Liddle said.

There was a tap at the door from the living quarters. It opened a fraction and Lady Wrathdale peeped in.

'Beattie!' Lewis said. 'Do come in.'

She glanced at Liddle. 'If you're busy, I can come back in a minute . . .'

'No, come in, it's all right.' Lewis turned to Liddle. 'We've finished for now, haven't we?'

Liddle nodded. 'Nothing else at the moment. I'll get this letter run off and delivered to every tenant by hand.' He fastened his attaché-case and left, nodding politely to Beattie as he went.

Lewis slipped the report into the centre drawer of the desk and stood up, crossing to his wife.

'I'm sorry I interrupted, Lewis.' She had a reticent manner that lent itself well to apology; even her clean good looks were geared to the softer expressions of regret and misgiving. At thirty-six Beattie Haddon was still well-known for her demure beauty, though she would have preferred to be admired for her intelligence. 'I always seem to be walking in on business,' she murmured.

'Nonsense.' Lewis took her hand and kissed her on the cheek. 'Did I tell you you're looking particularly lovely today?'

'No.'

'Well, you are.'

'Thank you.' Beattie gave him a mock-wary look. 'What brought that on?'

'Just seeing you standing there in the doorway.' He frowned. 'And guilt, probably. I neglect you.'

'Nonsense.'

Lewis kissed her cheek again.

'I came in,' Beattie said, 'to see if you were going to be at home for dinner tonight.'

Lewis pulled a face. 'No, I'm afraid not. Wretched JPs' meeting. I mentioned it, didn't I?'

'I couldn't remember if it was tonight or tomorrow night.'

Lewis moved away from her, going to the desk and shuffling papers as if he were looking for something. 'Does that cause you problems?' he asked after a moment.

Beattie shook her head. 'Not a bit. But Betty Seward rang. She's got a spare ticket for the Hallé concert tonight and she asked me if I'd like to go with her. I said I'd see what you were doing and let her know.'

Lewis looked up. 'What are they playing?'

'Some Mozart, I think.' She paused. 'And the Sibelius Second.'

'Oh, no!' Lewis groaned. 'Damn! I wish I'd known. Maybe I could've cried off. But it's too late now.' He smiled gently at Beattie. 'The Sibelius Second. Remember?'

'Of course,' Beattie said.

'Whatever happened to that recording we had of it?'

'We've still got it.'

Softly, Lewis said, 'We haven't played it for ages.'

'No.' A small sadness crossed Beattie's features, then she straightened, smiling brightly. 'I'll tell her I'll go then, shall I?'

'Of course.'

Beattie came across and kissed Lewis, then she made for the door. Pausing there she said, 'Will you be late?'

'Well . . .' Lewis sighed heavily. 'You know how these JPs go on. I expect you'll be home before I am. Don't wait up.'

Beattie studied his face intently for a few seconds, then she smiled sympathetically. 'Poor Lewis,' she said.

When she had gone Lewis turned to his desk again. His face was troubled. He shifted papers, aligned pencils and straightened the blotter. He was suddenly very angry with himself.

Frank Scully had spent two hours typing invoices before keeping an appointment with Donald Harper at the CorVol plant. Frank would have preferred to stay at the office and put in some work on the next issue of *The Messenger*, but there had been a prior arrangement to visit the CorVol plant with Donald on Monday morning. Lunch was part of the arrangement. It had been an uneven kind of Monday morning. The invoicing had given him some respite from the unpleasant traffic with the printers downstairs, but it was tedious work.

There had been one intriguing moment, however. Rummaging through the ledgers in the old office safe, trying to confirm the details on a proof entry form, Frank had found a small framed snapshot wrapped in a piece of burgundy-coloured velvet. The frame was made of leather, inlaid with silver; the picture was of John Wesley Banner, looking less formidable than usual, and beside him was a smiling Fiona Neave. Judging from Fiona's hairstyle and dress, the picture was probably three or four years old. Frank stared at it for a couple of minutes, wondering about it. Finally, none the wiser, he wrapped the frame in the velvet again and put it back behind the ledgers.

The visit to the plant had been interesting, but it had also been steadfastly unenlightening. Donald obviously wanted a piece written about CorVol, but Frank hadn't found one hook to hang a story on. Even the animals he had spotted in the laboratory cage had turned out to be there for simple, uncontroversial reaction tests. Donald might not have welcomed a story about experiments on live animals, but it would have been something.

The uneven pattern of the morning persisted into the

59

early afternoon. Donald had taken Frank to lunch at Micklethorpe's best hotel restaurant. The food had been excellent, but Sylvia had invited herself along and her innuendoes throughout the meal had taken on a bolder than usual edge – bold enough to keep Frank from enjoying the meal.

A piece of news that emerged over lunch left Frank wondering if he was pleased or not. Later in the week, Donald was going to Dublin for two days and he was taking Sylvia with him. The prospect of temporarily being able to relax in the house, without the constant pretence, did feel like a small blessing to Frank – especially since he and Sylvia were now lovers again, an escalation of deceit that he didn't let himself dwell on for any length of time. But the news also produced an unmistakable sense of impending loneliness. Frank decided not to dwell on that, either.

Now, in the middle of the afternoon, Frank was sitting in a rickety kitchen chair outside the back door of Ravensfell House. He was reading a three-page, handwritten manuscript; opposite him, on a bench, Miss Banner was plucking a white chicken, throwing the feathers down on to a piece of sacking spread out before her on the ground. A bulky envelope was lying on the bench beside her.

When Frank had finished scanning the manuscript he looked up at Miss Banner. The air around her was full of feathers. She paused and looked back at him.

'I said I'd give you something for *The Messenger*, didn't I?' she said.

Frank nodded. 'The title,' he said slowly; '"Tales of the Dale" . . .'

'Or whatever you think best. You'll need to go through it anyway. For spelling and the like.' She resumed plucking the chicken. 'I'm not much at writing. But folk around here like that kind of thing.'

Frank shrugged. 'I'm grateful for any contributions.

Especially feature stuff. It's a hell of a job filling those centre pages.' He thought for a moment. 'Country Crafts finishes this week. This piece would fit in that spot nicely.'

'Only if you like it,' Miss Banner murmured.

'It's your newspaper.'

'I know that.' Her fingers worked steadily, ripping out the feathers, throwing them at the sacking. 'But you're the editor. You must decide. Not that I think you'll reject it, mind.'

Frank smiled. He found her directness refreshing. 'No, I doubt if I will.'

'When it goes in,' Miss Banner said, 'I don't want my name on it.'

'Oh? Why?'

She glanced at him. 'Because, like you said, *The Messenger* is mine now. I don't want folk to think I'm taking advantage of that.'

'A pen name then,' Frank said.

'That'll do,' Miss Banner nodded.

'Anything in mind?'

'I'll leave that to you.'

Frank folded the manuscript and put it in his jacket pocket. 'People might ask what the writer's real name is,' he pointed out.

Miss Banner nodded again. 'Most likely. But you won't say, will you?'

'If that's the way you want it.' Frank cleared his throat. 'Uh, usual rates?'

'I don't want paying.'

'In that case,' Frank said, 'your contribution's doubly welcome. But since we're on the subject of money, I'm not that generous.'

Miss Banner turned over the chicken and started attacking a fresh patch of feathers. 'Your wages,' she grunted.

'Yes. The last time I was here you said you'd give the

matter some thought.'

'And I have.'

Frank waited for her to say more. But she didn't. 'What do you have in mind?' he asked her tentatively.

Miss Banner looked up. 'You take what you need,' she said.

Frank stared at her. 'I take what I want?'

'No. What you need.'

'From where?'

She continued plucking more slowly now. 'Money in, money out. That's in your hands now. I've talked to the bank about it. They're expecting you.'

'Are they?' The presumption needled Frank. He folded his arms defensively. 'Well, I'm not sure I want that responsibility.'

'Probably not,' Miss Banner said calmly. 'But there's no one else, is there?'

Frank remained silent for a moment, thinking it through. He sighed. 'I just help myself to my salary? Is that the idea?'

Miss Banner dropped a wad of feathers near his feet. 'That's right.'

You're taking a bit of a risk, aren't you?'

'I don't think so.' Miss Banner paused, resting her hands on the plumpness of the chicken. 'I'm not saying you're an honest man. Not altogether.' She put her head on one side, examining his face. 'But you're not a thief. And you've got a lot of pride. A proud man'll make do on as little as he can, so I'll not be wronged either way.' She went back to her chicken.

'I still think you're taking a chance,' Frank said, shaking his head.

'It's not one I'll lose any sleep over.'

Frank sat and watched the old woman, running her words over in his head. One thing rankled; in spite of himself, he had to ask her. 'In what way am I dishonest, do you think?'

'With yourself, mostly,' Miss Banner replied, without looking at him. After a pause she said, 'Still putting up at Rawdon End, are you?'

Frank shut off any speculation about what she meant. He stood up, frowning. 'Well,' he murmured, pushing back the chair, 'thanks for the vote of confidence.'

'Sit down,' Miss Banner said sharply. 'I'm not done yet.' She pushed the chicken aside and reached for the envelope lying on the bench beside her. Glancing at Frank she said, 'I've something else for you.'

Chapter Nine

The gatehouse of Aynsgill Castle, though much smaller than the lodge, was an elegant, superbly designed 17th-Century house set back from the road and nestling alongside the west gate of the castle grounds.

The furnishings in the sitting room had been chosen with care, though with no great expense, to reflect the period and atmosphere of the house. The one touch of incongruity was a music centre, set into an alcove by the stone fireplace with shelves of record albums underneath.

The lights had been dimmed. A table in one corner of the room was laid for dinner; there were two settings and between them was a simple, attractive floral decoration with a solitary candle at its centre.

Fiona Neave came through from the kitchen, glass in hand. She was wearing a dark blue, full-skirted dress; her hair had been combed out of its normally severe style so that it hung in soft waves to her shoulders. She stood for a moment looking round the room, breathing softly through barely parted lips. An observer, had there been one, would have said there was an air of suppressed excitement about her.

She took a sip from her glass them put it down on the table. Striking a match, she lit the candle and stood back, smiling at the soft, intimate effect.

From the kitchen there was the sound of the back door closing quietly. Fiona glanced at her watch, then stood watching the kitchen door, still smiling.

Lewis appeared in the doorway. 'Hello,' he murmured.

'Hello.' Fiona's smile widened. She moved towards him

then stopped, looking past his shoulder. 'Did you . . .'

'Yes,' he said soothingly, 'I locked it.' He closed the kitchen door and beckoned to Fiona. 'Come here.'

She went to him and he took her in his arms. They kissed and embraced until Fiona moved gently away, breathless. 'I'll get you a drink,' she said.

'Great,' Lewis said. 'I could do with one.' He sat down on the sofa, yawning and stretching.

Fiona went to the drinks cabinet and poured a large whisky, watching Lewis from the corner of her eye. 'It's been like that, has it?'

'Not especially,' he said. 'Maybe I'm just getting old.'

Fiona brought him his drink. She leaned down over the back of the sofa and put her cheek against his. 'I'll let you know later,' she said playfully. She crossed to the table and picked up her glass. 'Cheers.'

Lewis raised his. 'Happiness.'

They sipped their drinks, then Fiona said, 'Which way did you come tonight?'

'Across the park. I left the car up at the castle.' He pulled a face at her. 'Stop worrying. No one saw me.'

'I'm not worried,' Fiona said. Wryly, she added, 'You're the one who worries about that kind of thing.' She came and sat down at the other end of the sofa.

'We have to be careful,' Lewis told her. It was a gentle rebuke, one he had issued before.

'Yes,' Fiona nodded, 'we mustn't frighten the horses, must we?'

Lewis stiffened visibly, frowning at her. He was about to say something when Fiona put up her hand.

'Sorry, Lewis. It was a slip of the tongue.' She smiled. 'Forget I said it, darling.'

Lewis accepted the apology. He glanced at her sideways. 'I've got some news for you.'

'Snap.'

'Oh? Really?' Lewis sat forward. 'What's yours?'

She shook her head. 'You first.'

'Well.' Lewis was prolonging the moment, watching the curiosity in Fiona's eyes. 'After we talked about you buying *The Messenger* I asked my accountants to make a few enquiries and get me some figures. I got their report today.'

Fiona nodded eagerly. 'And?'

'You were right. Bought at a fair price, it would be a very good investment.'

'Didn't I tell you?' Fiona was delighted.

'So,' Lewis went on, 'if you're still keen on putting in a bid, the money's there whenever you need it.'

Now it appeared to be Fiona's turn to prolong the moment. She looked at Lewis for several seconds, then she said, 'Thanks. I appreciate your offer. I really do.' She moistened her lips. 'But I won't need to borrow the money now. That's my news.'

'Oh.' Lewis was intrigued. 'Come into a fortune, have you?'

'Well yes, as a matter of fact I have. A small one, anyway.' She reached out and squeezed Lewis's arm. 'I had a visit from a solicitor this afternoon. John Wesley Banner's left me fifty thousand pounds.'

Lewis gaped at her. 'You're not serious?'

'I couldn't believe it either. Not at first.'

'Fifty thousand . . .' Lewis looked appalled. 'Why?'

'I don't know.'

'You must have some idea.'

Fiona shook her head firmly. 'It came as a complete surprise.'

Lewis didn't seem prepared to accept that. 'You never even got any kind of hint from him that you were in his will?'

'Never. We weren't that close.'

'Close enough, it would seem,' Lewis said. 'Good friends, anyway.'

'Not even that.' Fiona's voice was level, matter-of-fact.

66

'As far as I was concerned he was just another customer. Of course the firm had been printing *The Messenger* for years before I took over. Half a century or more. Maybe that's the reason.'

Lewis shook his head. 'You don't leave fifty thousand pounds to your printers – however long you've been associated with them. Besides, he didn't leave it to the firm. He left it to you. A personal bequest to someone he's known for what, ten years?'

'Not much more.'

Lewis leaned towards Fiona. 'There was *no* explanation?'

'I told you. None.'

'No message?' Lewis had the insistence of a prosecuting counsel. 'No conditions? *Nothing*?'

'No,' Fiona sighed, 'not a word. I asked, but apparently all it says in the will is that I'm to get this sum of money out of his estate.'

Lewis gazed across the room, as if an answer might be lurking in the drapes. 'How much is his estate worth, for God's sake?'

Fiona shrugged. 'I've no idea. I didn't dare ask that. And the solicitor didn't say. Only that Miss Banner is the principal beneficiary.'

'Well that's something I suppose.' Lewis jiggled his glass agitatedly then drained it and stood up. 'At least he didn't leave you the lot.' He went to the drinks cabinet and started pouring himself another scotch.

'It was what he wanted, Lewis.' Fiona sounded bewildered. 'Being of sound mind and all that. For whatever reason. Maybe it was just a whim.'

'A *whim*?' Lewis stared across at her. 'A whim might have got you five hundred pounds, if you were lucky. As a token of esteem or whatever. Fifty thousand is a hell of a sight more than a token. And it's an indication of more than just esteem.'

67

'I told you,' Fiona said patiently, 'I hardly knew the man. We got on all right, mostly. We had a few blazing rows over the way we were handling *The Messenger*. He was very demanding. But when we were on speaking terms we chatted occasionally and I met him from time to time at this function and that.' She spread her hands. 'But that's it.'

Lewis was swirling his drink and chewing fretfully at his lip. 'It doesn't make any sense. Unless . . .' He shook his head and took a gulp from the glass.

'Unless what?'

'It doesn't matter,' he mumbled, staring at the carpet.

'Yes it does.' Fiona was beginning to get angry. 'Unless what?'

'Well . . .' Lewis looked up. 'Unless you're not being totally frank with me.'

Fiona got to her feet. 'Unless I'm lying, you mean.'

'I didn't say that.'

'It's what you're suggesting.'

'Not at all.' Lewis softened his tone a shade. 'I'm suggesting that maybe you're, well, being protective.'

'Protective?'

He nodded. 'Out of misplaced loyalty or whatever.'

Fiona was frowning at him, puzzled. 'Who am I supposed to be protecting?' She inhaled sharply, realizing suddenly what he meant. 'Banner! You think I'm protecting Banner!'

'You could be,' Lewis said, making it sound as if the assumption were perfectly reasonable. 'Maybe Banner wasn't quite everything a Methodist preacher ought to be. Maybe he pestered you from time to time. More than pestered you. Got a bit too free with his hands.' Lewis was examining the carpet again. 'Maybe he was a dirty old man and he upset you more than once. Propositioned you, even. And this is his way of making amends and you're keeping quiet about it to protect his reputation.'

'Oh, Lewis.' Fiona sounded almost sorry for him. 'That's

ridiculous. There was never anything like that. John Wesley was a model of propriety. As far as I remember he never even touched my arm or brushed past me. If anything he seemed to go out of his way to keep some distance between us.'

Lewis sighed and shook his head. 'Then I just don't know.' He looked straight at Fiona. 'Whatever his motive, he's put you in an impossible position. You could always refuse the bequest, of course. Or better still, announce that you're going to give the money to a charity. The Wrathdale Children's Home, perhaps.'

Fiona was astonished. 'Give it away? Why?'

'Darling,' Lewis said, 'I accept what you say about your relationship with Banner. And if you say you're not trying to protect him – well, OK, I accept that too. Without reservation. But what do you imagine other people are going to think?'

'I don't care very much,' she said coldly.

'Well you should. In a place like Wrathdale there'll be all kinds of gossip. It'll be the talk of every village.'

Fiona shook her head, dismissing the notion. 'There's no reason why anyone else should know,' she said. 'Apart from Miss Banner. I thought I'd go over and see her tomorrow. Talk to her about it. She might know why her brother left me the money. Maybe he discussed it with her.'

'I doubt that,' Lewis said impatiently. 'It's common knowledge they weren't on very good terms, isn't it? He treated her extremely badly, by all accounts. So he's not likely to have taken her into his confidence about something like this, is he?'

'I suppose not.'

'And I don't think you'll get a very warm welcome. After all, you've taken a damn great chunk of Miss Banner's inheritance away from her, and the odds are she's thinking what just about everyone else will think.'

'And what's that?'

69

'Oh, don't be naive.'

'That I was his mistress?' Fiona laughed, but the sound was forced, strained. 'That's ludicrous!'

'Maybe. But that's the construction most people will put on it. And can you blame them?'

'But it's not true.'

'You try convincing anyone of that,' Lewis said scathingly.

'I just have,' Fiona reminded him quietly.

'That's not fair.'

'I hope not.'

Lewis moved towards her, putting his hand lightly on her arm. 'Fiona, you know what I mean . . .'

'But why *should* it become common knowledge?' She sounded hurt, offended, as if Lewis's foreboding had already become a fact. 'A will's something that's usually very private.' She eased away gently, removing herself from his touch. 'I wish now I hadn't said anything to you about it. Then you'd have been none the wiser.'

Lewis drank the remainder of his scotch and put the glass down. 'Wills are kept on record, you know. Anyone can get a copy if they want to.'

'Why should anyone bother?'

'People do, believe me. Out of interest. Nosiness. Besides, in a community like this you can't keep anything a secret. The solicitor mentions it to his wife, she passes it on to a friend . . .'

'It wasn't in the hands of a local solicitor,' Fiona interrupted him. 'John Wesley had his will drawn up by a firm in Harrogate.'

'All the more reason for curiosity,' Lewis said, almost sadly. He moved forward again and took Fiona in his arms. 'Think about what I've said. Please. For your own sake.'

Fiona peered closely at him. 'For my sake?'

'Of course.'

'But even if I did give the money to charity,' she said,

70

'that wouldn't alter the fact that John Wesley willed it to me in the first place.'

'No, but it would leave the gossips floundering a bit. Take a lot of the sting out of the wagging tongues.'

Fiona moved away from him. She turned and stood looking at the candle in the centre of the table. A third of it had burned down already. 'Oh, God, I don't know. Maybe you're right. But then again . . .'

'What?'

'There may not be any gossip. It may never come out.'

'It only takes one malicious person to stir things up.'

'All right,' Fiona said petulantly, 'I'll think about what you've said.' She turned and went back to Lewis.

'Don't let's talk about it any more this evening. We don't have enough time together for arguments, do we?' She kissed him on the cheek, then crossed to the kitchen door and opened it. 'Let's eat. Put some music on, eh?' She started to go into the kitchen then paused in the doorway. 'There's one thing, of course . . .'

Lewis looked at her expectantly.

'If the worst comes to the worst,' she said, 'it's better the locals should think I was John Wesley's mistress than find out I'm yours, isn't it?' She turned and went into the kitchen.

Lewis moved slowly to the alcove by the fireplace and squatted by the record shelves. He selected an album and stared at the sleeve for a moment, then he took out the disc and put it on the turntable.

He lowered the pick-up arm gently on to the first groove and stood back, watching the disc revolve. His face grew pensive, sombre, as the music washed over him and the room was gradually filled with the majestic opening of Sibelius's Second Symphony.

Chapter Ten

At ten o'clock on Wednesday morning Frank Scully came into the printing works carrying two sheets of copy. He walked across to the bench where Fiona Neave and Reuben Flaxman were examining the layout for an advertising brochure.

'May I cut in?' he asked Fiona.

'Of course.'

Frank handed Reuben one of the sheets of copy. 'It's been confirmed now that the council's going ahead with the new car park,' he told Reuben, 'so we'll make that the lead story this week.'

Reuben glanced at the copy, nodded and dropped it on the bench.

'And this,' Frank said, 'is the second lead.' He handed Reuben another piece of copy then looked at Fiona. 'Congratulations, by the way.' He turned back to Reuben and said, 'You didn't do too badly either, did you?'

Puzzled, Fiona watched Reuben as he started to read the copy. The familiar scowl began to spread. Reuben looked up at Frank for a moment, then read some more.

'Where did you get this from?' he demanded finally.

'You know the stock answer to that,' Frank said. 'A reliable source. Why? What's the problem?'

Reuben waved the sheet of paper below Frank's nose. 'It's no one else's business,' he said angrily.

'What is it?' Fiona said.

Reuben straightened the paper and began reading it aloud. '"Among the bequests in the will of John Wesley Banner, the late owner and editor of *The Messenger*, is a gift of ten thousand pounds to the Ebenezer Methodist Chapel, Micklethorpe."'

'Oh, no,' Fiona breathed. She took the paper from Reuben and read the rest of the article. It was laid out clear and plain, a concise piece of journalism with no ambiguities.

The bulk of Mr Banner's estate, which exceeds £210,000 net and which includes proprietorship of The Messenger and title to the six acres of land known as Lower Common, is inherited by his sister, Miss Sybil Banner of Ravensfell House, Micklethorpe.

Other beneficiaries are Mr Reuben Flaxman of Hithergate Street, Micklethorpe who receives £5,000, and Mrs Fiona Lytton Neave of The Gate House, Aynsgill Castle, to whom Mr Banner has willed £50,000.

There was more, most of it about John Wesley's career and his close links with the Methodist Chapel, but Fiona didn't take any of it in. She handed the sheet back to Reuben.

'That's private,' Reuben snarled, shaking the copy at Frank again. 'Well, it's personal, anyhow.'

'It's a matter of public record,' Frank corrected him.

'Even so,' Fiona said, 'Reuben's got a point. Why is it going in the paper?'

'It's local news. And this is the local newspaper. Banner was a prominent figure in these parts. People will be interested.'

'You're right,' Reuben said bitterly. 'They will be. Very interested.'

'Well then,' Frank said brightly. 'And it *is* true, isn't it?'

'Truth's got nothing to do with it!' Reuben blustered.

'Yes,' Fiona said quietly. 'It's true.'

'Then why does it bother you?' Frank asked her. 'Good luck to both of you, I say.'

'Thank you, Mr Scully,' Fiona retorted icily. 'And what the hell makes you think I'm bothered?' She turned and walked quickly away to her office.

Frank turned to Reuben. 'Set both pieces up. And I want that picture I took of the site to go in with the car park story.' He went off the way he had come, through the door to the shop.

Tom Holliday came across from the press he was operating. He looked questioningly at Reuben.

'Take a look,' Reuben said, handing him the copy.

Tom read it slowly then looked up, shaking his head.

'Do you reckon I have to set that?' Reuben asked him.

Tom sniffed. 'He's the editor.'

'More's the pity,' Reuben growled.

Upstairs in the dark, ill-furnished editor's office, Frank Scully was standing by the window, looking across at the portrait photograph of John Wesley Banner on the opposite wall. After a minute he went to the desk and dug out the safe keys from the bottom drawer.

He went to the safe and unlocked it, then carefully took out the velvet-wrapped photograph in its leather and silver frame.

He unwrapped the picture and took it across to the window, studying it carefully in the weak sunlight. Like any other photograph it was a slice of time past, and not a particularly informative slice. Two people, one old and the other young, standing in front of a camera in the open air somewhere. Their expressions told the viewer nothing, beyond the fact that they weren't unhappy. It was a snapshot no more exceptional than millions of others.

Even so, the more Frank looked at it, the more he felt the picture had something to yield. As yet, it said nothing to him. But he was sure it would, if he persevered.

On weekdays the market square on Micklethorpe High Street was used as car-parking space. Just after noon on Friday Fiona Neave got back to the town after visiting a customer at Hunderston. She found herself a space in the

74

square and eased the MGB into it.

She got out, locked the car, and was making her way across to the printing works when she was confronted by Mrs Rawlings. The woman was tall and bulky, with a face as unlovely as her personality. Sensitive people had a tendency to avoid Mrs Rawlings; caught there on the pavement's edge, with the woman smiling grimly at her, Fiona had no chance of avoiding her at all.

'Morning, Mrs Neave.'

'Oh, good morning, Mrs Rawlings,' Fiona said pleasantly. 'How are you?'

'I'm very well, thanks.' The dry lips pursed for an instant. 'No need to ask how you are though, eh?'

Fiona blinked at her. 'Sorry?'

'Just about every day'll be a good one for you from now on, I'd say.'

'I'm sorry, I'm not with you . . .'

'I've just been reading about you in *The Messenger*,' Mrs Rawlings said. There was a predatory glint in her eye. 'Nice little windfall, eh?'

Fiona nodded, feeling her cheeks grow warm.

'Not that fifty thousand pounds goes very far these days. The way prices are now, you can hardly buy a decent house for that.' She paused, her head waggling as she leaned closer. 'Not the kind of house someone like you or me would want to live in, that is.' She narrowed her small eyes and said, 'What are you going to do with it?'

The effrontery left Fiona dry-mouthed. 'I haven't decided,' she said huskily.

'Well, there's not much point in saving money with inflation going up all the time, is there?' Even the woman's small talk carried a trace of malice.

'I suppose not.' Fiona looked at her watch, trying to conjure some urgency that would get her away from Mrs Rawlings. When she glanced up, the woman was staring straight at her.

'Who would have thought it, eh? About old man Banner.'

'Thought what?' Fiona said sharply.

'Well, him having so much to leave.'

'Yes, well . . .' Fiona looked at her watch again and started backing away. 'I must be going, Mrs Rawlings. It was nice talking to you.'

'And such a surprise you being named in his will,' Mrs Rawlings went on, checking Fiona. 'I mean you not being a relation or anything. Come as a surprise to you, did it?'

'Yes. A complete surprise.' Fiona could feel herself start to tremble.

'Still, you'd known him for quite a while, hadn't you?'

'He was a customer,' Fiona said, louder than she had intended. 'A tenant of mine. We worked in the same building.'

'Yes, of course.' Mrs Rawlings leaned close again, her face an unpleasant, sanctimonious rebuke. 'And you'd have done little things for him from time to time, I imagine, and he obviously appreciated it.'

Fiona began moving away.

'Well, I mean, you must have been very good to him for him to leave you all that.'

'Good day, Mrs Rawlings.' Fiona moved along the pavement, watching for a break in the traffic.

'Don't spend it all at once,' the big woman's voice rasped after her. 'You know what they say – easy come, easy go.'

Fuming and hardly able to control herself, Fiona stepped into the road, waiting for a car to pass. She glanced across the street to the newsagents. Two women were standing outside, looking at her. One whispered something to the other, then they both giggled.

Close to tears, Fiona stamped across the road, almost running the few yards to the printing works. 'To hell with them!' she hissed. 'To hell with everybody!'

A few minutes before Fiona reached the works, Reuben

and Tom had gone off for their customary Friday lunchtime in the pub on the corner of High Street.

At the bar, Reuben offered to buy Tom a drink, but Tom preferred to stick to the usual independent arrangement.

'I'll buy my own, thanks,' Tom said firmly.

'Please yourself.' Reuben beckoned to the barman. 'Pint of best and a pie.'

'I'll have the same,' Tom said.

Two men at a nearby table had been watching them and smiling. Now they got up and crossed to the bar. One leaned on the counter beside Reuben.

'Well,' he said, jerking his thumb at his companion, 'I don't know about him, but I'll have a whisky, thanks.'

Reuben stared at him.

'You're buying, aren't you?' the man said. 'A rich man like you . . .'

Reuben returned his gaze to the row of bottles behind the bar.

'Bet your boss isn't being so tight with her friends,' the man persisted, to the great amusement of his companion. 'Although, come to think of it, maybe that's why she got all that money. Being tight. If you know what I mean.' he winked. 'I like 'em tight, myself.' Both men started laughing. Reuben and Tom ignored them.

When the barman had set out the plates with the pies and began pulling the beer, Reuben called out to him.

'We'll take the drinks in the snug, thanks. It's getting right rancid in here.' He jerked his head at the man beside him, who was still laughing. 'Give Fred here a Lysol on me. He's got a dirty mouth.'

With slow dignity, Reuben and Tom walked off to the snug.

That afternoon Fiona drove out to Ravensfell House. She had intended to pay the visit at the weekend, but since her encounter with Mrs Rawlings she had been agitated, depressed and ultimately so confused that she decided there was an urgent need for some stable point of focus.

Driving through the countryside she recalled Lewis's warning about visiting Miss Banner. The reception might be chilly, as he had said, but it was a risk Fiona was prepared to accept. Before, her curiosity about the money had been secondary to her pleasure at receiving it – she had simply thought she *might* go and see the old woman. Now, the visit was an imperative. Fiona badly needed to know why John Wesley had remembered her so generously in his will. As things stood, there was nothing she could use to defend herself against the local reaction.

She parked her car in front of the house. Getting out, she crossed to the front door and rang the bell. She waited a minute but there was no response. She pressed the bell again.

After a third attempt she gave up and went round to the back of the house. There was no response to her knocking on the back door, either. She peered through the kitchen window; there was no sign of anyone.

Slowly, Fiona walked back along the side of the house. She felt deflated. On the way she had rehearsed her approach and conditioned herself to withstand rejection. She had even thought of a few ploys to soften whatever hard front she might encounter. Now she was going to have to go back to Micklethorpe with nothing resolved; everything, for the time being, would remain as it was.

She was ten feet from the car when she stopped, shocked. After a second she started moving again, slowly, staring at what had been done. She drew level with the car, feeling her stomach churn.

Four glassy-eyed, newly-shot wood pigeons had been thrown over the windscreen. The splayed wings and lolling heads hung obscenely; slimy, half-congealed blood was streaked on the glass and across the bonnet.

For an instant Fiona thought she was going to be sick.

She turned away from the car, breathing carefully, feeling her resentment mount steadily, displacing the nausea.

She glared across at the house, certain that she was being watched. The dominant feelings were etching themselves across her face – indignation, outrage, anger. She let her features betray every growing tendril of animosity in her. And she let her sudden defiance show, too.

Chapter Eleven

Frank parked his Marina alongside Donald Harper's Volvo and walked round to the back of the house. As he came in through the kitchen door, Sylvia was taking a tray of ice cubes from the refrigerator.

'Ah, you're just in time.' Sylvia tipped the cubes into the ice bucket and handed it to Frank. As he took it, she let her fingers wrap around his for a moment. She gave him an intimate, secretive smile, then turned away.

Frank took the bucket into the sitting room and set it down on the drinks trolley. Donald was pouring whisky into three glasses.

'Good day?' he asked Frank pleasantly.

'In between.' Frank tossed his copy of *The Messenger* on to the settee. 'How about you?'

'Hectic.'

Sylvia came in and crossed slowly to the settee. 'Go on, pity him,' she said to Frank. 'It's hell being a big executive, you know.' The mocking tone was harsher just lately, or so Frank believed. Donald didn't seem to notice. 'Decisions, decisions,' Sylvia sighed. 'And all that looking over your shoulder.'

'She's got no respect,' Donald murmured, turning to them with their drinks. 'Don't know why I married her.'

Sylvia took her drink and sat down. 'It's because you thought I'd go well with your suits, darling,' she said sweetly. She held up the newspaper and nodded to Frank. 'Fascinating reading this week. Fascinating. How about the Banner will sensation then? I must say you kept it very close to your chest. You didn't even mention it last night.'

Frank shrugged. 'You're not interested in local matters, remember?'

'I am when there's a nice juicy scandal.' She glanced at the headline. 'This'll have set all the biddies chuntering in their byres.'

'Apparently,' Frank murmured.

Donald laughed. 'Touché.'

'No,' Sylvia protested, 'You're way off target.' She threw the paper back on the settee. 'Fiona Neave's love life is no concern of mine. Can't say I admire her choice, though. John Wesley never turned me on. But *chacun à son goût*, and all that. If you're into geriatrics, why not?' Bitchily, she added, 'There's money in it, obviously.'

'Is that how you see it?' Frank asked her.

'Oh come on!' Sylvia made a derisive mouth. 'So do you. Otherwise why use the story at all? You know what sells newspapers.'

Frank nursed his drink with both hands. 'I know what sells some newspapers. But I'm a stranger in these parts. And would you believe it – my first thought was that maybe they were related in some way.'

Sylvia laughed low in her throat. 'They were,' she said. 'Obviously. Intimately on occasions.'

'There's no family connection,' Donald said to Frank. 'Mrs Neave isn't even local. She hasn't lived here all that long – ten or twelve years at most. She came to Mickle-thorpe when she got married.'

'And where's Mr Neave?' Frank asked.

'Good question,' Sylvia said. 'Went walkabout one day, by all accounts, and never came back. Ask her some time, why don't you? I'd love to know what really happened.'

Frank smiled. 'Just as an interested bystander, of course.'

'Of course,' Sylvia retorted, feigning innocence. 'It's not up to me to make judgements.'

'That's true,' Donald said lightly. He sat on the arm of

81

the settee and picked up the paper. 'By the way, Frank, you've got a reprieve. We're not putting you into solitary for the next couple of days after all.'

Frank looked at him, puzzled. 'What do you mean?'

'Syl's not going to Dublin with me after all.'

Frank shot a look at Sylvia.

'No,' she said, 'I've cried off.'

'At the last minute?' Frank said. He wasn't sure if the news pleased him or not. His ambivalence about their relationship seemed to get stronger every day. 'Why?'

'It's reunion time,' Donald said, smiling fondly at his wife. 'You're going to have company.'

'I had a telephone call this morning,' Sylvia told Frank. 'It was from an old friend of mine. My best friend, really. I've known her for years.' She glanced at Donald. 'She came to our wedding, didn't she?'

Donald nodded. 'Yes. And she's quite something. If you can take the Australian accent.'

'She married an Australian,' Sylvia explained. 'Been out there for quite a while. But she and her husband are in London at the moment. Just for four days. They've stopped over on their way back from New York. She was very disappointed when I told her I was going away and I'd so like to see her again, too. And Donald doesn't mind. He's glad to get me off his back, I think.' She looked across at Donald, who was reading the newspaper. 'Isn't that true, Donald?'

Donald looked up vaguely. 'What?'

With overdone patience Sylvia said, 'You're glad to get me off your back, aren't you?'

'At least I won't feel guilty about neglecting you,' Donald replied.

Frank was staring at Sylvia. 'Your friend,' he said, 'she's coming here, is she?'

'Yes, she's driving up tomorrow.' Sylvia's eyes weren't quite meeting Frank's. 'I did offer to go down to London, but she's never seen this part of the country and she said she'd like to.'

'Is her husband coming too?'

Sylvia shook her head. 'No, unfortunately he can't get away. I gather he's going to be up to his eyes in work.'

Frank was still staring at her.

'Excuse me,' Sylvia said, getting up. 'I must start doing something about dinner.' She went through to the kitchen.

Donald stood up and offered Frank a refill.

'A small one,' Frank said. They moved to the drinks trolley.

'Going back to what we were talking about a minute or two ago,' Donald said as he poured the drinks, 'you know the thing that interested me most about Banner's will?'

'What?'

'That bit about Lower Common, the piece of land he's left his sister. Just recently, that acreage has come up in conversation a couple of times at CorVol.' He handed Frank his glass. 'It's the ideal site for a new factory we're thinking of building.'

'Oh, really?' Frank looked surprised. 'You're expanding. I got the impression from you that CorVol might pull out of Micklethorpe altogether.'

Only if the grass was greener elsewhere,' Donald said. 'And certainly not if we managed to buy that land. But we were under the impression, from its name, that it was a public common. It's certainly used that way.'

'What's so attractive about it?' Frank asked him,

'It's right on the river and we need lots of water for cooling purposes in a particular process of ours. And I mean lots.'

'That might not go down too well with the locals,' Frank said dubiously. 'The conservationists wouldn't like it. And you wouldn't be too popular with the big landowners, either. Not if you interfered with the trout fishing.'

'Oh, we're used to opposition. And there are generally

ways of working round any objections – or overcoming them. Especially these days, with unemployment so high.' Donald sipped his drink thoughtfully. 'It's a very interesting development. An entirely new departure for CorVol. I've got a copy of the architect's sketch plans in the study. I'll show you.' He put down his glass and went through to the hall.

Frank turned and went to the door of the kitchen. Sylvia was slicing a tomato. She looked up.

'I must say you don't seem very pleased,' she pouted.

'It's a very elaborate lie, isn't it?' Frank said coldly.

'Had to be something out of the blue,' she replied, shrugging. 'It was the best I could come up with.'

'Why bother?' Frank was almost whispering. 'You said yourself that you'd insisted on going to Dublin with him.'

'I did.' She smiled. 'But that was arranged before you walked back into my life. Now I've got better things to do.'

Frank shook his head. 'I should've moved on that first day.'

Sylvia's eyes hardened a fraction. 'Probably,' she said. 'But you didn't, did you? I wonder why?'

Donald came back from the study, carrying the rolled plans. He crossed to the dining table with them.

'Frank's having a fit of conscience,' Sylvia called through to him. Frank glared at her, startled.

Donald was spreading the plans on the table. 'Oh? What about?'

'You tell him,' Sylvia said to Frank. Her face was challenging, mischievous.

Frank stared at her for several seconds. He started to say something, but Sylvia spoke first.

'He meant to buy some wine on the way home, but he forgot.'

Donald came across, laughing. 'You're joking,' he said. 'You're not really worried about that, are you, Frank. We've got plenty of wine in.'

'Yes, I know,' Frank said lamely. His eyes flickered

84

momentarily to Sylvia. 'But this was to be a contribution from me. It seemed like a good idea.'

'Some other time them, if you feel you must.' He slapped Frank's shoulder and started moving back to the dining table. 'But it really isn't necessary. What's mine is yours.'

A small, triumphant smile curled Sylvia's lips. 'Feel better?' she said to Frank.

He turned away and followed Donald.

The plans covered the entire table. Donald bent down over them, tracing the lines with his finger. 'Now these are only first thoughts, of course,' he said to Frank, 'but they'll give you a general idea of the overall concept . . .'

Frank nodded, as if he were listening. His heart rate hadn't settled to normal yet. For one desperate moment he had believed Sylvia was forcing it all into the open. She hadn't, but she had shown him she was capable of doing it. Frank had glimpsed a hard core of ruthlessness in her little joke.

'It would be a light industrial complex,' Donald was saying, 'totally integrated into a rural environment and enhancing rather than detracting from it . . .'

The uneasiness in Frank would dog him right through the evening; he knew that and he knew Sylvia would detect it. He suddenly thought of the two days they would be alone in the house together. The prospect of that made the uneasiness rather worse. He would have to do something. He would have to stop going with the tide. He folded his arms and sighed quietly to himself, frowning and trying to concentrate on what Donald was telling him.

On Saturday, while Sylvia was at the airport seeing Donald off to Dublin, Frank called on Miss Banner. They discussed that week's edition of *The Messenger*, and inevitably Frank had to mention the strength of local reaction to the item about John Wesley's will.

He was standing at the sitting room window, looking out

at the garden. Miss Banner was in her chair, her hands resting in her lap.

'It's caused something of a stir,' Frank said. 'Muddied the waters somewhat.'

'Has it?' Miss Banner sounded mildly surprised.

Frank turned and faced her. 'You must have known it would.'

'My brother made his money out of Wrathdale,' she said bluntly. 'Only right that Wrathdale should know where it's gone.'

'There's a lot of gossip,' Frank said.

'I dare say. Folk are like that. Hurtful. With truth or lies.' Miss Banner said it with a finality that Frank now recognized. The matter was dismissed. She clasped her hands and looked at him levelly. 'Have you read my piece?'

'Yes. It's good.'

'It'll be read.'

'I made one or two small changes when I typed it,' Frank said. 'Just to tidy it up.'

Miss Banner made one slow nod of the head. 'You've the right.'

'And I've changed the title, too. I'm calling it "Wrathdale Remembered".'

'If that's what you want.'

'By Chronicler', Frank added. 'That's the pen name I chose.'

Again, Miss Banner nodded. 'That'll do.'

Turning to the window again, Frank remarked casually that perhaps Miss Banner's piece could become a regular feature.

'If you think so,' she said quietly.

'Oh,' he murmured, 'that'll be up to the new editor.'

'You've a while to go yet.'

Frank turned to her, shaking his head. 'Only two weeks.'

Miss Banner regarded him for a moment in silence. 'You said you'd stay until I found someone.'

86

'I said I'd stay for a month.'

'Until I've found someone,' Miss Banner said stubbornly. 'That's my understanding.'

'We agreed on a month,' Frank insisted, coming across and standing in front of her chair. 'Are you looking for someone?'

Miss Banner looked at her hands. 'It's not easy, finding someone who's right.'

'Well, there's not much time left.'

She looked up. 'You fit in nicely.'

'I've other things to do.'

'So you said.' The steadiness of the old woman's eyes was slightly unnerving. 'Have you not done with running?'

He frowned at her. 'What's that supposed to mean?'

'You can't run from yourself, you know.'

'I'm not running from anything,' Frank snapped.

'Are you not?' The eyes seemed to look beyond his stance, beyond the image of himself he projected.

'No,' he said. He was finding it almost impossible to look at her now.

'If you were running,' Miss Banner said reflectively, 'Wrathdale's maybe the place to stop for a breath.'

'Just two more weeks. I can't stay any longer.'

'Why?'

'There are reasons.'

'There always will be. Anywhere.' Miss Banner's voice was stern. 'You make them yourself.'

'If you say so.' Frank buttoned his jacket, preparing to leave.

'I'm right. You know it.'

'Two more weeks,' Frank muttered. 'And that's it.'

'Until I've found someone,' Miss Banner insisted. 'That's what you said.'

'All right then!' Frank was suddenly angry. 'Until you find someone!' He stamped across the door and opened it. 'So long as it doesn't take more than a fortnight!' He went out, shutting the door firmly.

Miss Banner remained where she was, unperturbed, looking towards the window.

That night Frank made long, intense love to Sylvia, meeting her hunger with the driving energy of his own physical need and a deeper, urgent craving to discharge the tensions that were accumulating in him.

When it was over he lay staring at the ceiling, feeling Sylvia's warm nakedness beside him under the covers.

'How are you going to explain your friend not turning up?' he asked. 'Or did she?'

'No,' Sylvia said dreamily. 'She couldn't make it in the end. Sad, isn't it? A migraine, perhaps. Or a family problem. I'll think of something convincing.'

'I don't doubt it.'

She nudged him. 'You're not complaining, are you? Two days and nights together. That was too good to be missed. And you're glad I didn't go, aren't you?' Her fingers trailed along his leg.

'Seems like it.'

Sylvia turned towards Frank, raising herself on one elbow and looking down at him. 'God, I'm going to miss you, Frank Scully! And not just for this, either, damn you.'

Frank squinted up at her. 'Then it's just as well I'm moving on,' he said.

'Do you really have to?'

He sighed. 'You're the second person to ask me that today. Miss Banner wants me to stay, too.'

'So there you are, then.' Sylvia brought her knee up slowly across his legs. 'You'd have a job. And me. What more do you want?'

Frank made a show of thinking it over. 'Self-respect?' he said finally.

'That's a luxury item. Sorry, can't help you.'

'If I did stay, I'd have to move out of here.'

'Of course.' She stroked his face. 'You'd need a place of your own. Just so long as you were around.'

Frank shook his head. 'It wouldn't work. Any of it.'

'We'd work,' Sylvia breathed. 'You know that. We always have.' She brought her face very close to his. 'And just in case you need convincing . . .'

She kissed him and her hand crept across his chest. At first Frank didn't respond, but gradually, as Sylvia went on kissing him and her hand caressed him more intimately, he found himself being slowly drawn in again, away from his misgivings, away from his determination to dictate his own course. He closed his arms around Sylvia and rolled over with her, letting himself slip.

Chapter Twelve

Jack Hennessey had an open, friendly face and a confident way of conducting himself. He was thirty-five, an age he believed to be ideal. A man was entitled to be taken seriously in his mid-thirties; at the same time he could display all the vigour and energy of youth. That thought was firmly to the fore as he pressed the bell-push on the front door of Ravensfell House.

His confidence slipped a little as the door opened and the old woman stood facing him. Her expression suggested he might be a trespasser. It also suggested she was quite capable of dealing with him if he was.

'Good morning,' Hennessey said, smiling valiantly. 'Miss Banner?'

She nodded.

'My name's Hennessey.' He waited for understanding to dawn, but it didn't. 'I wrote to you.'

'Did you?'

'Yes, some days ago as a matter of fact, but I didn't get a reply. As I had to be in the area today I thought I'd look in on you.'

Miss Banner moved back, silently instructing him to follow her. Hennessey stepped into the hall, nervously fingering the knot in his tie. When Miss Banner had closed the door he followed her into the sitting room. She didn't offer him a chair.

'Did you get my letter?' he asked. Miss Banner had positioned herself with her back towards the window, so that he had to squint to see her clearly.

'I may have done.'

'It was about the vacancy on *The Messenger*.'

'Oh yes.' Miss Banner's tone of voice didn't suggest she recalled the letter; it implied, rather, that Hennessey should explain himself further.

He cleared his throat. 'The job appeals to me very much.'

'Does it?'

'Yes, very much indeed.' Hennessey was beginning to flounder. 'I think I've got all the right qualifications. I'm with *The Echo* at the moment. Chief sub. Been with them five years.'

'And you're looking to better yourself, are you?'

'Well . . .' He had to clear his throat again. The woman made him feel like a schoolboy, a rather grubby one at that. 'I've not got a bad job now. *The Echo*'s a highly respected newspaper. But an editorship's what I'm after, and I think *The Messenger*'s just the kind of challenge I'm looking for.' He didn't seem to be making any impression on Miss Banner at all. 'I know the district well,' he added hopefully. 'I was born and brought up in this part of the world.'

Miss Banner shook her head slowly, like a solemn condemnation. 'Not in Wrathdale, you weren't.'

'Ah, no,' he said hastily. 'But very near by. Staithdale.'

'What gave you the idea that I need someone for *The Messenger*?'

'Well, *The Echo* ran a piece about Mr Banner's death and I just assumed . . .'

'I see.'

Hennessey had the distinct feeling he'd been rebuked for being so presumptuous. 'I'm not looking for a large salary,' he said.

'Are you not?'

'No.' He shifted his weight from one foot to the other. 'As I said in my letter, what attracts me to the job . . .'

'You've wasted your time,' Miss Banner interrupted him. 'I'm suited.'

Hennessey was truly surprised. 'You've found someone?'

'I was never looking. I've got an editor.'

'At the moment, yes. I realize that. But he's just standing in for now, I understand.'

'Oh? And who told you that?' Miss Banner demanded sternly.

'I can't remember now.' Hennessey knew it sounded too vague, too false. 'I heard it somewhere. Someone told me it was just a temporary arrangement.'

'Did they?' Miss Banner glared at him. 'Well, they told you wrong. There's nothing temporary about it. It's for as long as may be.'

Less than an hour later, Jack Hennessey was sitting in Lord Wrathdale's office at Aynsgill Lodge. He explained the outcome of his brief visit to Miss Banner, while Lewis sat behind his desk and listened carefully.

'She's just not interested,' Hennessey concluded.

'Well,' Lewis sighed, 'you did your best. As I said, it would only have been for a few months. Six at most. Then you'd have been free to take up that job in London. Still.' He smiled at Hennessey. 'You won't have to wait now.'

Hennessey looked crestfallen. 'I'm not sure I should take it now,' he said. 'After all, I didn't keep my side of the bargain.'

'You were willing to and you tried,' Lewis pointed out. 'I can't ask for more than that.'

'Well, that's very fair of you, Lord Wrathdale.' Hennessey stood up. 'And I do appreciate you putting me up for the London job.'

Lewis came round the desk and shook his hand. 'Believe me, I wouldn't have done if I didn't think you could handle it.' Crossing to the door with Hennessey he said, 'You're sure Miss Banner was adamant about the present editor staying on?'

'Absolutely,' Hennessey said. 'As far as she's concerned, he's a permanent fixture.'

'Really.' Lewis held open the door for Hennessey and

watched the man leave. When he had closed the door again and gone back to his desk, he sat and stared at the wall for several minutes, deeply preoccupied over Mr Frank Scully. It was hard to be dispassionate about the new editor of *The Messenger*; apart from any other consideration, he was probably the only other person around Wrathdale who knew about Lewis and Fiona Neave.

Chapter Thirteen

Tuesday morning was the official opening of the Wrathdale Arts and Crafts Centre. It was a new building, set in attractive, sloping grounds on the northern outskirts of Micklethorpe. Attendance at the event was by invitation, but the customary contingent of gatecrashers and freeloaders had turned up in plenty of time to enjoy the exhibits and the free food and drink.

By eleven o'clock most of the church and civic dignitaries had arrived to mingle with the leading and lesser lights of the artistic community. Lord and Lady Wrathdale were there as principal guests, circulating in the company of the mayor, his wife and a handful of councillors.

Fiona Neave's presence at the event was less conspicuous. She stayed close to the wall-mounted exhibits, speaking to other guests only when they spoke to her, and occasionally casting discreet glances in Lewis's direction. From time to time she watched Frank Scully, too. He was wandering round the building with his battered Nikon slung around his neck, taking pictures and occasionally scribbling down notes.

At 11.15 Mrs Dace, the chairman of the Arts Centre Committee, called for order. People immediately grabbed extra glasses of sherry from the waitresses, then gathered near the centre of the main exhibition room to hear the inevitable speeches.

Mrs Dace spoke of the six long years of hard work and occasional struggle by determined people to make the Centre a reality. There had been doubts, she said, disappointments and even despair; at one time she had personally feared that if the place ever did open, it would be as a memorial to herself and the others who had first proposed its creation.

In conclusion, Mrs Dace declared herself delighted with the venture. There was just cause, she said, to celebrate. 'I now call on the man without whose encouragement, support and financial arm-twisting on our behalf this project would, despite all our efforts, have remained nothing more than a dream. Lord Wrathdale.'

There was loud and sustained applause as Lewis stepped forward. He looked around the gathering, being careful to pause and smile at the moment when Frank Scully photographed him.

His speech was neatly constructed to flatter, inform and be readily quotable. He said that the Centre provided an ideal setting where the people of Wrathdale, and visitors, could fully appreciate the wealth of local artistic achievement represented by the opening exhibition. He implied that the Centre would be no less than life-enhancing, in addition to providing strong encouragement for aspiring artists and craftsmen.

'If that is the case,' he concluded, 'then I know that you, Madam Chairman, and the members of your committee will be more than satisfied. Now, it is with the utmost pleasure that I declare the Wrathdale Arts and Crafts Centre well and truly open.'

Lewis stepped back to more ecstatic applause and shook hands with Mrs Dace.

The waitresses moved in with freshly charged trays of drinks as the guests began to circulate again. Fiona Neave detached herself gracefully from the edge of the throng and crossed to a side table laden with bowls of olives, nuts and other nibbles. She put down her empty glass and looked about her uncertainly. A waitress offered her another drink, but she declined.

'Hello, Mrs Neave.'

Fiona almost jumped at the closeness of the voice. She

turned and saw Frank Scully, helping himself to a Twiglet. 'Mr Scully,' she said, acknowledging him coolly.

'I didn't expect to see you here,' he said.

'Oh, really?'

Pointedly, Frank looked across to where Lewis was standing, still talking to Mrs Dace. Fiona followed the direction of his eyes. She frowned at him as he looked back at her.

'But then,' Frank said, grinning, 'your hobbies do get you about a bit, don't they?'

'I'm on the committee,' Fiona said stiffly.

'Well, that explains it, doesn't it? You'd have to be here, wouldn't you?' Frank glanced across to the opposite end of the room. 'Excuse me,' he murmured, 'I must get a picture of the mayor. He collects them.'

Lewis saw Frank move away from Fiona. He immediately excused himself to Mrs Dace and began crossing the room, not too quickly, collecting two fresh glasses of sherry on the way. He took a zig-zagging route, nodding to people and smiling, then when he was close enough he went up to Fiona. He addressed her brightly in a voice that was loud enough for the others nearby to hear, if they chose.

'Mrs Neave! How nice to see you. You're well, I hope?'

'Yes, thank you,' Fiona said just as brightly, then in a lower, barely audible voice she said, 'Hello, Lewis.'

Maintaining the charade, Lewis said, 'Would you like a sherry?'

'Thank you.' Fiona took the glass he offered her.

Lewis was beaming, as if he could scarcely contain his delight. 'You and the other committee members really are to be congratulated,' he said, still using his public-address voice. 'Quite apart from anything else, you made an excellent choice for the first exhibition.' He pointed to a framed oil painting near the door, where nobody else was standing. 'I'm particularly taken with this landscape.'

They moved to the spot together and stood side by side, studying the picture.

Softly, without taking his eyes from the canvas, Lewis said, 'Are you really all right?'

'Yes, I'm fine.'

'Have there been any more adverse reactions to that wretched will business?'

Fiona glanced cautiously to either side before she spoke. 'As far as I know,' she said, 'nobody's planning on running me out of town. And I haven't been denounced from any pulpit yet.' She raised a hand and pointed, as if she were discussing a particular feature of the painting. 'But you were right, of course. The majority verdict is that I was John Wesley Banner's mistress. I'm not giving that money away, Lewis. Having it's the only consolation.' She smiled tightly. 'Do you know, I've even had a veiled hint from one member of the Rotary Club that he'd be only too willing to come to a similar arrangement to John Wesley's.'

Lewis glanced at her for a moment, shocked. 'You're not serious!'

'Very. And so was he, I think.'

'My God. What did you say?'

'I told him you weren't into sharing.'

Lewis almost choked on his sherry. When he had settled himself, he murmured, 'I'm putting in a bid for *The Messenger* next week, ostensibly on behalf of a friend. Your name won't be mentioned.'

Fiona sighed. 'As things stand, Miss Banner certainly wouldn't sell it to me and that's for sure.'

'She might not be interested in selling it to anyone.'

'Yes,' Fiona nodded, 'that's a possibility, I suppose.'

'In which case,' Lewis said, moving closer, 'it would be helpful if you were to drop a broad hint to Scully that you're not at all keen to renew the printing contract when it runs out. If that happened, there's only one other place around here that's equipped to take on that kind of work.

The Echo. And I doubt if they'd be very eager to saddle themselves with it. What's more, their printing works is forty miles from here. And that's not viable.'

Fiona gave him a worried look. 'I'm not sure I could do that, Lewis. It would be taking unfair advantage.'

'It may not be necessary, but if it is, well . . .' Lewis shrugged. 'That's what business is all about.'

Fiona wasn't convinced. 'Let's talk about it on Thursday,' she murmured.

'Thursday's off, I'm afraid. I can't make it.' He glanced at Fiona uneasily. 'Something's come up.'

Fiona swung round angrily, facing him.

'Hello, Mrs Neave,' a pleasant female voice said.

Lewis turned smoothly, meeting his wife with a smile. It took Fiona a few seconds to compose herself.

'I'm sorry to butt in,' Beattie said, moving closer.

'Nonsense,' Lewis said. 'You're not butting in at all. Mrs Neave and I were just admiring this picture.'

Still a little flustered, Fiona touched her hair and forced a smile. Her eyes, she knew, were betraying the way she really felt. But Beattie didn't appear to notice anything out of place.

'I'm so glad you're here,' she said to Fiona. 'I've been meaning to give you a ring.'

Fiona swallowed. 'Oh?'

'Yes, it seems ages since I last saw you. And you and I have got to have a chat.' She paused, looking squarely at Fiona. 'It's long overdue.'

Fiona could feel her face tensing. Lewis was glancing nervously around the room.

'A chat?' Fiona said. 'Well, of course, Lady Wrathdale. Any time.' She couldn't stop her eyes flicking to Lewis for an instant. 'About something in particular?'

Beattie smiled. 'About this year's Aynsgill Meet. I want your advice on what the theme should be. You will help me out, won't you?'

'If . . . if you really think I can,' Fiona stammered.

'I'm sure of it. Your idea was such a success last year. You must come up to the lodge for dinner one evening very soon.' Beattie turned to her husband. 'We'd like that, wouldn't we, Lewis?'

The relief was visible on Lewis's face. 'Very much,' he said.

'How are you fixed for this week?' Beattie asked Fiona. 'Not Thursday, though. Lewis is away on Thursday, aren't you, Lewis?'

'Unfortunately,' he said gruffly.

'Any other evening, though,' Beattie assured Fiona. 'Friday, perhaps?'

The encounter was putting too much strain on Fiona's powers of pretence. 'This week's a bit difficult,' she said. 'I'm rather tied up. Maybe next. Would that be all right?'

Beattie said that would be fine. 'See how you're fixed then give me a call and we'll arrange something.'

'Yes, I'll do that.' Oddly, speaking to Beattie had produced the same effect on Fiona as the kerbside run-in she'd had a few days earlier with Mrs Rawlings. The two women couldn't have been more different, but the sense of threat was identical. Guilt, Fiona thought; her sense of guilt was turning on her, making her imagine something that wasn't there.

'Everything all right at the gatehouse?' Beattie asked.

Fiona nodded, perhaps too firmly. 'Fine.'

Beattie inclined her head, smiling at Fiona. 'You know,' she said, 'I've often thought, on those evenings when I've been on my own, that maybe I'd just stroll across the park and drop in on you and say hello.'

'You should,' Fiona said, hoping she wasn't looking as stricken as she felt. 'That would be nice.'

'Well, one of these evenings I might just do that and surprise you.'

'Good,' Fiona said. 'I'll give you a call then.' She managed a smile. 'Excuse me.' She turned and walked off, pushing her way through a group of people by the door.

Lewis and Beattie watched her go. 'Such a charming woman,' Lewis said to his wife, warily checking her reaction.

'Yes, she is,' Beattie agreed. Thoughtfully, she added, 'And I just don't believe what they're saying about her.'

Frank Scully was at a table on the other side of the room, packing his camera bag. He was talking to David Gibbs, a local schoolteacher. David had written to Frank the previous week, asking if there was anything in the old files at *The Messenger* that might be suitable for dramatizing for the school play. Frank hadn't found time to reply, but now he was discussing the request with David.

'Ideally,' David was saying, 'the item we want would be something tied into an historical event. The kids like that. And keeping it local, they relate to it better. Last year Mr Banner came up with a story about a strike at the old lead mines.'

Frank was nodding, trying to think of something suitable. He had spent a few hours with the files, on and off, but most of the material he could remember had been too trivial to turn into a play, even a one-acter. While he was thinking, he caught sight of Fiona Neave leaving the building. She didn't look at all happy.

'I'm sorry,' Frank said to David Gibbs, finally. 'I can't help you – not off the top of my head, anyway. I'm not really up on local history. I'm a foreigner.'

'Me too,' David said. 'Lincoln.'

Frank did up the buckles on the bag and lifted it off the table. 'At least you're from the north of the Wash,' he said. 'That has to be an advantage. You probably even speak the language.'

David laughed. 'Do you like it round here?'

'Yes, as a matter of fact I do. By and large.'

'Are you thinking of staying on?'

Frank smiled at him. 'It's been suggested.'

'Why not, then?'

'It's not that simple.' Frank began moving towards the door. 'You're welcome to come down and have a look through the file copies of the paper yourself. Or there's the local guide book. Bound to be snippets in that.' He looked at his watch. 'It's time I was off.'

'And me. Back to school.'

They walked out into the car park together. On the way across to his Marina, Frank had an idea. He turned to David. 'This item you're after, does it have to be historical. I mean, you know, from way back?'

'Not necessarily. Why?'

They reached the Marina and Frank put his bag in the boot. He leaned on the side of the car and folded his arms. 'I might have something for you, after all. A sort of local parable. A tale with a moral in it. How would that suit?'

David nodded. 'It sounds promising. What do you have in mind?'

'Well,' Frank said, 'I'm starting a new feature in *The Messenger* this week. "Wrathdale Remembered". Nothing more than fifty years back I wouldn't think, any of it. But the first story is quite a good one. Charming's the word, I think. I quite like it anyway. It's most likely apocryphal, but it'd go down well with the managers of a Church of England school, I'd say.'

David looked fascinated. 'What's it about?'

'Apparently it happened just after the war.'

'Well,' David said, 'that's history as far as Junior Four are concerned. And me, for that matter.'

Frank told him the story. It concerned two farmers from the dale who, from their earliest days, had been great rivals. Each tried to better the other at everything – farming, sport, drinking. At one time, they were both even chasing the same girl.

When the time came for one of the annual livestock and agricultural shows, one of the rivals discovered that his prize ram had disappeared. He was convinced the other man had stolen it, to keep him from winning the contest. But he had no way of proving it. Late at night, drunk and angry, he sneaked into the other fellow's farm and set fire to the barn. The weather was dry and warm and the building soon burned to the ground. It seemed to the farmer, in his intoxicated state, that he had exacted a fitting and justifiable revenge.

By the time he got home he had sobered up considerably, but he still felt pleased with what he had done. Then his wife told him that his rival had called at the house earlier to say that he had found the ram up on the dale, stuck in a hole between some rocks. It had obviously broken loose, as rams often do, and run off in the hills and fallen into the hole.

The rival had left a message with the farmer's wife. 'Tell Dick not to worry,' he had said. 'The animal's all right. He can pick it up in the morning. It's locked up snug and safe in my barn.'

David Gibbs was enthusiastic. 'I like it,' he told Frank. 'I like it very much.'

Frank went to the driver's door and opened it. 'You'd probably need to pad it out. Add some more characters, maybe.'

David nodded. 'It's certainly got possibilities. But what about copyright? Who wrote it?'

'Don't worry about that,' Frank told him. 'I'm sure I can get permission to use it if it's right for you.'

'I'd like to read it. It's in this week's edition, is it?'

Frank got into the car and started the engine. 'Yes, but if you want I could let you have a proof copy later today. Drop into the shop later, I'll leave one there for you.' He waved to David Gibbs and drove off.

Before he reached the end of the road, Frank had forgotten about the story. Instead, he was thinking about Fiona Neave. He was wondering, in particular, what had happened at the opening of the Centre to make her go frowning off like that, as if she had inherited somebody else's woes on top of all her own.

Chapter Fourteen

Alec Metcalfe was in the lounge bar of the pub on High Street, holding forth to a group of his cronies. He was a fleshy, affable man, a local councillor who owned a builders' merchants firm in Micklethorpe and was successful enough to command an audience whenever he wanted one.

Alec had just reached the conclusion of a long, hilarious yarn about a fisherman friend. His listeners were roaring with laughter when Reuben Flaxman came into the lounge. He spotted Alec and made his way across to him.

'Now then, Reuben,' Alec greeted him.

'Mr Metcalfe,' Reuben mumbled, nodding to Alec and his companions. He touched Alec's arm, a small gesture of urgency. 'Can I have a word? In private?'

'Of course,' Alec said. He led Reuben to the far end of the bar and leaned there, mildly intrigued. Reuben looked agitated, but then there was always some unsettled expression or other sitting on that broad face.

'I came looking for you over the weekend,' Reuben said.

'Me and the wife were down south,' Alec told him. He nodded at the beer pumps. 'Will you have a drink?'

'No, I'm not stopping.' Reuben took a folded sheet of proof paper from his pocket. 'I brought you this.' He handed it to Alec.

Bewildered, Alec took it. 'What is it?'

'That's going in *The Messenger* this week,' Reuben said, keeping his voice low. 'I thought you ought to read it now, though, seeing that you're Jack Jefford's brother-in-law.' He sighed heavily. 'Maybe there's something you can do about it between you. There's nowt I can.' He glanced across at the others. 'And I was never here, mind.' He nodded a curt farewell and left.

Alec stared at the folded paper in his hand, looking more intrigued now and faintly concerned. He unfolded the proof and started to read it.

Jack Jefford was supervising two men who were repairing the dry stone wall that formed the boundary along the west side of his land. Jefford was a big, florid-faced man in his early sixties, a farmer who had prospered from hard work and aggressive dealing. As he watched the workmen he issued a steady stream of instructions, even though they knew exactly what they were doing. It was Jack Jefford's principle to assert his authority at all times, even when there was no need.

As he was climbing over to the roadside after inspecting the support stones on the inner side of the wall, he saw his brother-in-law's Land Rover approach and draw up a few yards away. Jack wiped his hands on the knees of his trousers and started walking towards the car. When he drew level, Alec Metcalfe wound down the window.

'Hello, Alec. What brings you out this way again?' They had spent some time together earlier in the day, talking over Jack's imminent election to the council.

'Get in,' Alec snapped. He looked grim.

Jack peered in at him. 'What's up?'

'Just get in.'

Jack went round to the other side and climbed into the passenger seat. He shut the door and looked at Alec. 'Well? What is it?'

Alec handed him the proof he had been given by Reuben Flaxman. 'Read that,' he said.

Jack opened the sheet and looked at it, bemused. '"Wrathdale Remembered",' he read aloud. '"The Rivals."' He pulled a face and thrust the proof back at Alec. 'I haven't got time for that,' he grunted. 'I've work to do.'

'Read it!' Alec said sharply.

Reluctantly, Jack took back the paper. He started to read it. Alec watched him and saw the change come over his brother-in-law's face. After a minute Jack looked up.

'Oh, my God,' he groaned.

'Aye,' Alec sighed.

'Where the hell did this come from?'

'Reuben Flaxman gave me it. It's going in this week's *Messenger*.'

'What?' Jack had turned white. 'But they can't . . .'

'I don't see why not,' Alec said.

Jack leaned back, staring sightlessly through the windscreen. 'There must be something we can do.' He sounded almost desperate.

Alec shook his head. 'What do you suggest? We go to this fellow Scully and tell him he can't print that. Likely he'd ask why. And then what do we say?'

Jack stared down at the paper as if someone had fouled it. 'Whoever wrote it, where did they get it from? Who is this Chronicler?'

'God knows.' Alec leaned close to Jack for a moment, studying his face. 'Who did you ever tell about it? Apart from me?'

'No one.'

'Not even Irene?' Alec's sister had been married to Jack Jefford for over thirty years.

Jack gaped at him. 'Don't be bloody daft! I'd no reason to tell *her*. Anyhow, you're not suggesting she wrote this, are you?'

'Of course not.'

Jack's eyes narrowed. 'Have you ever said anything to anyone?'

'Oh, yes, I'm likely to have, aren't I?' he said scathingly. 'Concealment. They can put you away for that, you know.'

'Then maybe it's just coincidence.' Jack sounded eager to believe that.

'Maybe,' Alec mumbled.

'And we're getting steamed up about nothing. Maybe folk'll not connect it.'

Alec was looking at him pityingly. 'Reuben Flaxman did. And so will a good few others.'

Jack was shaking his head, not wanting to accept what was obvious. 'But this is about . . .'

'It's as like the truth as makes no difference,' Alec said flatly.

'But I didn't burn down Ted Watkins' barn with one of my own rams in it!'

'More's the pity,' Alec said, watching the first lines of despair deepen around his brother-in-law's eyes.

Frank Scully was at the table by the window in his office, sorting through the photographs he had taken at the opening of the Arts and Crafts Centre. He heard the door behind him open softly and he turned. Sylvia Harper had come in.

'Hello, darling,' she said.

She went to Frank and raised her arms, ready to put them around him. He sidestepped her and went to the door and closed it.

'You don't seem exactly overjoyed to see me,' Sylvia pouted.

'I'm sorry. It's a busy day. Is there something I can do for you?'

'Yes, I'm looking for a lift home. My car's in for a service.' She crossed to where Frank was standing.

'You'll have to hang on a bit.'

'Not too long I hope.' She put her arms around his neck. 'We'll be on our own until eight-thirty.' She kissed him, working her lips sinuously on his. Frank was slow to respond and he broke the embrace after a few seconds. As he eased away, he noticed an attractive diamond brooch on Sylvia's jacket lapel. It was shaped like a shamrock.

'Do you like it?' Sylvia asked.

'Very nice.'

'Donald brought it back for me from Dublin.'

Frank nodded, going over to the table again. 'What is it? A good-conduct medal?'

Sylvia laughed. As Frank started going through the photographs again she began wandering round the office. She stopped in front of the framed picture of John Wesley Banner and studied it.

'Did you know,' she said, 'that man once named a woman an adultress to her face, in front of the whole chapel congregation?'

Frank glanced over his shoulder at her. 'It doesn't surprise me. But I shouldn't worry about it, if I were you. He's dead. And anyway, you're not a Methodist.'

Sylvia went on gazing at the picture. 'Sanctimonious old sod. And those eyes! They're a real turn-off. They give me the shudders. I say Fiona Neave deserved every penny of the fifty thousand she got out of him.'

She moved to the desk, casually examining the clutter, then she noticed a bundle of estate agents' brochures on top of the overflowing in-tray. She picked them up and leafed through them. 'House hunting?' she enquired archly.

Frank turned, cursing himself. He had forgotten the brochures were on display. He went across to the desk. 'I'm thinking about it,' he admitted. 'It's quite an attractive idea. And it's what you want, isn't it?'

'Yes, of course,' Sylvia said. 'So long as I'm the attraction. But if you're thinking of moving out . . .'

'It's not on, Sylvia. If I stay I couldn't continue living with you and Donald. Not when you and I are . . .'

'Carrying on, as they say,' she prompted him, smiling. 'That's such a lovely expression. Typically English.' She moved closer to Frank. 'We only picked up where we left off.'

'Well, we couldn't continue that way. Not right under Donald's nose. Not in his house.'

'Oh, I don't see why not,' Sylvia said airily. 'It adds something, don't you think? A little spice?'

'My God, you're incredible.' There were times when she genuinely shocked Frank. 'Don't you have any shame?'

'I gave it up. Years ago. And don't tell me that you're suddenly getting a conscience.'

'What makes you think I haven't had one up to now?' Frank asked her.

'Because,' she replied levelly, 'it hasn't been all that noticeable.' She glanced at the brochures again. 'Still, I suppose you having a place of your own might have some advantages.' She smiled. 'It'd be a change of scene, at least.' She made to put her arms around Frank again but he backed off.

'I've got to take some pictures down to Tom for block making,' he said.

'And then you're finished?'

'More or less.' He went back to the table and picked up the pictures he had selected, then went to the door.

'Don't be too long,' Sylvia said. 'Time's awasting.'

Frank went out and Sylvia turned her attention to the house details again, examining them critically.

The Jeffords' kitchen, like most other farmhouse kitchens in the region, was the hub of the house. It was practical and comfortable; its furnishings and fittings reflected Jack Jefford's success.

The colour television set in the corner was switched on, but nobody was watching it. At one end of the long table Irene Jefford was working on some dress material. There was no need for her to economize by making her own clothes, Jack had told her that plenty of times. Just as many times, Irene had told him that she enjoyed dressmaking. It had nothing to do with economizing.

At the other end of the table Jack was going through the motions of cleaning his rifle. Twice in ten minutes he had laid the gun down and stared off into space. Now, as he did it a third time, Irene glanced at him.

'You all right, Jack?'

Her voice snapped Jack out of his reverie. 'What?'

Irene was an intelligent, down-to-earth woman. It showed in her clear eyes and in the firm set of her mouth. Nothing much ever escaped her. 'Something troubling you, is there?'

'No,' Jack said irritably. 'Nothing. What makes you think there is?'

'Well, you've not said more than a dozen words since you got home. And you look a bit off colour.'

Scowling, Jack stood up and threw his cleaning rag on the table. 'I'm perfectly all right!' he shouted at his wife. 'If I've stayed quiet it's because I've got nothing to say! Just leave me in bloody peace, woman!' He turned around and stormed out into the hallway, slamming the door behind him.

Donald Harper got home shortly after eight-thirty. Sylvia was laying the table for dinner and in the sitting room Frank was standing with a glass in one hand and a record sleeve in the other, listening to an Errol Garner record he had just put on.

'On your feet!' Donald called, coming in through the kitchen. 'The lord and master's home!'

'Worn out, no doubt,' Sylvia said, pecking him on the cheek as he paused by the dining table.

'Well, I wouldn't say no to a fairly stiff drink.'

Sylvia preceded Donald into the sitting room and went to the drinks trolley to pour him a whisky. Donald tossed his briefcase on to the settee. He nodded to Frank.

'Keeping you at it, are they?' Frank asked.

'It's this conference that's coming up. There's a hell of a lot to be done.'

Frank moved to turn down the volume of the music.

'No, leave it,' Donald told him. He dropped into an armchair, looking genuinely exhausted. Sylvia brought him his drink and he sipped it. 'Been in long?' he asked Frank.

'Ages,' Sylvia said. 'Both of us. And we're worn out, too.'

'What have you been doing, then?'

'Screwing,' Sylvia said. 'We only got out of bed ten minutes ago.'

Donald laughed but Frank's face stiffened. 'That's not funny, Sylvia!' he said sharply.

'She thinks it is,' Donald said.

'It was a damned stupid question,' Sylvia murmured. She leaned down to Donald and gave him another peck, on the forehead this time. 'What do you think we've been doing?'

'You've just told me.'

'Idiot! Oh, by the way, Frank's got some news for you.'

Frank stared at her blankly as she went back to laying the table.

'Oh, really?' Donald said. 'What is it?'

Frank shrugged. 'You tell me.'

'Oh, come on,' Sylvia said impatiently. Addressing Donald, she said, 'He's decided to stay on at *The Messenger*.'

'Have you?' Donald looked delighted.

'Apparently.' Frank crossed the room and perched himself on the arm of the settee.

'That's great. Good thinking. Have you told Miss Banner yet?'

'No, but I think she knows already, anyway.'

'Probably,' Donald said. 'It wouldn't surprise me.'

'He's looking for somewhere to live,' Sylvia said.

Donald put on a critical, disapproving face. 'Is he? Oh, I

111

see, we're not good enough for him now that he's got a regular job, is that it?'

'So it would seem,' Sylvia drawled.

'Seriously,' Donald said, 'you don't have to move out, you know.'

Frank nodded. 'I realize that. But this was only a temporary arrangement and . . .'

'Of course, I understand. You looking for something to rent or to buy?'

'To rent, ideally.'

Donald thought for a moment. 'That's not going to be easy,' he said. 'Rented accommodation's pretty thin on the ground in these parts. Most of it's for summer letting – there's a lot more money in it that way and no hassle about getting people out. I'll ask around at CorVol. See if anyone there knows of anything that's going.'

'Thanks,' Frank said.

'We'll miss him, won't we, Syl?' Donald said wistfully.

'He'll still be around,' she replied.

'Of course,' Donald murmured. 'Only maybe not quite so accessible.' After a pause, he said, 'And that's a shame, isn't it?'

Frank was vaguely disturbed by the remark. He glanced at Donald. His face betrayed nothing. He appeared to be absorbed in his glass. He took a sip from it and leaned back in his armchair, closing his eyes and relishing the taste of the whisky. Frank took a gulp from his own glass, swallowing it quickly, not bothering about the taste.

Chapter Fifteen

Fiona Neave was at the desk in her office, checking some figures with a calculator, when Frank Scully tapped the door and looked round the edge.

'May I?' he said.

'Yes, of course.'

Frank came in and closed the door. Instead of approaching the desk, as Fiona had expected, he went to the wall at the right and looked at a photograph hanging there. It was a study of a pair of curlews.

'This is new isn't it?'

'Not really,' Fiona told him. 'It's only just been framed, but I took it last summer.'

Frank stood back, gazing admiringly at the other prints on display. 'You're building up quite a collection.'

'Slowly,' Fiona said. 'What can I do for you, Mr Scully?'

He went to the desk, taking a small velvet-wrapped bundle from his pocket. He handed it to Fiona. 'I thought you might like to have this.'

She held it on her palm, hefting it, running her thumb across the soft texture of the cloth. 'What is it?'

'Take a look. It was in the safe upstairs.' he watched her as she slowly unfolded the velvet. 'It's really a part of old man Banner's estate, I suppose, but I don't imagine that anyone else would want it.'

Fiona uncovered the picture frame and held it between her hands, looking at the photograph of herself and John Wesley Banner. 'Good Lord!' she smiled. 'I remember this. It was taken at Wrathdale show about three years ago. Or was it four?' The smile faded. 'This was in the safe, you say?'

'That's right,' Frank said. 'Tucked away in a corner.'

Fiona put the picture down on the desk. 'What on earth was it doing in there? And why did John Wesley keep it, anyway? I didn't even know he had it.'

Frank pointed at the velvet wrapper. 'Lovingly preserved,' he murmured.

Fiona's face hardened. 'What are you suggesting?'

'That it obviously meant a great deal to him.' Frank's voice carried no other implication; neither did his face.

'If you're thinking what . . .'

'I'm not,' Frank cut in quickly. 'I never have.'

'Well, most of Wrathdale does.' Fiona looked down at the picture again. 'After that story you put in *The Messenger* about Banner's will . . .'

'I only reported the facts,' Frank said firmly.

Fiona looked at him. For the first time, Frank could see the full vulnerability behind her eyes. 'You must have realized the interpretation a good many people would put on those facts,' she said quietly.

It would have been easy and straightforward to issue a barrage of standard quotes from the ragbag called journalists' ethics; Frank thought, in the circumstances, that Fiona deserved a little more than that. 'There's no way you can stop readers from interpreting a news item any way they like, to suit their prejudices,' he said. His tone was almost regretful. 'They do it all the time.'

Fiona started to say something but stopped.

'You can't allow for it,' Frank said. 'And it doesn't alter the facts. No editor can be held responsible for dirty minds.'

Fiona was looking at him steadily. 'In this instance,' she said, 'it might have been fairer if you'd just taken them into account.'

'If you're looking for an apology, forget it. That's what the paper's all about, local news.' He paused, caught for an instant by the genuine hurt he could see. More gently, he

114

said, 'But I am sorry the way the story's been twisted. And I do owe you something for that.'

'Well,' Fiona sighed, 'I might just call that debt in some time.'

'I hope you will.' Frank crossed to the door and stood there, grasping the handle, looking at Fiona. 'What are you doing this evening?'

'Why?'

'Have dinner with me?'

Fiona shook her head. 'Sorry,' she said, sounding as if she meant it. 'Not tonight. I'm booked.'

Frank nodded and smiled wryly. 'Yes, of course. I understand.'

The softness that had edged into Fiona's manner vanished. She sat up stiffly in her chair and shot Frank a look of clear resentment. 'No, I don't think you do understand,' she said crisply. 'I'm going to a meeting of the Trades Association in Hunderston.'

Frank looked unconvinced. 'That sounds like fun,' he said, opening the door and going out.

Fiona looked at the picture curiously for a few minutes after Frank had gone. Finally, still looking puzzled, she slipped it into the desk drawer, together with the piece of velvet.

At eight o'clock that evening Frank came into the printing works and went to where the last two stringed bundles of the new edition of *The Messenger* were lying on the floor. Reuben Flaxman and Tom Holliday were by the door, getting out of their overalls. Frank's suggestions for speeding up production meant, now, that the men got home an hour earlier on Thursdays, and Tom was openly grateful. Reuben, on the other hand, had simply moaned about people coming along and upsetting his routine.

'This is the lot, then?' Frank said, hoisting the bundles.

'Yes, that's it, Mr Scully,' Tom said.

Frank crossed to the side door with the papers. 'I'll be on my way, then. Goodnight, Tom. 'Night, Mr Flaxman.'

'Goodnight,' Tom called out.

Reuben, reaching for his jacket, simply snorted. As the door closed behind Frank he glared at it. 'Smarmy bugger,' he growled.

The back of the Marina and the seat beside Frank were piled high with newspapers. He drove out on to High Street and turned right, feeling the engine drag. These delivery trips had taught him a few new things about driving. He had learned a lot about the effect of weight distribution on a car's suspension, too.

The first two deliveries were made inside thirty minutes. Now that he was familiar with the route, and with the techniques of jerk-lifting papers and throwing them into doorways instead of carrying them, Frank could complete deliveries in a third of the time it had taken him on that first night. He even took a mild pleasure in doing the job; it rounded-off and underscored his weekly achievement of getting an edition out and into the shops.

At nine-thirty, travelling along the bleak stretch of road between Brorston and Feltry with only one bundle of papers remaining on the back seat, Frank reduced speed as he spotted something up ahead. Drawing nearer, he saw it was a woman standing by a car, waving. He dropped the engine into bottom gear and pulled in opposite the other car. It was only when the woman stepped into the full beam of his headlights that Frank realized it was Fiona Neave.

He rolled down the window.

'Oh!' Fiona said, surprised. 'Hello.'

Frank grinned at her.

'It's not funny. There hasn't been another car along here for more than half an hour.'

Frank got out of the car. 'What's the trouble?'

He followed Fiona to her MGB. She went to the front

116

and pointed. The offside tyre was flat. There was a large gash in the tread.

Frank sighed. 'All right, then. Where's the spare wheel?'

Fiona looked at him sheepishly. 'It's being repaired,' she said.

Seeing that she looked cold and miserable, Frank resisted the temptation to laugh. Instead, he led her to his car and held the door open for her. 'I'll get you to a 'phone,' he said.

Ten minutes later, from an isolated telephone box, Fiona called her garage in Micklethorpe. They promised they would pick up the MGB in the morning. She went back and got into the Marina beside Frank.

'Tomorrow,' she said, 'first thing.'

'What about your meeting in Hunderston?' Frank asked her.

Fiona shrugged.

'I've only got one more delivery to make, then I'll run you there if you like and wait for you.'

'Well, that's very good of you, but . . .' Fiona looked at her watch. 'It's not really worth it now. I was late anyway and they finish at nine.' She smiled at Frank. 'Thanks all the same.'

'Think nothing of it.' Frank flipped his cigarette out of the window and started the engine. 'I hope you're hungry,' he said, grinning. 'I certainly am.'

He drove to the Swan Hotel, an establishment five miles from Micklethorpe where the standards of decor and cuisine were as high as the prices.

They were given a corner table in the opulent, soft carpeted dining room. For the first few minutes they said hardly anything to each other. It was a period of quiet transition; the delicate first phase of a friendship was crystallizing.

When they had each had some wine and were started on

117

the main course, Frank paused with his fork in the air for a moment, watching Fiona eat. She combined all the outward signs of a hearty appetite with an elegant, assured table manner. He found it strangely endearing.

'Is that good?' Frank asked her.

'It's delicious!' Fiona said enthusiastically. She put down her knife and fork and picked up her wine glass. She took a sip and looked around the room. 'This place is living up to its reputation. Frankly, I'm surprised we got in without a reservation. They're usually fully booked.'

'The power of the press,' Frank said.

'Oh. I see.' Fiona looked impressed.

Frank shook his head, smiling. 'It's not true. They'd just had a cancellation.'

Fiona laughed. For just a moment Frank saw a small girl in her, someone carefree, good-natured, totally happy with the world. In the same instant he acknowledged to himself that he could like this woman very much.

They ate in silence for a few more minutes, then Frank said, 'I gather you don't come from this part of the world. Originally, I mean.'

'No. But I was born not too far away. In Darlington.'

'Is your family still there?'

Fiona shook her head. 'Both my parents are dead. They were killed in a road accident eleven years ago.' Her eyes turned sad as she told him.

'I'm sorry,' Frank said.

'So am I.' Fiona looked down at her plate absently, as if the memory had temporarily made her forget what she was doing here.

'Brothers and sisters?' Frank asked brightly.

'No. I was an only child.' She looked at Frank. 'How about you?'

'Father, mother, two brothers and one sister. All alive and well as far as I know. I haven't seen any of them since God knows when.'

'That's a shame.'

'Maybe,' Frank said. He had some sad memories of his own. 'I don't think they'd agree with you.'

Fiona was studying him now, much the same way he had looked at her while she was eating. 'So how do you enjoy being with *The Messenger*?' she asked him.

'Very much. Enough to want to stay on. For a while, anyway.'

Fiona nodded. 'Yes. I thought you would.'

Frank was surprised that she should have thought that. 'Did you? Why?'

'Oh, I don't know.' She smiled, and Frank felt warmed by it. 'Intuition, maybe.' She moved a segment of meat thoughtfully with her fork. 'What if the newspaper changed hands? How would you feel about that?'

Frank sat back. 'Still thinking of buying it, are you?'

Fiona gave him a puzzled, slightly worried look.

'You as good as told me,' he reminded her. 'That day in your office.'

She remembered. 'That was before anyone knew that Miss Banner was planning on keeping it. It seemed like a good idea at the time.'

'But not now?'

'The question doesn't arise,' Fiona said. 'It's not for sale, as far as I know.' She was studying him again. 'But if it were, and I did buy it – would that bother you?'

Frank thought for a moment. 'I don't know,' he said. Then, with his eyes on hers, he murmured, 'Yes, I think it would.'

They both concentrated on their food again. After a while, without looking up, Frank asked, 'When are you going bird-watching again?'

Fiona put down her knife and fork and dabbed her lips with her napkin. 'Saturday,' she said, then waited until Frank looked up from his plate. 'Want to come?' she asked him.

Chapter Sixteen

Jack Jefford drove his Land Rover round to the back of the farmhouse and parked it by one of the outbuildings, as he did every day at lunchtime. He crossed the yard and went into the kitchen, wiping his boots on the mat by the doorway.

He saw Irene at once. She was sitting slumped in an armchair by the fireside with a crumpled copy of *The Messenger* in her lap.

Worried suddenly, Jack took a step towards her. 'Irene!'

She turned her head to him slowly. Her face was drawn and pale. 'It was you,' she said. She sounded stunned. 'All those years ago. It was you killed that man up at High Top Farm.'

Jack pretended he didn't understand what she meant. Irene held up the paper. He took it from her, scanning the lines he had read before on the newspaper proof.

'Don't be bloody daft, woman,' he blustered. 'This isn't about me, it's about . . .'

'I know it's about you, Jack.' Irene's voice was cold, certain. 'And so will other folk. It's about two fellows who grew up together in these parts and were great rivals.' She pushed herself up in the chair. 'That's how it was with you and Ted Watson. And you were great rivals, the pair of you . . .' She pointed at the paper Jack was holding between clenched, trembling hands. 'It tells in there about a race the two men had. I recall you and Ted had a race through the snow one winter. From pub to pub until you fell down dead drunk just a couple of paces in front of him and had to be carried home on a paling. That was common knowledge at the time and still is.'

Jack shook his head violently, as if he was trying to dislodge something. 'It's not about . . .'

'It's about how they were both courting the same girl,' Irene cut in, her voice rising, 'and the tricks they got up to, to put the other in a bad light with her.' She stood up, confronting her husband. 'Well, I'd have married Ted Watson if it hadn't been for you painting him so black and talking me out of it. And it's about a prize ram and how one of them thought the other had stolen it from him to stop him from winning with it at the local show.' Irene narrowed her eyes. 'Only it wasn't a ram, was it? It was that sheepdog of yours. The one you were so cocksure about beating everyone else's at the trials . . .'

'Damn it, woman!'

Irene wouldn't be stopped. 'You swore it was Ted that poisoned the dog so that his would win, didn't you? You'd no proof but you were dead certain of it. Well . . .' She stabbed a finger at the newspaper. 'In that story, the fellow whose ram it was got drunk and set fire to the other fellow's barn in revenge. And Ted Watson's barn was burned down with all his winter hay in it, wasn't it? And you'd had a good few drinks the night that happened.' Irene nodded with slow, grim conviction. 'Now I know for certain. And everyone'll know. It was you put a match to it. It was you that burned that tramp to death.'

Jack was panting now, as if he had been running. Ashen, wild-eyed, he looked as if he was going to start bellowing at her.

'Oh, for God's sake,' Irene said. 'You can't deny it. It's all there in black and white for them that can put two and two together.' She watched as the fire suddenly went out of Jack and he turned to the table, lowering himself slowly into a chair.

'I didn't know,' he said. His voice was low, bled of anger and denial. 'There was no way of telling he was in there.

He'd hidden himself away.' He stared across at Irene. 'You don't think I *knew* he was there, do you?'

'No,' she said coldly, 'But you were in such a rage over that dog, and with all that beer in you I doubt you even looked to see if there was anything else in that barn aside from hay. Livestock, maybe.' She glared at him. 'So knowing wasn't important, was it? You really didn't care.'

'I wasn't thinking,' Jack groaned. His eyes were searching her face pathetically, looking for one small sign of forgiveness or compassion. 'All right, so I didn't look. I just opened the door and dropped a match inside. But I've paid for what I did then.' Tears welled in the corners of his eyes. 'I've lived with knowing that I killed that man for thirty-five years, and there are still nights when I wake up in a sweat from dreaming about it.'

'I wouldn't wonder,' Irene said. 'And what's to happen now?'

'The coroner's verdict was accidental death,' Jack said glumly. 'It's on record that the old man set fire to the place himself. There's no one can prove anything different. Not after all this time.'

Irene came forward and leaned her hands on the table. 'Maybe not in any court that could send you to prison for it. But there'll be another verdict now.' She picked up the newspaper Jack had dropped on the table and held it in front of him. 'This is all the proof Wrathdale needs. The mischief's done.'

Jack stared at the words that swam beyond the film of his tears. 'THE RIVALS'. He lowered his head to the table and let out a long, despairing moan.

Fiona Neave and Frank Scully were concealing themselves behind a cluster of rocks. Fiona had her binoculars to her eyes, watching a bird slowly quartering the ground over a field to the south of them.

It was a clear, bright Saturday morning. Sunlight bathed

the dale, enriching the dozen natural colours of the fields and hillsides and throwing the craggy rises into sharp relief. To Frank, it seemed as if he and Fiona were the only people in that glorious landscape. For possibly the first time in his life, he had an inkling of what was meant by contentment.

Fiona lowered the glasses and handed them to Frank. 'A short-eared owl,' she said. She took up her camera and propped her elbows on the rock, focusing the long telephoto lens carefully.

Frank watched the bird through the glasses, panning slowly with it as it continued its slow-flapping flight over the field. 'That's amazing,' he said. 'Out in broad daylight.'

Fiona had her eye against the viewfinder and her finger poised over the shutter release. 'More often than at night,' she said. 'It's hunting. Looking for voles.' She pressed the release and kept her finger there. The shutter fired and the motor drive went into action, taking three more shots before she lifted her finger again. 'It's only in the past twenty or thirty years or so that it's bred this far south.' She sat back, pointing. 'There he goes. He's off.'

Frank smiled and looked at her. 'You're really into this, aren't you?'

'I think it's fascinating.' She moved back, putting her camera on the grass and sitting down with her back against the rock. From her anorak pocket she took a notebook and made an entry in it. Frank came across and sat beside her.

'The spring's the time to see the short-eared owl,' Fiona said, putting the notebook back in her pocket. 'It puts on quite a display.' She waved her arms in front of her, illustrating the bird's movements. 'It circles high up over its territory, glides on the air currents and makes a strange kind of booming noise. Then, suddenly, it'll twist its wings right under its body and drop like a stone, clapping them together as it falls. Just as you think it's going to hit the ground it shoots its wings out and climbs back up and starts all over again.'

'Impressive,' Frank said, a little teasingly. He grinned at Fiona. 'Who could resist a come-on like that?'

Fiona made a mock-reproving face. 'You know, I'm not sure ornithology's really your scene, Mr Scully.'

'Frank, please.'

She hesitated for a moment, then nodded. 'All right.'

Frank sniffed the air and sighed. 'I'm enjoying today,' he said.

'That's good.' Fiona trailed her fingers idly through the grass. 'I don't think you're out here out of any scientific interest, though.'

Frank grinned again. 'Chemistry comes into it.'

'Yes.' Fiona nodded without looking at him. 'I don't doubt that.'

'It's more my field.'

Again she nodded. 'Elementary or advanced?'

'I'm on a research project at the moment,' Frank said. 'Into reaction. Testing a theory.'

'Which is?'

'That two seemingly incompatible elements can be made compatible.'

Fiona pulled a blade of grass and twirled it between her fingers. 'Interesting thought. And what are your findings so far?'

'Too early to say yet,' Frank said weightily. 'But the signs are good.'

Fiona looked at him. 'Just take care,' she said. 'The trouble with chemistry is that experiments can sometimes blow up in your face.' She picked up her camera. 'Shall we? There are some grey wagtails up by Corrie Gill. I'd like to get a shot of them if I can.'

They got to their feet, brushing grass and loose earth from their clothes. As Fiona made to move off, Frank detained her with a light touch on her shoulder. 'Tell me something,' he said. 'Why did you ask me to come along?'

Fiona's eyes wavered a little. 'I just thought that if you

had nothing better to do . . .' She shrugged. 'Besides, it's nice to have company.'

'And you were short on that today?'

'It's in very limited supply.'

Frank looked out over the fields. 'Maybe you should shop around more.'

'Lower my standards?'

'No,' Frank said easily, 'not necessarily. Just try the free market. You might find company easier to come by there. That's good advice, believe me.'

Fiona looked at him thoughtfully, then nodded. 'I'll bear it in mind.'

She moved off, leading the way out of the rocks. Frank stood watching her for a moment, then slowly began following her.

When Alec Metcalfe arrived at the Jefford farm he found his sister, Irene, standing by the door looking tense and anxious. She led Alec into the kitchen where they stood facing each other.

'The telephone's not stopped ringing,' Irene said. She glanced across at the instrument as if it were a malignant intruder. 'Usually, people hardly ever ring us at all. Now folk we don't see from one year to the next are all suddenly wanting to know how we are. Nobody says anything about the piece in *The Messenger*, but they hint at it just the same.' She shook her head and drew her hand across her forehead. Alec could see that her fingers were trembling.

'Are you all right?' he asked her.

'No,' Irene said. 'It's no good pretending I am. I feel sick and I haven't been out, not since. Not even to the village. I can't bring myself to.'

Alec looked about him, feeling awkward in the warm, quiet room. 'How's Jack?'

'He's not spoken today at all.' Irene sighed shakily. 'It's like he's sort of turned in on himself. Didn't come to bed until three this morning and then I don't think he slept.'

Alec nodded, as if Jack's behaviour was something to be expected. 'Did you tackle him with it?'

'Yes. And he admitted it.' She looked at her brother, her eyes still mirroring her shock. 'It was him who killed that man, Jack.'

'I know.' Alec saw the sudden accusation on Irene's face. 'What would have been the point of telling you? It was done. Your knowing wouldn't have changed anything.' The look she was giving him reminded Alec of their childhood, when she had always been slow to forgive, no matter how much he flattered or bribed her. 'It was an accident, Irene.'

'Don't give me that!' she said angrily. 'An accident's when I burn my hand on the iron. It wouldn't be an accident if I chucked it through your front room window and hit you on the head with it. Even if I didn't know you were sitting there.' She held up a finger for emphasis. 'The least harm I'd've meant you was a broken window. And the window and your injuries couldn't be weighed separately.'

Alec sunk his hands in his pockets, looking properly chastened. 'What are your feelings, then?'

'I've told him I'll stick by him,' Irene said. 'But it can't ever be the same between us, and he knows it.'

'Well,' Alec said slowly, 'what I've got to say to him isn't going to help.'

'What is it?' Irene asked, then guessed almost at once. 'The Committee?'

Alec nodded.

'Well, I can't say I wasn't expecting it,' Irene said. 'They want him to stand down from the election, I suppose.'

'More than that,' Alec said. 'They want him to resign altogether.'

'Oh no! But that's not right.' Irene was indignant. 'That's too much! It was so long ago. And anyhow it's only what people are saying. You and I know for certain what he did, but for other folk it can't be more than a suspicion. Even after that story in the paper.' In spite of everything, her loyalty to Jack was persisting; she was prepared to clutch at every straw in his defence. 'And there's no one who would dare accuse him to his face, is there?'

'The Committee's not saying anything about what was in *The Messenger*,' Alec sighed. 'They've not given that as the reason. Nor will they, ever. They've just decided he's not suitable.'

Irene's face was scornful. 'Not suitable! After how many years?'

'You know how they are,' Alec said, shrugging. 'Any hint of a scandal and they take fright.'

'And what if he won't resign?' Irene knew the possibility was remote, but she was prepared to raise it, nevertheless.

'Then they'll just vote him out. And that'd be worse.'

Irene stared at the window for a moment. 'I reckon he'll feel there's not much worse could happen to him than this,' she said gravely.

Jack nodded. 'Where is he?'

'Out the back somewhere.' Irene sat down at the table and covered her face with her hands.

Alec looked at her, feeling helpless. He turned and crossed to the back door. 'I'd best have a word with him,' he said. He went out and walked slowly across the yard in the direction of the barn.

He rounded the corner of the barn and saw Jack Jefford, leaning on the rail that surrounded the sheep pen. His eyes were fixed in the direction of the animals, but he didn't appear to be seeing them.

Alec crossed to him and put a hand gently on his arm. 'Jack,' he said softly. Jack turned his head and the sight of his face shocked Alec. He was haggard, like a man sinking into a terrible illness. He appeared to have shrunk.

'Jack . . .' Alec moistened his lips, suddenly fearful, wondering how he could do it, how he could pile more misery on to this man, when he already looked as if he was carrying more than he could bear.

Fiona Neave and Frank Scully were crossing a wide field, making their way back to the lay-by where Fiona's car was parked. The bird-watching expedition was over, and Frank was looking exhilarated.

'I see what you mean now,' he said to Fiona as they trod through the short grass. 'It *is* fascinating.'

Fiona glanced sideways at him. 'Are you just being polite?'

He shook his head. 'That's not one of my failings. Will you ask me to come out again?'

'No,' Fiona said, after a pause. 'I'll let you take the initiative from now on.'

They reached a dry stone wall. Frank clambered over it and held out his hand to Fiona. She took hold of it and let him help her over. 'Thank you,' she said demurely.

'My pleasure,' Frank smiled, still holding her hand.

Fiona stood close to him, waiting for her fingers to be released. 'Still experimenting?' she asked softly.

Frank nodded slowly, keeping his eyes on hers. 'I think it's all coming together.' He was on the verge of kissing her, and he could see she would probably let him. But a mixture of technique and natural caution intervened; he let go Fiona's hand and they began walking down the road towards the car.

As they reached the side of the MGB a Range Rover was approaching. Fiona recognized it before Frank did and she smiled faintly. As the vehicle drew nearer they could both clearly see the driver, Lord Wrathdale, looking at them with undisguised curiosity. As he passed he smiled and waved, but the hard look in his eyes cancelled the cordiality of the gesture. Fiona smiled and waved back. Frank made a small, mockingly-deferential half bow. When the car had passed he began laughing.

128

'Well,' he said, vastly amused, 'now we're square.' He looked at Fiona. He could see she was quietly enjoying the moment. Frank found that very reassuring.

They drove back to town. As Fiona was parking the car in the market space, Frank turned to her. 'Are you in a rush to get to the office?' he asked her.

Fiona braked and switched off the engine. 'What did you have in mind?'

Frank pointed to the tea rooms up the street. 'Fancy a cup of tea?'

'Why not?' Fiona said without hesitating. 'Good idea.'

They got out of the car and started walking side by side up High Street.

Above them, at the window of Frank's office over the printing works, Sylvia Harper was standing looking down street. She watched as Fiona and Frank walked up the tea rooms. Her mouth tightened a little as Fiona laughed at something Frank said. She went on watching until they had gone into the tea rooms.

Sylvia turned from the window, crossed to the desk and picked up her handbag. As she left the office she was smiling, but it wasn't a smile of amusement or pleasure.

Irene Jefford poured boiling water into the teapot and covered it with a floral cosy. She glanced at the clock on the mantelpiece. It was just after 4.30. Irene sighed and crossed to the oven. She opened it and looked at Jack's lunch on the top shelf, covered with a plate. It would be ruined now, she was sure. She turned off the oven and closed the door.

She went into the yard and looked about her.

'Jack.'

There was no response to her call. Irene walked down towards the barn and called out again. There was still no reply. She went round to the front of the barn and saw Jack's Land Rover. The barn door was half open.

Irene crossed to the door and paused, listening to a small

sound coming from inside. It was a slow, rhythmic creaking. Puzzled, she stepped into the gloom. The creaking was louder now. Irene looked around, waiting for her eyes to adjust to the low light. Her foot touched something and she looked down. It was a step ladder. She looked up suddenly, staring at the rafters. 'Oh, my God . . .'

Jack was hanging by his neck from a rope tied round one of the beams. His body swayed gently, revolving by slow degrees. Irene clamped a hand over her mouth, hearing the scream build inside her head as Jack swung round towards her, his face deep purple, his sightless eyes glazed and bulging.

A few miles away, at Ravensfell House, Miss Banner had settled down with her afternoon tea in the sitting room. On her lap she had the sampler she was working on. She her tea and looked at the words, frowning a l

BURNING FOR BURNING,
WOUND FOR WOUND,
STRIPE FOR STRIPE.

The first line had been fully embroidered. Miss Banner set her cup aside carefully and took up her needle and cotton. Slowly and with great care, she made the first stitch in the first letter of the second line.

Chapter Seventeen

Sylvia had lowered the heat under the coffee and was transferring the jug to the spirit warmer when Frank came hurrying in from the hallway. His jacket was hanging from one arm and he was trying to get a knot in his tie.

'Morning,' Sylvia said casually. She reached across and turned off the radio.

Frank got the rest of his jacket on and ran his fingers through his hair, which was standing up in clusters. 'It's practically noon,' he muttered, staring accusingly at his watch.

'Hardly. It's not ten yet.'

Frank groaned. 'Forgot to set the bloody alarm, didn't I?'

'I was about to come up and wake you,' Sylvia said.

Frank drew his hands down over his eyes, blinking at her. 'You left it a bit late.'

'Obviously. Pity.' Sylvia faced him, putting her hands on her hips. 'Bacon and egg?'

Frank was buttoning his jacket. 'No, nothing, thanks.'

'A cup of coffee, at least,' Sylvia insisted. 'I've just made some fresh.'

Frank looked at her stubborn little pout. 'Well, half a cup, then.' When she had poured the coffee he crossed and took the cup from her. 'That's fine. Thanks.' Abruptness was something he couldn't avoid in the morning. This morning, he was finding it harder than usual to be civil.

'Sugar and milk on the table,' Sylvia said.

Frank shook his head. 'Just as it is.' He sipped the coffee, wincing as the hot liquid hit his tongue.

'And where were you last night?' Sylvia asked him.

'In Leeds,' he said. 'Talking to the local radio people. Fixing myself up as their Wrathdale reporter. The meeting went on a bit.' He rubbed his temple gingerly. 'They're a boozy lot.'

Rather too casually, Sylvia said, 'You weren't with Fiona Neave, then.'

Frank looked at her sharply.

'I saw you in town with her yesterday,' Sylvia explained. 'Getting out of her car together and going into the teashop. You looked very chummy.'

'You should have joined us,' Frank said.

'I nearly did.'

'Pity you didn't.' He swallowed some more coffee. 'We could've split the bill three ways then.'

'Yes, I thought it was like that.' Sylvia made an effort to look suddenly bored by the topic. 'Not that I care, one way or the other.'

'Really.' Frank smiled thinly. 'I'm glad to hear it.'

'And if you fancy her . . .'

Frank arrested the cup halfway to his mouth. 'I have your permission?'

Sylvia couldn't mask the aggrieved look in her eyes. 'There's not much I could do about it, is there?' she said.

Frank drained the cup and put it down. 'If you really believed I was having an affair with her, you'd think of something.'

'Probably.'

Frank nodded. 'I'll bear that in mind.' He moved to the back door, but Sylvia blocked his way, pushing her body at him and putting her arms around his neck.

'That was silly of me,' she said in a small voice. 'I shouldn't have said anything. Forgive me, darling. I was only teasing anyway. You don't really have to rush off, do you?'

'Yes, I do.'

She tightened her grip, pressing her breasts hard against

132

'No.'

'You knew I would the last time I was here, didn't you?'

'Aye,' she nodded. 'For certain.'

Her prescience irritated Frank a little. 'How could you be so sure?'

Miss Banner's lips tightened for a moment, then she said, 'I reckon you're not without some good sense.' She paused. 'What about a place to live?'

'Well, I'm all right where I am at the moment.'

'Are you?' Her eyes had narrowed the merest fraction. 'I'm looking around . . .'

'There's no need,' Miss Banner said. She picked up the bunch of keys from the table and held them out to Frank. 'My brother let it to holidaymakers, but it's mine now and I don't hold with that. Not when there's local folk who need a roof.'

Frank was surprised. He stared at the bunch of keys dangling in front of him.

'Take them then,' Miss Banner said sharply. 'If it's the rent you're worried about, I'll not rob you. I know what you earn.'

Frank took the keys and shoved them in his pocket. 'That's very good of you,' he said. He gave her a small, mischievous smile. 'What if I don't like it?'

'Then maybe I'm wrong about you and you're all fool,' Miss Banner said gruffly. 'And that being so, you'd best be moving on.'

Frank looked at her, still smiling, realizing that was probably the closest Miss Banner would ever come to having a joke with anybody.

Towards noon, Fiona went into Frank's office to speak to him. She stood just inside the door for a moment, listening to him talk on the telephone, then she moved across the room and stood looking at the framed portrait of John Wesley Banner.

'It was suicide, I suppose?' Frank was saying. 'No, of course not. But an accident maybe?' He paused, frowning at the mouthpiece. 'Oh, I see. Was there any note? No, I appreciate that. No, of course not. Just a couple of lines for now.' He scribbled something on his notepad. 'When is the inquest?' he asked his caller. 'Yes, I'd be grateful. Thanks for getting on to me, Inspector. 'Bye.' He put down the telephone and sat back.

Fiona turned to him. 'What inquest?' she asked.

'On a fellow named . . .' Frank consulted the pad; 'Jack Jefford. Know him?'

Fiona nodded. 'Vaguely.'

'Well, his wife found him hanging in a barn on Saturday.'

'Oh, no.' Fiona looked shocked. 'How awful. Why did he do it?'

'That's up to the coroner to decide,' Frank said. 'Money problems, maybe. General depression. An illness, perhaps. Who knows?'

Fiona pointed at the pad. 'I can come back later if you want to get that typed up.'

'No it can wait.' Frank stood up and came around the desk. 'I was coming down to see you anyway. How are you today?'

'Mystified,' Fiona said.

'Oh? Why?'

Fiona glanced aside for a moment, then she said, 'That photograph you found in the safe. The one of John Wesley Banner and me . . .' She hesitated.

Frank was nodding, encouraging her to go on.

'Well, is there anything else in there that concerns me?'

'Like what, for instance?'

Fiona looked away again. She wasn't being cagey, Frank decided; rather, she was having trouble broaching some point or other. 'Oh,' she said vaguely, 'I don't know. Anything.'

'Should there be?'

'Of course not. But . . . Well,' she sighed, 'I was just wondering.'

Frank went behind the desk again and opened the bottom drawer. He took out a bunch of keys and crossed to the safe with them. When he had opened the door he stood back. 'Look for yourself, if you want to. But I can assure you there isn't anything in there that's even remotely connected with you. I went through everything just a couple of days ago and sorted out the junk. Why were you wondering?'

'Because,' Fiona said hesitantly, 'there was more than one photograph in that frame. I accidentally broke it this morning – knocked it over with my briefcase.' She took two snapshots from her pocket and handed them to Frank. 'I found these tucked down behind the other picture.'

Frank looked at them. The prints were some years old, and they were obviously the work of an amateur photographer. One showed a happy, grimy little girl gazing up at the camera from a sandpit. The other was of the same girl but she was much older, wearing a school uniform and standing in a garden hand in hand with a man and woman.

'Who's that?' Frank asked.

'Read what's written on the back.'

Frank turned the prints over. On one it said *Fiona aged four*; the other said *Fiona on her eleventh birthday*. Frank flipped them over again and stared at the child. 'That's you!' he said, grinning.

'A good few years ago,' Fiona said patiently.

Frank pointed to the man and woman. 'And who are they?'

'My mother and father. That picture was taken in our garden.'

Frank nodded. 'So where's the mystery?'

'Where did Banner get them from?' Fiona said quietly, frowning at the snapshots.

'You didn't give them to him?'

'Of course I didn't. Why would I? Besides, I hadn't seen them before.'

'I see.' Frank murmured. 'It is a bit mystifying.' A thought occurred to him and he glanced up. 'Did Banner know your parents?'

Fiona looked doubtful. 'If he did, he never said anything to me about them. And they never mentioned him either.' She shook her head. 'No, it's not at all likely.'

'Could someone else have given him the pictures?'

'Who?'

'Well . . .' Frank turned the prints thoughtfully in his hand. 'Your ex-husband, perhaps.' He caught the sudden, defensive narrowing of Fiona's eyes. It was the first time he had made any reference to her marriage.

'No,' Fiona said firmly. 'I told you, I've never seen those before. And there's no way Geoffrey could have got hold of them. Besides, even if he had, why would he give them to Banner?'

'If he'd asked for them, maybe . . .'

Fiona shook her head. 'He didn't get them from Geoffrey. I'm positive about that.'

'Well, unless he took them himself,' Frank said, 'he must have got them from someone. From somewhere.'

'Yes, but from where?' Fiona looked across at Banner's portrait again. She had the look of someone suffering a nagging, worrying pain. 'And why did he want them?'

Frank leaned back on the desk, bracing himself on his arms. 'There's only one explanation as to why, isn't there?' He looked faintly amused. 'You may not have been aware of it, but old JWB must have had one hell of a thing about you.'

Fiona glared at him. 'That's nonsense!'

'Is it?' Frank held up the snapshots. 'These. The photograph frame wrapped in a piece of velvet and locked away in his safe. The money he left you. It all fits, doesn't it?'

Fiona wasn't going to accept the notion without resisting. 'I'd have known if he felt that way about me,' she said. 'Instinctively.'

'With a younger man, perhaps,' Frank said. 'With someone you were on your guard against, anyway. And besides, how often did you see him?'

'Not often. But when we were together he never as much as hinted at anything like that to me. Not once.' She looked down at her hands for a moment, considering the theory Frank had put forward, weighing the evidence. 'Still,' she said grudgingly, 'that would make some crazy sense of it all.' She looked up at Frank. 'And it's possible, I suppose.'

'Of course it is. You should be flattered.'

'Should I?' Fiona said indignantly. 'Well I'm not. To tell you the truth, I'd feel better about it if he'd been in the habit of pinching my bottom from time to time. At least his ambitions would have been out in the open. I could have coped with that. But this . . . .' She gestured at the photographs. 'It's like finding out some dirty old man's been peering through a keyhole at you for years. And having photos of me as a *child*, that has to be sick. And there's still the question of how he came by them.'

Frank nodded towards the safe. 'And you thought the answer might be in there.'

'There was just a chance.'

'Sorry,' Frank said.

Fiona took back the snapshots from him and looked at them. 'Now I don't suppose I'll ever find out. Ah, well.' She put the prints back in her pocket. 'Just another of life's unsolved puzzles.'

'I could ask Miss Banner about the pictures if you like,' Frank suggested.

'No,' Fiona said hastily, 'I don't think that would be a good idea. It would just confirm her worst suspicions about me. As a matter of fact, I'd rather you didn't say anything to anyone. Please.'

Frank assured her he wouldn't.

'Thanks.' Fiona looked at her watch. 'Time's flying. I believe you wanted to see me about something.'

'Ah, yes,' Frank nodded. 'Are you doing anything special at lunch time?'

'Nothing special. Why?'

Frank put his hand in his pocket and pulled out the bunch of keys Miss Banner had given him. 'I may have found myself a place to live,' he said. 'I'd like your opinion. And your advice.'

At 12.30 they drove out in Fiona's car to Half Mile Cottage. It was a small house standing alone in a neglected garden fronting on to the main west road out of Micklethorpe. It was a cheerless looking place, and for a couple of minutes Frank was convinced he wouldn't be able to live there. But Fiona encouraged him to go inside and look around before he made up his mind.

The front door led directly into the living room. There were a few sticks of old, battered furniture and one dusty-looking rug in the middle of the floor. A door on the far wall concealed the stairs, and another led through to the small kitchen.

After a cursory examination of the bedroom and kitchen, Fiona made her pronouncement.

'You could do a lot with it,' she said.

Frank pulled a face. 'Maybe.' He stepped into the living room and looked around. 'A woman's touch. That's what it needs.'

'The right carpet and some curtains,' Fiona said, nodding. She sounded enthusiastic. 'They'll make all the difference. And would Miss Banner object if you took that fireplace out?'

'I don't know.' Frank stared glumly at the soot-blackened cavity under the chimney breast.

'If not, one of those new wood-burning stoves would go well there.'

'I'll have a word with her,' Frank said, watching Fiona go through to the kitchen again. He looked at the ruptured armchair and the dilapidated sofa. 'The furniture's a bit sparse.'

'Yes,' Fiona said, coming back into the room. 'You'll need to buy a few bits and pieces.' She came and stood beside Frank, rubbing her hands, running a critical eye over the walls and ceiling. 'There's an auction tomorrow at Feltry. We printed the catalogue for it. The dealers will be after the best of it, but you could probably pick up one or two nice things quite cheaply there. I was tempted to look in myself.'

Frank turned and looked at her. 'We'll go together then, shall we?'

Fiona gave him the look he had seen before, questioning, evaluating. Then she smiled. 'Why not? I'd like that. I've nothing else planned.'

'That's encouraging,' Frank said, returning her smile.

Chapter Eighteen

The old boathouse stood remote, shrouded by trees at the side of the river that wound for miles through the Wrathdale estate. Fiona and Lewis were on the landing stage, a few feet within the entrance. They were embracing. As they drew apart, Lewis smiled with careful humility.

'Thanks for coming,' he said.

'You said it was important on the telephone.' Fiona, although she was glad to see him, couldn't avoid sounding cool.

'It is.' Lewis took her arm and led her to where they could look out at the wide curve of the river as it turned north, half a mile from where they were standing. Easing his arm around her shoulder, he said, 'It's important for me. I want you to know how sorry I am about Thursday night.' He sighed, staring into the distance. 'Everything was fine. I'd kept the evening entirely clear as usual. And then, out of the blue, I suddenly find that I'm going to have to stand in for the Lord Lieutenant at a boring reception. There was no way I could get out of it.'

Fiona looked at him. 'It's the old, old story, isn't it? I half expect it now. Every time.'

'Nothing's going to interfere with next Thursday,' Lewis whispered, nuzzling her hair. 'I've made absolutely sure of that.'

'We'll see,' Fiona said flatly. 'Wednesday might interfere.'

Lewis moved back, frowning at her. 'Why should it?'

'She knows, Lewis.' Fiona's eyes were steady, certain.

'About us?' He looked startled. 'Whatever makes you think that?'

'Why do you think she invited me?'

'To discuss the Aynsgill Meet,' Lewis said. 'She's very keen to get you involved with it again. She told me so.'

Fiona shook her head. 'She's going to warn me off. In the nicest possible way, of course. But that's what she has in mind.'

'Beattie?' Lewis was wide-eyed, disbelieving. 'She's not that . . .'

'Clever?'

'Oh,' Lewis said, 'she's clever enough. Devious is the word I had in mind.'

A cold breeze swept across the river and Fiona turned away from it, wrapping her arms around herself. 'She's a woman. So she's devious. We have to be to survive in your world.'

'But *you're* not.'

Fiona shot him a pained, indulgent look.

wis murmured, 'only because of the way things are between us.'

'Don't you believe it,' Fiona warned him. 'Besides, she could claim the same extenuating circumstances.'

'You're wrong, darling,' Lewis moved close to her again. 'I promise you. All right, so she may have her fair share of deviousness, but Beattie doesn't play that kind of game. If she suspected anything, she'd bring it out into the open then and there. I know.'

'From experience?' Fiona asked him, smiling faintly.

'Exactly. From being married to her for seventeen years. She'd never embarrass me like that.'

Fiona studied his face for a long moment before she said, 'Heaven forbid.'

Lewis drew her to him, trying to coax some warmth from her. 'If you really believe what you're saying, why are you coming on Wednesday? You could have found some excuse and declined the invitation.'

Fiona pulled away from him. 'For how long?' Her face was very serious. 'Sooner or later the excuses run out, don't they?'

'It's all in your imagination,' Lewis said. 'I'm sure of that.' He moved forward to take her in his arms again.

'Let's walk for a while,' Fiona moved towards the entrance. She paused and looked over her shoulder. Lewis was hesitating. 'It's all right,' she told him patiently, 'there's no one about.'

Lewis nodded and followed her, but he still looked uncomfortable. 'I can't stay too long,' he muttered as he fell into step beside her.

'Now where,' Fiona said, 'have I heard that before?'

The auction was being held in a large country house overlooking the village of Feltry. Dealers, collectors and bargain hunters had turned up early; they roamed the rooms and stairways, examining the lots and making notes, muttering to each other and fingering inlays and ~~~~~~~ a way that struck Frank Scully as almost ~~~~~. Ten minutes among the opulent, regimented arrays of furnishings and ornaments had depressed him. Nothing made a man feel more excluded, he believed, than the outward display of heritages and lifestyles he knew nothing about.

Fiona, on the other hand, was enjoying herself. Frank watched her as she steadily checked items against their descriptions in the catalogue and nodded, as if she were playing a guessing game – and playing it very well.

On a half landing above the main hall they stopped before a handsome long-case clock.

'Isn't that beautiful?' Fiona breathed.

'Yes it is.' Frank smiled at her. 'It would go all right in the sitting room, wouldn't it?'

'Yours or mine?' Fiona peered at the sticker on the side. 'What number is it?'

'Lot a hundred and twelve.' As Fiona turned the pages of the catalogue Frank sighed. 'Look at that workmanship. It'll go for a fortune.'

Fiona found the entry. She read it, then looked up at Frank and nodded sadly. 'You're right. It's Georgian.' She read from the catalogue; '"An extremely rare example".'

'Ah, well.' Frank shrugged at the clock. 'I wouldn't have wanted it anyway. It's slow.'

They moved on down the stairs. At the bottom they turned towards the dining room and almost bumped into Lady Wrathdale.

'Hello, Mrs Neave.' Beattie looked surprised and delighted.

'Hello,' Fiona said, a little stiffly.

'Have you got your eye on something special, or are you just browsing?'

'There's lots of things I'd like,' Fiona said. 'But I could never afford them.'

Beattie nodded sympathetically. 'I know the problem.' She turned her attention to Frank, who was waiting to be introduced.

'Oh, I'm sorry,' Fiona said. 'You haven't met, have you? This is Frank Scully, the new editor of *The Messenger*. Lady Wrathdale.'

There was only a momentary frown as Frank reached out and shook Beattie's hand.

'It's nice to meet you, Mr Scully. I've seen you about, of course. You were at the opening of the Arts and Crafts Centre, weren't you?'

'Yes,' Frank said. Rather jokily he added, 'And I have to tell you, Lady Wrathdale, that you're a photographer's dream.'

'Oh, how kind. I must say I was very pleased with the one you put in the paper. I looked quite human for a change.'

'I'll let you have a print,' Frank promised her. It was a trivial exchange, weightless and largely without much point, but Frank had been learning that it got a person by in Wrathdale society a lot better than meaningful conversation.

Beattie was looking delighted again. 'Thank you. Why

don't you bring it to the Lodge one evening? Lewis and I have been meaning to ask you up for a drink, but he's been out such a lot lately.' She paused, and her eyes met Fiona's for the briefest instant. 'I think he's going to be a bit more settled from now on, though.' She beamed at Frank. 'I'll give you a call, shall I? We'll make a date.'

'Fine,' Frank said. For Fiona's sake, he felt it was time to move along. 'I'll look forward to it.'

A large group of people came past, jostling them; Beattie moved to an empty space by the bottom of the stairs and Frank and Fiona, unable to do anything else, followed her.

Beattie didn't appear to be in any hurry to part company with them. 'Are you here in your editorial capacity?' she asked Frank.

'No,' he laughed, 'just bargain hunting. Mrs Neave and I are setting up home together.'

'Oh, really?' Beattie said.

Frank had intended it as a light joke, but Fiona's sudden frown and Beattie's interested expression made him wish he hadn't said it.

'Mr Scully's moving into a cottage,' Fiona said testily. 'I'm helping him choose some furniture for it.'

Beattie smiled at her. 'Oh, that must be a lot of fun. I envy you.' To Frank she said, 'And you couldn't be in better hands.' She turned to Fiona again, her smile unwavering. 'From what I hear, you've done a marvellous job furnishing the Gatehouse.'

'It's easier when you've only yourself to please.' Fiona said. She could quite manage to return Beattie's smile.

'Is there anything here that takes your fancy, Lady Wrathdale?' Frank asked, forcing her off the subject of domestic arrangements.

'Yes.' Beattie lowered her voice. 'There's a wonderful old terrestrial globe. Eighteenth century. It's Lewis's birthday in a couple of weeks and he's always wanted one.' She looked at her watch and became brisk suddenly. 'I must be getting back.'

'Aren't you going to bid for it?' Frank asked her.

'No.' Beattie's voice went even lower. 'Whenever I bid at a local auction the price rockets. But fortunately the vicar of our parish church is here. So he's going up to my limit for me. He's eighty-four and rather threadbare. I'm hoping the auctioneer will take pity on him.'

Frank laughed and Fiona managed a polite smile.

'Well,' Beattie said, moving off towards the front door, 'goodbye, Mrs Neave . . .' She nodded to Frank. 'It was nice meeting you, Mr Scully. I'll be in touch.'

They watched her go, but just as they were about to move into the dining room Beattie stopped and came back to them.

'I've just had a thought,' she said to Frank. 'Mrs Neave's coming to dinner with us on Wednesday. We're going to talk about the Aynsgill Meet, but that won't take very long. And three's never been my favourite number. So why don't you come along as well?'

Frank suddenly felt he was out on a shaky limb. He glanced at Fiona.

'It's a good idea, don't you think?' Beattie asked Fiona. 'Since you're obviously friends. And it would make a better balance, wouldn't it?'

Fiona swallowed. 'Yes, it's a very good idea. If Mr Scully hasn't any other plans.'

'Free as a bird,' Frank said awkwardly.

'Well, that's fine then.' Beattie started moving away again. 'Seven-thirtyish. And don't dress up, for God's sake.' She gave them a little wave and moved off into the crowd.

Fiona stared after her for a moment, then she turned to Frank. 'I'm sorry about that. It's not going to be a very relaxing evening for either of us, is it?'

'Oh?' Frank said with assumed innocence. 'Why?'

'You know damn well why!' Fiona snapped, startling him with the harshness of her voice.

By Tuesday afternoon, Frank was finally installed in Half Mile Cottage. With the help of Donald and Sylvia Harper he moved in his collection of books, a bed and the furniture Fiona had helped him select at the auction. With fresh curtains, a new carpet and strategically placed lamps, the old house was transformed into a cosy, welcoming home. Frank felt, after all, that he would truly enjoy living there.

The change of base, even the anticipation of the change, had brought with it an altered viewpoint. Frank had the sense of being his own man: he found himself working more efficiently and energetically, and his sense of direction began to harden. So, oddly, did his sense of belonging, which at one time he believed had deserted him for good.

On the few occasions during that week when confrontations with Sylvia had been unavoidable, Frank found himself being automatically distanced, as if a self-protective drive in him came into action the moment the woman appeared. Nothing there was resolved yet, but Frank had the clear feeling that he was moving by stages towards a neat, reasonably clean break. The establishment of his own territory was making it easier for him to withdraw from Donald Harper's.

As if to counter his growing sense of buoyancy, dinner on Wednesday evening with Lord and Lady Wrathdale left Frank deflated. He was treated with charm and generosity. So was Fiona Neave. But the overwhelming atmosphere of togetherness and family solidarity – Frank couldn't be sure if it had been deliberately engineered by Beattie or not – left him with considerable pity for Fiona.

For almost an hour during the meal Beattie had talked about the children, and she had drawn Lewis into an enthusiastic series of predictions about the young people's future.

After dinner, as they all sat round the coffee table, Beattie brought a framed picture to show Frank.

'Our children, Mr Scully.'

Frank gazed at the smiling group, and just for an instant he glanced up at Fiona and saw the bleak, dispossessed look on her face.

'That's Peter,' Beattie was saying, 'he's the eldest. He'll be sixteen in November. And that's Philippa. She's the middle one. And here's the baby of the family. Lewis junior.'

Every word, Frank thought, every name was an extra anchor on Fiona's isolation. She was being given an outsider's view of a compact family with a long, deep-rooted heritage. Beattie was telling her, whether deliberately or not, that the unity of the Wrathdales was unassailable.

It got no better. As they sipped their brandy the talk moved to the castle, to Lewis's responsibility to share his inheritance with the public, at least for part of the year, and his obligation to tutor his sons in the unique complexities of *noblesse oblige*. Then there was the matter of Lewis's mother – still alive, returning soon on a visit to England after years in Italy – the matriarchal reminder of duty and honour who was obviously adored by her son. Fiona was being shown, in all its compact richness, a world where she would never be permitted to belong.

All the time, while Beattie talked about the family and the multitude of responsibilities the Wrathdales' position forced on them, Lewis played chorus to her. There was some evidence of reluctance, though not much. To Frank it was obvious how small and separate Fiona's place was in that man's life; to Fiona herself, he realized, the revelation must have been agonizing.

Just before they left, Beattie took Fiona aside to discuss the Aynsgill Meet. The two men moved to the other side of the room, where the drinks were laid out on a table.

'Armagnac?' Lewis asked Frank, holding up the bottle. 'That'll do nicely.'

As Lewis was pouring the drinks he said, 'I understand you're planning on settling here, Scully.'

Frank shook his head. 'Not settling. Just staying on for a bit.'

Lewis nodded slowly. 'You like this part of the country, do you?'

'It has its attractions.'

Lewis handed Frank his glass. There was no mistaking the small flash of resentment in his eyes. 'I'd have thought you would have found it a bit dull, after London.'

To Frank, for whom the whole evening had been such a pain, the opportunity to do some needling of his own was irresistible. 'On the contrary,' he said, smiling broadly. 'I find it fascinating.' He sipped his brandy. 'There's such a lot going on.'

Again, the resentment from Lewis was unmistakable.

Later, as they were about to get into Fiona's car outside the Lodge, Frank paused and looked at her across the hood as she fumbled to get her door open. She was grim-faced, seething.

'I'll tell you something for nothing,' Frank said quietly. 'If you're looking for any kind of future there, you haven't a hope in hell.'

Fiona glared at him angrily, then jerked open the door and threw herself into the driving seat. She had the engine started before Frank was inside the car. He still had his door partly open when she let out the clutch, swung the car in a tight circle and roared off down the drive.

Chapter Nineteen

On Thursday morning Donald Harper left on an overnight visit to Brussels. That evening, while Frank Scully was getting out another edition of *The Messenger*, Sylvia Harper let herself into Half Mile Cottage. She used a key she'd had made from Frank's, during the confusion of moving in.

She stood for a minute in the warm silence of the sitting room, watching the weak moonlight slant across the carpet. There was a pleasing sense of permanence about the little house, a solidity that felt protective. Although Sylvia enjoyed taking risks, she could also take equal pleasure in feeling hidden away, snug and secure. She smiled at the darkened room, then crossed and drew the curtains before switching on the light.

The impression of welcoming warmth grew suddenly. The mute, informal arrangement of the bookcase, the leather settee, the desk and the armchairs was friendly. The pictures on the walls evoked peace without inviting scrutiny. Sylvia believed in auras, and this place had an aura that she had never been able to conjure in her own home.

Still smiling, she crossed to the kitchen and put on the light. There was time, she hoped, to prepare a small welcome. It would be fun to do, the more so because it would be unexpected.

A couple of miles away, in the similarly warm and cosy sitting room of the Gatehouse, Lord Wrathdale had already encountered his own surprise. The table was laid as expected, the lights were low and there was a seductive aroma from the kitchen. Fiona, also as expected, was looking as beautiful as ever. But her ultimatum had come as an unpleasant shock.

Lewis was staring at her, shaking his head. 'You can't be serious!' he said.

'I'm perfectly serious.' Fiona was staring back at him. There wasn't a trace of uncertainty on her face. 'I want you to leave your wife. Tonight.'

'Be reasonable, Fiona. That's not possible . . .'

'Why?'

'Because it isn't.' Lewis looked devastated. 'I can't walk out, just like that.'

'It's what we planned,' Fiona said firmly. 'From the very beginning, from the first night. It's what you said you wanted. To leave your wife. For us to be together.'

'And I still want that.'

Fiona's eyes hovered between disdain and anger. 'You don't want it enough, apparently.'

'As much as ever,' Lewis insisted. He looked around the room, seeking all the markers of security, endurance. He had never suspected it could be withdrawn from him so easily or completely. 'I swear, Fiona . . .'

'Then do it.' There was finality in her voice, cold and unswerving. 'Now.'

'With no plans made? Nothing arranged?'

'We've made plans,' Fiona said. 'We've talked about it endlessly. And whatever arrangements you think are necessary you can handle from here or anywhere else, just as well as you can from the Lodge.'

'Darling . . .' His voice had turned soft and pleading. 'Be patient. That's all I ask.'

'I've been patient. For two years I've been patient. God knows how patient I've been.' She glanced at the dining table and its neat settings. It seemed to underscore her tolerance, her time of waiting. She looked back at Lewis. 'But no more,' she said. 'My patience has run out. So it's either now, or we forget the whole thing and you walk out of that door and leave me in peace.'

Lewis was shaking his head slowly, trying to placate her. 'You don't mean that. You're just upset. But you won't tell me why. What brought this on anyway?' He stood back from her a little, his face stiffening with self-righteousness. 'It was nothing I said, that's for sure. I'd hardly opened my mouth before you blew up. And it's such a waste, darling. I didn't come here this evening to . . .'

'Of course you didn't,' Fiona snapped. 'We both know why you're here this evening, Lewis. For the same reason as all the other times. Only for too long I've been kidding myself that that wasn't the only reason.'

'And you know damn well it isn't.' His voice dropped almost to a whisper. 'I love you.'

'Then prove it. That's what I'm asking. For you to prove just that.' Fiona sighed, and for the first time since Lewis arrived she began to look vulnerable. 'I'm tired,' she said. 'Tired of having to meet you in secret. Tired of half-hour conversations snatched in lonely places out of sight. Tired of being careful, tired of being disappointed, of excuses.'

'Darling . . .'

'Tired of making love three times a month provided you can get away from home for long enough,' Fiona went on, not letting him interrupt. She drew her hand across her forehead, and when she looked at Lewis again there was a hint of moisture in her eyes. 'I want more than that. Much more. I want to share your life with you. To build up memories together that we can shout from the rooftops if we feel like it. I want to be part of you. For you to be part of me. But not just on Thursdays and not in hiding. Out in the open. And with dignity. And if that's not possible from this moment on, then I'm sorry. I just don't want to know any more.'

Lewis tried to take her in his arms, but Fiona pulled away. 'Fiona, darling. Just give me . . .'

'No,' she said gravely. 'No more time, Lewis. You've had all the time I can spare.' She looked at him squarely. 'What's it to be?'

'Try to understand,' Lewis said, his voice agonized. 'Please! I can't. Not now. Not tonight.'

The impasse had been reached. Fiona was unmovable. Lewis stood looking at her for a minute, seeing more strength in her than he had ever suspected. There was nothing more he could think of; she had left him no room for bargaining or compromise. He walked to the kitchen door and pushed it open. 'I do love you, you know,' he said simply.

Fiona was on the verge of tears, but she was determined to go through with it. 'Goodbye, Lewis,' she said firmly.

At Half Mile Cottage, Sylvia had taken off her shoes and was curled up on the settee with one of Frank's books. She was still waiting to deliver her surprise welcome. It was after nine; Frank, she was sure, would be home any minute.

Sylvia looked at her watch. Time had a tendency to crawl. It was an observation she had made dozens of times, during the long days when she was at home alone and bored. The great irony, of course, was that when she was with Frank and enjoying herself, time flew.

She returned her attention to the book, trying to force the meaning off the page and into her head. It was difficult. After a couple of minutes she gave up trying and simply let her eyes glide over the print, while her head occupied itself with the time ahead, an entire night alone with Frank Scully in his new home, in his new bed.

When Lewis had gone, Fiona sat on an arm of the settee, staring at the dining table, its untouched place settings, the floral arrangement. After a minute she emitted a long shuddering sigh and lowered her head, closing her eyes tightly.

Outside, Lewis was halfway to the castle where his car was parked when he stopped and looked back at the Gatehouse. His mind was churning. The sight of the little house and the sharp, poignant memory of what it had meant for two years brought a sudden onrush of decision. He started walking back down the path towards the Gatehouse.

He was a hundred yards from the house when he saw a car approaching. He stood and watched as it pulled up in front of the Gatehouse. Puzzlement gave way to a fresh wave of indecision. Lewis had an image of Beattie, as sharp and heart-gripping as the picture he held of Fiona. He heard the car door close and saw someone go up to the front door of the Gatehouse.

Sighing, Lewis turned and began making his way up towards the castle again.

Frank Scully rang the bell and waited. There was no response. He reached for the bellpull again but as he did the door opened. The smile died on his lips. Fiona looked as if she had received tragic news.

'I was just passing,' Frank faltered, 'and I thought . . .' He could see she was barely able to control her expression. 'I should've telephoned first,' he murmured, moving away. 'Some other time . . .'

'Come in,' Fiona said flatly.

Frank was uncertain if he should, but when Fiona stepped back from the open door he followed her inside.

In the sitting room Fiona made a fierce effort and turned to Frank with a wide, over-bright smile. 'Would you like a drink?' she asked him brittly. 'Of course you would.' She went jerking towards the drinks table like a puppet. 'What would you like? Whisky? Gin? Brandy? Vodka? Some wine perhaps? I've got some very nice wine.'

Quietly, feeling rather embarrassed, Frank said, 'I'll have

155

a whisky, thanks.'

Fiona snatched up the bottle. She had trouble unscrewing the cap, and when she held up a glass to pour the drink her hands shook so badly that the bottle and glass rattled together.

Frank crossed the room quickly and took the bottle from her, setting it down on the table. He took a gift-wrapped package he had been carrying under his arm and handed it to Fiona. 'I brought you this.' He removed the glass from her other hand and started pouring himself a drink.

Fiona stared at the package. 'Oh, how nice!' she exclaimed, too gaily. 'A present!' She put the package on the table and started fumbling at the coloured string. 'Have you eaten?' she asked Frank. 'There's plenty of food. Pity to waste it.' She jerked at the string, failing to break it. 'Damn! I can't get it open.' She started tearing off the wrapping. 'What is it?'

'Nothing much,' Frank said. 'Just a thank-you for your help over the cottage.'

'Oh, how kind of you. But it wasn't necessary. You shouldn't have done that.' She finally managed to open the box and take out the contents. It was a delicate piece of porcelain, fashioned in the shape of a tree with two birds nesting in its branches and two others flying around the trunk. Fiona placed it gently on the table. Her hands were still shaking.

'I hope you like it,' Frank murmured.

'Oh. It's beautiful!' Her breath caught as she tried to go on. 'But you really shouldn't . . .' She broke down suddenly, burying her face in her hands and beginning to sob.

Frank put down his glass and crossed to her. Fiona turned to him and he took her in his arms. 'What is it? What's the matter?'

She stared dumbly at Frank, tears streaming down her cheeks and her lips trembling. Frank gazed at her for a minute, reading the look in her eyes, seeing the pain and the alienation, and then before he knew it he was kissing her, tasting her tears and feeling her arms close tightly around him. His concern evaporated in the path of sudden, galvanizing hunger as Fiona pushed her hips at him and whimpered urgently against the pressure of his lips.

Sylvia stirred and woke up slowly, taking a moment to remember where she was.

She sat up on the couch and shivered. The lamp she had been reading by was still burning. She looked across the room and saw daylight glimmering beyond the curtains; she looked at her watch. It was after seven o'clock.

At the curtains she peered out carefully before opening them, screwing her eyes against the onslaught of the light. She went back to the settee and switched off the lamp, then went to the bottom of the stairs.

'Frank? Are you there?' She climbed the stairs and stood on the landing. 'Frank?' The bedroom was empty. Sylvia went back downstairs, frowning.

She was slipping her shoes on when a sudden thought struck her. Hurriedly, she put on her jacket and went out, slamming the front door after her.

It took her less than ten minutes to drive out to Aynsgill Castle. She stopped the Volvo by the end of the road leading down to the Gatehouse. Frank's Marina was parked outside.

Sylvia wound down her window and stared at the car, feeling her anger grow alongside her hurt. It was the kind of anger she had felt years before, when Frank had walked out on her – a cold, vengeful sensation low in her stomach.

After a minute, she wound up the window again. She started the Volvo and turned it in a wide circle, then drove slowly back in the direction she had come.

At Ravensfell House, Miss Banner's morning was proving to be as infuriating as Sylvia Harper's. The postman had brought a pile of bills and one large, bulky envelope, addressed to John Wesley. The bills were irksome enough, but it was the journal in the large envelope that appeared to spark real anger in Miss Banner. It was the current edition of an evangelist quarterly called *Gospel Tidings and Dissertations.*

Miss Banner stood in the sitting room, riffling the pages, scowling at the journal as if it intended her immediate and serious harm. She glanced towards the bookcase cabinet, then threw the journal on the middle of the table. She strode across to the cabinet and after some searching in the drawers she found the key to the glass doors.

She stood with the doors open wide, staring at the long row of old journals, a collection she had overlooked in her haste to purge the house of her brother's belongings. Simply looking at the books seemed to intensify her anger. She began scooping them up until she had her arms full, then she took them to the table and dumped them there.

Returning to the cabinet for more, she caught sight of the large, immaculately bound family bible. The sight of it made Miss Banner pause. Hesitantly, she reached into the cabinet and took it out.

She went to her favourite chair and sat down with the bible on her knees. For a while she simply gazed at the cover, then she undid the clasp and slowly opened the book.

On the first two pages, in careful handwriting in various styles, there was a date list of the births, marriages and deaths of the members of the Banner family, dating back to the middle of the eighteenth century.

Miss Banner stared at the last entry on the list, her own: *Sybil Banner, born 14th April, 1921.* Suddenly, with a stifled, angry sob, she ripped the pages out and tore them to shreds, letting the big bible crash to the floor. She scattered the pieces into the air and sat back, breathing harshly through her mouth as the shreds fluttered unheeded on to the carpet.

After a few moments, as if to console herself, she sat forward and looked at her embroidery frame, lying on the table by the chair. Almost half the lettering in the text was completed. She sighed at it, gradually gaining control of her breathing again.

Lying beyond the frame was the photograph from which Miss Banner had lopped off the image of her brother. Her eyes moved to it. She sat there looking at it for a long time, her gaze lingering on the smiling face of Fiona Neave, which was now ringed heavily in ink.

Chapter Twenty

Fiona was standing by the window wearing a short bathrobe, sipping her coffee and gazing thoughtfully out across the fields beyond the Gatehouse, watching the early ground mist beginning to clear. Behind her, the table was still set for dinner; the porcelain ornament that Frank had brought the previous night was sitting near the centre of the table, where Fiona had left it.

Frank came down the stairs and into the sitting room carrying his jacket over one arm, doing up the button on his shirt cuff. He stopped just inside the door as Fiona turned to face him. There was a slight awkwardness between them, even some embarrassment on Fiona's part.

'Hello,' Frank said, smiling.

Fiona's smile was no more than a twitch of the lips.

'Have you been up long?' he asked her.

'No, not very long. Are you hungry?'

'Not a bit.' Frank came further into the room, still fumbling with his cuff.

'Are you sure?' Fiona's voice had some of the brittle edge he had noticed the night before. 'It's no bother. And it's usual, isn't it? Bed and breakfast. I mean they go together, don't they?'

Frank frowned at her. 'Just some coffee, thanks.'

Fiona went to the table, put down her own cup and started pouring one for Frank. He threw his jacket down on a chair and crossed to her.

'You'll have to forgive me,' Fiona said, concentrating too hard on what she was doing. 'I'm a bit hazy on morning-after etiquette.' She put down the coffee pot and handed Frank his cup. 'But then you see, I'm not used to anyone staying so long. Midnight goodbyes are more my style.'

Frank took one sip from the cup and put it down. 'Are you finished?' he asked her.

Fiona stared at him sharply, then she shook her head self-reproachfully. 'I'm sorry.'

'Who are you trying to hurt, anyway?'

'Well – certainly not you.' Her smile was easier now. 'Believe that.'

Frank tried to put his arms around her, but she drew back smartly.

'Listen,' she said, 'you must understand. About last night . . . You walked in at a bad moment for me.'

Frank nodded. 'I know.'

She was looking down at the table, tracing a pattern with her finger on the cloth. 'I needed someone. I desperately didn't want to be alone. But that's it. I wouldn't want you to think . . .'

'What wouldn't you want me to think?'

She looked at him. 'That there was anything more to it than that.'

Frank picked up his cup again and stared glumly at the dark coffee, swirling it. 'I was just handy,' he said flatly.

'Yes, to be honest.'

'It could have been anyone.'

Fiona shook her head. 'No, I wouldn't want you to think that either.'

'Well,' Frank murmured, 'that's something.'

'And you'll settle for it?'

'Looks like I'll have to.'

Fiona sighed. 'Thank you.'

'For now, anyway,' Frank added.

Fiona gave him a troubled little look as he sipped his coffee. In the morning, with the softness of sleep still on her face, her feelings were more transparent. She was aware of that and she looked away as Frank's eyes met hers.

'So what happened before I arrived?' he asked her.

161

Fiona stared into her cup.

'You don't want to talk about it?'

She lifted her head, looking at him cautiously. 'It won't help, if that's what you're thinking. But if you really want to know, I decided to prove that you were wrong.'

Frank blinked at her, not understanding.

'You told me,' Fiona said, 'that I hadn't a hope in hell of any kind of worthwhile future with Lewis. Remember?'

'I shouldn't have said anything.'

'Oh,' Fiona said lightly, 'I'd have put it to the test sooner or later, anyway. Now I know for sure.' Her voice hardened. 'The bubble's burst. It blew up in my face.'

After a pause, Frank said. 'He was that honest about it, was he?'

'Hardly. Men never are, are they? But the message came over clear enough.' She made a resigned gesture with her hand. 'So it's over.'

'After how long?'

'Twenty-two months, eight days, twelve hours and thirty-six minutes.' She sniffed. 'Give or take a minute.'

Frank shook his head slowly. 'You can be that exact?'

'It was that important to me,' Fiona said. 'A special kind of calendar.'

'Was?'

Fiona nodded and pointed towards the kitchen. 'Right up until the moment he walked out of that door.' She checked herself. 'No, that's not true. For a little longer than that. Until . . .' She broke off, staring at Frank for a moment, then she turned and went back to the window. 'Now it's just another calculation, though,' she murmured at the glass. 'Of so much wasted time. So much spent emotion.'

'Are you sure of that?' Frank asked softly.

'Absolutely. I wish I wasn't. Because that's what really hurts. All that waste. And I'm not a kid any more. I just can't afford to be that generous.'

Frank looked at her. Even without seeing her face, he could measure the pain in her, the gnawing of the aftermath. 'You chose the wrong man, that's all,' he said.

'I seem to make a habit of it.'

'Next time it'll be different.'

Fiona turned to him. 'I'm not going to be looking for a next time, Frank. Nothing even halfway permanent, anyway.' Her mouth tightened for an instant. 'In fact I'll be guarding against it.'

'Just as and when,' Frank said, narrowing his eyes cynically. 'All very casual. That's the way it's going to be, is it?'

'Something like that,' Fiona nodded. 'For amusement only. Much the same way you play it.'

Frank raised his eyebrows. 'We're ideally matched then, wouldn't you say?'

'Maybe.' Fiona sipped her coffee and came back towards the table. 'So long as it's clearly understood that from now on I'm going to be playing to new rules.'

Frank took that in slowly, then he put down his cup, crossed the room and put on his jacket. 'To tell the truth,' he said, 'I'm rather tired of games.'

'Then the answer's simple,' Fiona told him. 'Don't deal yourself a hand.'

At ten o'clock Frank called on Miss Banner to collect her weekly piece for *The Messenger*. He found her in the garden, standing among her beehives. She had taken the top off one and was examining a honeycomb. Bees were crawling on her hands, arms and face.

'Don't they ever sting you?' Frank asked her. He was standing several feet back, not wanting to go any closer than he could avoid.

'Why should they?' Miss Banner said. 'They've no cause. I'm gentle with them, so they're gentle with me.'

Frank started flailing his arms wildly as a couple of bees

flew around his head, investigating him.

'And they won't hurt you, either,' Miss Banner assured him.

Frank retreated a couple of feet, still waving his arms. 'I don't have your confidence.'

'Not when it was me that called you down here, they won't,' Miss Banner murmured, turning the comb over in her hands.

Frank smiled, in spite of his nervousness. 'Ah, but do they know that?'

'Aye,' she said, replacing the comb. 'Of course. I told them.' She put the top back on the hive and walked over to Frank. 'You'll have come to collect what I've written for next week.'

Frank nodded. 'Yes please.'

They started walking towards the house. 'Casual sales are up again this week,' Frank said. 'And the newsagents are taking a lot more regular orders, too. Your weekly piece is a real winner. I hope you're not running out of material.'

'You've no need to worry on that score,' Miss Banner said. 'I've a lot to tell yet.'

When they got to the house Miss Banner led the way to the sitting room. On the table was the familiar lined pad and lying across it, six detached pages covered with Miss Banner's handwriting.

'Everyone's very curious now,' Frank said as the old woman went to the table. 'There's not a day goes by that two or three people don't ask me who Chronicler is.'

'They haven't guessed then?' she said, then added, 'Even though you said they would.'

'They will. Sooner or later.'

Miss Banner fanned the pages, gazing at them. 'I doubt there's many as remember I can read and write.' She looked across at Frank. 'And anyhow, you'll not confirm it, will you?'

It seemed, Frank reflected, that Miss Banner needed

constant reassurance on that point. 'Not without your permission' he said.

'And you'll not get that.' She held out the sheets of paper to him. 'Here's more for you, then.' Her look, Frank noticed, had a trace of pride; it was the look of someone who knew she was doing a good job.

That evening, just after six o'clock, Frank went down to the printing works and looked in on Fiona. She was sitting at her desk, frowning at a sheet of figures. Frank tapped the door and she looked up.

'Nothing heavy,' he said. 'Just a friendly visit. Can I come in?'

She nodded. 'Of course.'

He crossed the room and eased himself on to the edge of the desk. 'About time you were packing it in, isn't it?'

'No.' Fiona was still frowning at the figures. 'I'm going to be here for a while yet, I'm afraid.'

'Problems.'

'One in particular.' Fiona sat back and looked up at him. 'We lost a good contract today. Bread and butter work. It's going to make a nasty hole in our figures. I'm just working out how nasty and seeing what can be done to plug it.'

Frank nodded sympathetically. 'Did they get a better quote?'

'Apparently not.'

'Then how come you lost it?'

'On a very feeble pretext.' Fiona scowled momentarily. 'The truth has to be that I'm no longer *persona grata* with the committee of the Daleswomen's Association. Or with the Secretary, anyway.'

Frank looked surprised. 'What have you done, for God's sake?'

'I've come into money,' Fiona said quietly.

It dawned on Frank at once. 'Oh no! Surely not!'

'Around here, yes. Even now. And with them in particular.' Fiona shook her head resignedly. 'I suppose I should really have anticipated it. Because there was no way they were going to see that as unearned income.'

Frank was appalled. 'But that's bloody monstrous! And if I hadn't printed that story about the will they'd have been none the wiser.'

'Oh, I don't know. It would probably have become public knowledge eventually, anyway.'

'And it might not have.' Frank drew his fingers through his hair. 'What can I say?'

'Nothing. We've been all over that and what's done's done. Anyway, it's not totally disastrous. The business'll survive it. Just so long as it isn't repeated too often.'

Frank was still looking apologetic. 'Is there anything I can do?'

Fiona smiled. 'How about starting another newspaper?'

The idea seemed to appeal to Frank. 'Or you buying *The Messenger*,' he said. 'Do you still want to?'

'I wouldn't mind. But I think that's a non-starter now.'

'Why?'

'Because Miss Banner would never sell it to me. The bid *was* going to come from Lewis. That's not on any more.'

Frank spread his hands. 'So I'll handle it for you.'

The possibility had never occurred to Fiona. 'Would you?'

'Why not?'

Fiona turned the thought over in her mind. As a proposition it shone, but she had been in business long enough to know that every deal had to be examined very carefully before it was agreed on. 'Let me think about that,' she said.

'Yes, you should.' Another idea had occurred to Frank in the meantime. 'Tell me, how much work do you do for CorVol?'

'Not much. Most of their printing's done down south.'

'Well.' Frank shifted on the desk, warming to the notion.

'I can't promise, but I might be able to do something about that. At least to push some of it your way.'

Fiona was nodding. 'Of course. You've got a good connection there, haven't you?'

'Yes, but I'm not sure printing's his province. Still, I'll have a quiet word with him.'

'Thanks. I'd be grateful.' Fiona was visibly brighter now than she had been when Frank first walked in.

'My pleasure,' Frank said, getting off the desk. 'I'll leave you to it, then.' He walked towards the door, then paused. 'By the way,' he said, 'are you doing anything tomorrow night?'

'I'm not sure,' Fiona said guardedly. 'Why do you ask?'

'I'm having a house-warming at the cottage. I was going to invite you last night. Will you come?'

Fiona twirled her pencil thoughtfully. 'Do you really think that's a good idea?'

'The Harpers'll be there too.'

'Just the same,' Fiona murmured. She was obviously in a quandary. 'Will you leave the invitation open?'

'Sure,' Frank said.

'OK. And if I don't make it, well, thanks for asking me anyway.'

Frank took that to mean Fiona wouldn't be coming. He gave her an understanding nod and left. As the door closed, Fiona sighed quietly and went back to her calculations.

Chapter Twenty-one

Donald Harper had arranged the miniature stacked stereo system on the centre of Frank's sideboard and put the little speakers at either end. After some fumbling at the power socket on the skirting board, he managed to get the plug in and the system's dials lit up.

'There we go!' Donald stood up, beaming at the shiny new equipment. Beside him, Frank and Sylvia were gazing at the lights like children looking in a toyshop window. Donald slipped a cassette into the tape deck and soft music began to fill the room. He patted Frank's shoulder and crossed to the table where half a dozen new long playing albums were lying. He held them up. 'These are to go with it,' he said. 'Just to get you started. Syl picked them out. She said she knows what you like.'

'And you can't deny that,' Sylvia drawled at Frank.

'How could I?' Frank said. He took the albums from Donald and smiled at Sylvia. 'Here's the proof.' He put the records down. 'Thank you. Both of you.' He moved to a small table by the fireplace where bottles and glasses were set out. 'What'll you have to drink?'

Sylvia asked for a brandy and soda and Donald said he would have a whisky. As Frank started pouring Sylvia wandered aimlessly around the room.

'This *is* fun isn't it?' she said.

Donald sat down on the settee, spreading his arms out along the back.

'The room's looking a bit different now, Frank.'

'It's a start,' Frank said modestly. To prepare for the small party, he had spent an hour going round with polish and a duster, and at the last minute he had even rearranged some of the furniture. It had amused him, afterwards, to realize that he was showing signs of becoming house-proud. 'Do you want anything with your scotch, Donald?'

'A little water, maybe.'

Sylvia scanned the row of bottles. 'You haven't brought any in,' she told Frank. He started to go to the kitchen but she checked him. 'I'll get it,' she said. 'I do so like to make myself useful.' She was halfway through the kitchen doorway when there was a knock on the front door. Sylvia paused, frowning.

'I'll get it.' Frank put down Donald's glass and went to the door. When he opened it he saw Fiona Neave standing on the doorstep, carrying a bottle wrapped in gold foil. There was a slim parcel under her arm. Frank didn't conceal his surprise.

'You did invite me,' Fiona said quietly.

'But you weren't sure about coming.'

'That hasn't changed. But I'm here anyway.'

Frank smiled. 'And I'm glad.' He stepped aside and ushered her into the room. Donald got to his feet immediately, smiling broadly.

Sylvia remained where she was, in the kitchen doorway, trying to look as if she was pleased. 'What a surprise,' she said brightly. 'You didn't say anyone else was coming, Frank.'

'Fiona wasn't certain she could make it,' Frank said. 'Now, have you all met before?'

Donald came forward, nodding. 'I don't know if Mrs Neave will remember, but we were introduced once.'

'Of course,' Fiona said. 'I remember. Hello, Mr Harper.'

'And when it's not important,' Sylvia said, maintaining her counterfeit smile, 'I use the same hairdresser as you do. I've seen you in there. That has to be almost as good as an introduction.'

'My wife Sylvia,' Donald said, shooting her a worried glance. 'And I'm Donald.'

169

Coolly, Fiona nodded. 'Good evening, Mrs Harper.' She handed the parcel to Frank. 'For the house,' she said.

Frank took off the wrapping. It was a framed enlargement of one of the colour photographs Fiona had taken the day they had gone birdwatching together.

'The short-eared owl. Remember?'

'Of course,' Frank said. He was delighted. 'It's beautiful. Thank you.'

'May I see?' Donald said, and Frank handed him the picture.

'This,' Fiona said, 'is my contribution to the celebration. It seemed appropriate.' She gave Frank the bottle.

He unwrapped it. 'Champagne,' he said, then emitted a low whistle. 'Krug sixty-six! This is very special.'

'It's a special occasion.' Fiona said, then looked across the room sharply as Sylvia turned on her heel and went into the kitchen.

Donald was shaking his head admiringly at the picture. 'This is delightful,' he said. 'Did you take it?'

Fiona was about to reply when Sylvia came back into the room, holding aloft a bottle of champagne.

'Snap!' she said triumphantly.

For an instant Frank looked bewildered. Then he understood. He glared at Sylvia.

'Where did you get that?' Donald asked.

'It was in the refrigerator,' Sylvia said. 'I put it there. Thursday night.'

'Well, that's that mystery solved,' Frank said, rather more lamely than he would have liked.

'I thought you spent Thursday curled up with a good book,' Donald said to Sylvia.

'This was earlier,' she said. 'I was bored. And I had nothing better to do.' She turned her attention to Fiona for a moment, issuing a hard, challenging look. 'You know how it is. So I came looking for company and brought a friend with me. But you weren't at home, were you, Frank?'

Her eyes flashed at Fiona again. 'He must have been out on the job somewhere.'

Fiona smiled charmingly. 'So you left the champagne for him. For tonight. Or some other time. That was nice of you.'

Sylvia nodded. 'And it proves that you and I have something in common, doesn't it?' She paused. 'A liking for champagne.'

Donald crossed and took the bottle from Sylvia, squinting at the label. 'You didn't miss much, Frank. This one's not nearly the same quality.' He grinned at Sylvia. 'But it'll do.' He started uncorking the bottle.

'I'll get some glasses,' Frank said, 'and let the Krug chill.' He went into the kitchen with the bottle.

Sylvia crossed the room and stood beside Fiona. 'That was our house-warming gift to Frank,' she said, pointing to the hi-fi unit. She glanced at the picture lying on the table, making a clear, undisguised comparison.

'Really,' Fiona said, maintaining the charm. 'It's very handsome.'

'But then he and Donald are old friends. And I've become very close to him since he drifted up here.'

The moment of tension was broken by a loud pop as Donald eased the cork out of the bottle. Frank came in on cue with a tray and four glasses. He put them on the table and Donald began pouring. He filled all four glasses then turned to Sylvia. 'It's just occurred to me,' he said, holding the bottle over the last glass; 'If Frank wasn't here when you came round on Thursday, how did you get in?'

Sylvia was visibly thrown by the question, but she recovered quickly. She looked at Frank. 'I've still got your spare key, haven't I?' She went to the sideboard and picked up her handbag. Removing the key she'd had cut, she crossed and handed it to Frank. 'I forgot to give it back to you. I don't suppose I'll be needing it again.'

Frank took the key and pocketed it. He gave Sylvia a

171

hard, warning look. 'I can't think why you should,' he said.

Sylvia returned the fleeting glare and turned away.

Donald brought the drinks on the tray and they each took one. 'To Frank and Half Mile Cottage,' he said, raising his glass. 'Happy days for both of them.' He took a sip and Fiona did the same. With obvious reluctance, Sylvia put the glass to her lips and removed it again, barely tasting the champagne.

'Thank you,' Frank said, and raised his own glass. 'To all of us.' As they all drank, Frank's eyes were firmly on Fiona. Sylvia was looking at her too.

Fiona cradled her glass and looked around the room. 'It's quite cosy, isn't it?' she said to Frank.

Frank nodded, but Sylvia broke in before he could say anything.

'You really must get another bed, Frank. Or a new mattress, anyway. The one you've got now is terribly uncomfortable.'

Donald laughed. 'I told you that's what she was doing when she slipped upstairs the first time we were here, didn't I? Checking the bed.'

Putting an edge in his own voice now, Frank said to Sylvia, 'That's all changed. Now it's your full interior-sprung luxury.'

'You obviously haven't been up there lately,' Fiona said smoothly to Sylvia.

Trying to smile, Sylvia fluttered her eyelids at Frank. 'You haven't been to another auction sale, have you?'

'No,' Frank said. 'Not this time.'

The music stopped, leaving a sudden stillness in the room.

'Oh, do play the other side, Frank,' Sylvia pouted. 'It's got some of the best tracks on it.'

As Donald went to the sideboard with Frank to show him how the tape deck worked, Sylvia crossed to the settee and ran her hand along the back of it in a calculated, proprietary movement.

'This is one of Frank's auction bargains,' she told Fiona. 'Do you approve?'

'Yes, I do,' Fiona said, smiling pleasantly. 'But then I have to really, don't I?' She waited for the incomprehension to spread across Sylvia's face before she went on. 'I helped him choose it. Didn't he tell you?'

Sylvia sipped her champagne, watching Fiona over the rim of the glass. Finding no suitable retort, she switched her attention to the two men. 'This is supposed to be a party, isn't it?' she said. 'Let's play a game.'

So softly that only Sylvia heard her, Fiona murmured, 'We are, aren't we?'

The rest of the evening was consumed with light conversation, drinking and listening to music. The two women continued to spar at every opportunity, although Fiona's obvious talent in that direction kept Sylvia from gaining any clear edge.

At eleven o'clock, Donald announced that he and Sylvia had to be going. Frank saw them to the door and thanked them again for their gift. He watched as they got into the Volvo; Donald waved, but Sylvia slid into the passenger seat without looking back.

As the car pulled away, Donald glanced sideways at his wife. 'You were being particularly bitchy tonight,' he said.

Sylvia was staring at the road ahead. 'I don't know what you mean,' she replied haughtily. 'I was just plain bloody bored. If anyone was being bitchy, it was that Neave woman.'

'You don't approve?'

'Who am I to approve or disapprove?'

'That's a point,' Donald said quietly.

Sylvia sniffed. 'I can't honestly say that I took to her, though.'

'She's a very attractive woman.'

Sylvia pulled open the glove compartment and took a

cigarette from the packet that was lying there. 'Old man Banner obviously thought that, too,' she hissed. 'But that's not much of a recommendation either.' She snapped the glove compartment shut and stabbed a finger at the cigar lighter on the console.

'Thank you,' Donald said wearily. 'But for your information, there's nothing to that story. It's just vicious gossip.'

'How can you be so sure?'

'Because it's part of my job to know what's going on locally,' Donald said. 'It's in CorVol's best interests.'

For a moment Sylvia was silent, then she said, 'Well, if you're right, then she's been in even less demand since her husband walked out on her, hasn't she? I mean, since we've been here I don't think I've seen her out with a man once.'

'Maybe there was no one around she fancied.' Donald smiled faintly. 'Till now.'

Sylvia snatched the cigar lighter from its socket and lit her cigarette. 'What's so attractive about Frank Scully, for God's sake?' she demanded.

'He must have something.'

'Well, it escapes me.'

Donald nodded slowly. 'Yes,' he said, 'so it would seem.'

Back at Half Mile Cottage, Frank had lowered the lights and put a disc on the turntable. The music was a favourite of his, Albinoni's Adagio in G Minor for strings and organ. He sat on the settee beside Fiona, letting the music wash over him. For as long as he could remember, the flowing symmetry of the piece had soothed him like old brandy.

After a while he turned his head slowly and looked at Fiona. Her eyes were closed. Frank leaned across and kissed her lightly on the lips. She opened her eyes and stared at him. Then she frowned and shook her head sadly.

'I'm sorry,' Frank said.

'So am I,' Fiona murmured. 'But only for you.' In one smooth, assured movement she turned and put her arms around him and began kissing him ardently.

Chapter Twenty-two

Two weeks after the house-warming, Frank was visited in his office by Councillor Ben Mayhew. It was no great event, although Mayhew's style was to make every occasion seem important, if not momentous. He was a bluff, self-regarding man in his mid-fifties who owned Micklethorpe's only Do-It-Yourself shop. He had come to the *Messenger* office to discuss an advertising feature planned to support his new venture, a larger and more ambitious DIY mini market.

Frank found the interview heavy going. Mayhew's up-to-the-minute ambitions were backed by a primitive bargaining-instinct that never missed an opportunity; prices had already been settled, but as they sat at the desk with the rough draft spread out between them, Mayhew still kept trying to knock Frank down a few pounds on trivialities. Frank resisted steadily, but it was exhausting.

After half an hour they managed to agree on the layout, but Mayhew had lingering suspicions about the smaller advertising spaces surrounding his own large spread.

'What about all these?' he demanded, scowling at the blank boxes.

'I'll be offering those spaces to your suppliers and whoever you've got fitting the place out for you,' Frank said patiently. 'You know the sort of thing; "Fix-It Tools wish every success to the new Mayhew's DIY Home Improvements Centre."'

Mayhew nodded slowly, watching Frank from beneath his bushy eyebrows. 'You'll be making a good few quid out of this, then. Wouldn't do you much harm to let me have my half page for nothing.'

'You must be joking.' Frank had to smile. It was Mayhew's boldest stroke yet. 'Look how many times you've got your name mentioned. And the copy for the feature'll be entirely dedicated to you and the new shop. Great publicity. Besides, you're getting the whole feature at the old advertising rates as it is.'

The whiff of a bargain brightened Mayhew visibly. 'You're putting the rates up, then?'

'Ten percent.'

'Well . . .' Mayhew rubbed his chin for a few seconds, then nodded sharply. 'So long as I'm not paying any more.' He studied the layout again, like a father scanning his newborn for blemishes. 'Will there be a photo and a piece on the opening in the paper itself? Like among the news items?'

'Well, a picture for sure,' Frank assured him. 'And maybe a paragraph or two.'

'Good,' Mayhew said. He sat back and folded his arms. 'I'm happy then.'

Frank could scarcely believe it. 'Fine,' he said. 'Then it's two more half pages after this with three six-by-four follow-ups pushing your special offers. Right?'

'Aye, that's it.'

Frank rolled up the layout, signalling that their business together was at an end, for the moment. He had a lot to do. As he stood up to put the layout on top of the safe, Mayhew took a cigar case from his pocket and offered him one.

'No thanks.' It looked as if the councillor was in a mood to linger. Frank sat down again, shifting his papers, trying to look as if he was under pressure.

'*The Messenger*'s doing all right then, is it?' Mayhew asked, cutting the end from a cigar and lighting it.

'No complaints. Sales are well up over the last five weeks.'

Mayhew nodded. 'You've got that "Wrathdale Remembered" to thank for that, I reckon.'

'Well, it's certainly helped.'

'We never got anything like that in John Wesley Banner's time. Clever.' Mayhew blew some smoke towards the ceiling. Trying for casualness, he said, 'Who is it that's writing it, then?'

Frank smiled. 'Chronicler,' he said.

'Aye, but who *is* Chronicler?'

'A lot of people have asked me that.'

'I don't wonder,' Mayhew grunted. 'And you'll not say?'

'I agreed not to,' Frank told him. 'The writer prefers to use a pen name.'

'Doesn't surprise me. Whoever it is, they know a thing or two.'

It was becoming clear that Mayhew would go when he felt like it; there was no point trying to rush him. Frank stopped shuffling his papers and folded his hands on the desk. 'You're following the series, are you?'

'Everyone is.' Mayhew studied the end of his cigar. 'It were the wife put me on to it. It's the first thing she turns to – but then, like all women, there's nothing suits her better than a good gossip. I reckon those little stories have put the fear of God into some folk in these parts.'

Frank looked surprised at that. He had thought of the articles as charming curiosities, nothing more.

'And the rest of us are learning a thing or two from them,' Mayhew went on. 'That latest one, for instance. Of course, everyone *thought* it were old George Carver what poured that stolen petrol into the drains during the war. And there's a few as didn't think he got a tip-off from someone in the police that he were going to be raided. Not that there were any proof, mind. Not then. But well . . .' Mayhew gestured with his cigar. 'Now we know for sure, don't we?'

Frank was frowning now.

'Of course,' Mayhew said, 'Carver's not named straight out in it. But then I reckon you're too smart for that, eh?'

He winked at Frank. 'Reading between the lines though, it were him all right.' He chuckled. 'They tell me he hasn't come out of his house since last Wednesday. He's been properly shamed.'

Now Frank looked shocked.

'And then there were that one that was really about Jack Jefford.' Mayhew shook his head with fleeting sadness. 'Bad business that. All round.' He stood up and moved the chair back. 'Still, like it says in the Bible, eh? "Be sure your sins will find you out." And I've nothing to hide.' He went towards the door, then paused. 'Time for a drink, have you?'

'I wish I had,' Frank said. He got up and crossed to the door, holding it open for Mayhew. 'I'm afraid I'm a bit pushed. It's press day.'

'Oh, aye. Of course.' Mayhew stepped out on to the landing. 'Ah well. Another time, eh?' He nodded cordially to Frank. 'Cheerio.'

Frank went back to his desk and tried to work. But he couldn't – not until he had taken the current issue of *The Messenger* from the file and read Miss Banner's piece again. He read it twice, then sat staring into space, realizing in sharp, painful stages how he had been as naive about the purpose of 'Wrathdale Remembered' as he had been about the motive behind the article on John Wesley Banner's will.

He started work again with the energy that can sometimes be generated by annoyance. It was double-edged; Frank Scully didn't much favour the kind of journalism that could damage or ruin human lives, and he disliked being used. He promised himself he would have words with Miss Banner.

Sylvia was in the Volvo, heading back from Micklethorpe to Rawden, when she rounded a bend and saw the crashed Range Rover a hundred yards ahead. It was on the left hand side of the road, angled over among the ruins of a dry stone wall. Its front wheels were off the ground and its drive shaft was resting on the footings of the wall. The skid marks clearly indicated that the vehicle had been travelling on the wrong side of the road. Sylvia began to slow down.

Beside the wreck a man from a local garage was attaching a tow rope from his breakdown truck while his mate, assisted by a farmer, was clearing the larger stones from under the Range Rover. Standing off from the activity and looking very bored by it all was Lillian, the Dowager Lady Wrathdale. She was an elegantly dressed, silver-haired woman of sixty-seven who made every effort to look half that age. A little way beyond her, just as fashionably dressed but looking a little more ruffled, her young companion Sergio stood gazing off across the fields.

'He's a bloody maniac, he is,' the farmer was muttering to one of the garage men. 'Driving on the wrong side, he were. Nearly ploughed into my tractor as I came out of the gate.'

Lillian saw the Volvo approaching and immediately began waving to it. She stepped into the road then turned towards the wreck and called out imperiously, 'Right, we'll leave you to it, then. I'll call in at the garage later. Or someone will, anyway. Meanwhile you have my name and address.'

The three men stared at her.

Lillian called out something to her companion in Italian, then the two of them moved towards the Volvo where it had drawn in on the opposite side of the road. Sylvia wound down the window.

'Would you be so kind as to give us a lift?' Lillian asked sweetly. She saw Sylvia looking at the wreck. 'Nothing to worry about,' she said. 'Nobody hurt.' She turned and said something else in Italian and her companion immediately opened the front passenger door and got in beside Sylvia. Lillian got into the back.

Sylvia gazed at them both, as amused as she was

179

surprised. Sergio was giving her his best smile while Lillian settled back in a regal pose by the window.

'Where do you want to go?' Sylvia asked, starting the car again.

'Well,' Lillian said in a low, confidential tone, 'we were looking for a decent pub, actually. Can you recommend one?'

Ten minutes later they were in the lounge bar of *The Malt Shovel*, a few miles outside of Rawden. Sylvia and Lillian sat at a table in the corner while Sergio got the drinks. Lillian had lit up a cheroot in an amber holder which she waved elaborately as the drinks arrived.

'Ah! Good boy!'

Sergio set out the glasses from the tray and was about to sit down when Lillian stopped him with an abruptly raised finger. She snatched up the notes from the tray then pointed to the remaining silver coins.

'You take that, Sergio darling,' she said in slow, careful English. 'Go and play on the machines. And take the tray with you.'

Sergio gave her a hurt look, then shrugged and picked up his glass again. He shot another smile at Sylvia then moved off with the tray and the money.

'He'll be perfectly happy playing with the space machines or whatever,' Lillian confided to Sylvia. 'He adores them.'

Sylvia, who was only just getting accustomed to the Dowager's bulldozing style, looked around her for a moment then said, 'I'm not sure they have any machines here.'

'Oh, they're bound to,' Lillian said airily. 'They're everywhere these days, aren't they? They've probably got them in the Vatican now.' She raised her glass. 'Cheers.'

They drank, Sylvia sipping her gin and tonic and noticing that the older woman was almost gulping hers – which was, she'd swear, a large measure of neat scotch. She also noticed, now that they were close to each other and in a good light, that Lillian's immaculate make-up couldn't quite hide the fact that her face had been lifted more than once.

Sylvia put down her glass and decided to give her curiosity a cautious airing. 'He's a good-looking young man, isn't he?' she said brightly.

'Yes he is,' Lillian replied. 'Very.' She was fixing Sylvia with a candid, sardonic look. 'But then gigolos have to be, don't they? Or they wouldn't eat.'

'Oh.' Sylvia was taken aback, though only a little. 'I'm terribly sorry, I didn't mean to . . .'

'Of course you didn't,' Lillian smiled. 'Have I shocked you?'

Sylvia shook her head. 'Not in the least.'

Lillian studied her openly for a minute, sipping absently from her glass, then she said, 'No, I didn't think so. But then, you don't really fit in around here, either.'

Sylvia was warming to the woman rapidly. 'Thank you,' she said. 'I take that as a compliment.'

Lillian nodded at Sylvia's hand. 'You're married, I see.'

'Yes.'

'How long?'

'Quite some time.'

'Happily?'

Sylvia hesitated. 'Do I have to answer that?'

Lillian's nod and the momentary narrowing of her eyes signalled her understanding. 'There'll be lovers then.' She put up her hand hastily. 'No, don't bother to answer that either. There's no need.'

Sylvia laughed. 'You can tell?'

'*I* can,' Lillian murmured. 'But don't worry. It's not some kind of stigma you carry around with you. It requires a very special kind of perception. And I do so envy you.' She sighed wistfully and took another swallow from her glass. 'Such a thing was quite out of the question for me when I was your age. I was far too restricted. I thought

181

about it a great deal, though.' She straightened, pulling herself back into the present. 'And what does your husband do, apart from boring you?'

'He's in public relations.'

'And dedicated to it, no doubt.'

Sylvia nodded. 'Totally.'

'And do you live in Wrathdale?'

'Unfortunately. You don't though.'

'No, I live in Venice.'

'Oh, really?' Sylvia was intrigued. 'I was in Venice once. It's lovely, isn't it?'

Lillian nodded dreamily. 'It's the only place to live, as far as I'm concerned. So many interesting people. And all of them so simpatico. Didn't you find that?'

'I wasn't there long enough to really get to know anyone,' Sylvia said. 'Besides,' she added, 'my husband was with me.'

'Pity.' The understanding was in Lillian's eyes again. 'You should spend some time there. Unencumbered. I'm quite sure you'd find it extremely stimulating. In every way.'

'I might do that.' Sylvia saw no reason why she couldn't, given Donald's preoccupation with work and his moderate indifference to what she got up to when she was out of his sight. She watched Lillian as she made further inroads on her drink, fascinated by the woman's self-possession. 'Are you married?'

'Widowed.'

'Oh, I'm sorry.'

Lillian shrugged. 'You've no cause to be. I'm not. He led me a hell of a dance.'

Sylvia nodded, showing some sympathy of her own. 'And are you just passing through?'

'Visiting. Though I suppose you could say I'm a native of sorts. Long time since I was last here, though. Fourteen years.' She looked round her, shivering theatrically. 'God but it's a dreary place, isn't it?'

'Incredibly,' Sylvia agreed. 'So why are you here?'

'Because,' Lillian sighed, swirling the remains of her drink, 'my son and his wife were planning on coming to me in October. It was the only time they could make it. And that would've been awkward. I've other plans for around that time. So this way they get their filial obligations over for another year. And I'm left with October free and no problems.'

Sylvia laughed. She found this woman thoroughly delightful. 'Are you staying with them?'

'Yes,' Lillian said grimly. 'And I've been cooped up in that house for the past four days. Oh, they're lovely people, really they are. But such sticks. You can't imagine how provincial they are. But then if you live locally I expect you've met them. My son is Lewis Haddon.'

'Then you must be Lady Wrathdale,' Sylvia said, wide-eyed.

'Thank God you didn't say the Dowager Lady. It makes me feel like some kind of relic.'

Getting over her surprise, Sylvia introduced herself.

The older woman nodded, smiling. 'Hello, Sylvia. I'm Lillian.'

'Donald and I have been invited to a garden party at the castle. I imagine it's to meet you, isn't it?'

Lillian sighed deeply. 'Indeed it is. Oh, I do wish they hadn't done that. It's going to be quite an ordeal. For you too, I imagine. Still, it's nice to know there'll be at least one other human being there.'

Their glasses were empty. The two women looked at each other, smiling. 'Now,' Lillian said, 'you will have another one, won't you?'

An hour later they emerged from the pub and stood for a moment in the forecourt. Lillian slipped half a bottle of whisky into her handbag and turned to Sylvia.

'My dear, I can't tell you how much I've enjoyed talking to you.'

'It's mutual,' Sylvia assured her.

'Now, if you wouldn't mind just dropping us off at the garage, I'll ring the Lodge and get my son to pick us up from there.'

They crossed to the car and Sylvia held open the back door for Lillian. 'I don't imagine your son's going to be too pleased.'

Lillian climbed in carefully and looked at Sylvia. 'Teach him to lock up the scotch, won't it?' She folded her hands in her lap and sat back, smiling. 'By the way, would you like Sergio to drive?'

Chapter Twenty-three

On the day before the garden party at Aynsgill Castle, Frank Scully made his usual weekly visit to Miss Banner at Ravensfell House.

According to ritual, Frank sat on the Victorian sofa in the sitting room while Miss Banner sat at the table opposite him, reading through the new edition of *The Messenger*. It had occurred to Frank that this was like having a weekly meditation session, motionlessly watching the top of the old woman's head for fifteen minutes as she read every page from top to bottom.

When she had finished, Miss Banner folded the newspaper neatly and placed it to one side. 'You're getting more advertisements in, I see,' she remarked quietly.

'Yes,' Frank said, 'there's a very healthy demand for space at the moment.' He leaned forward. 'I've put the rates up ten percent, by the way.'

Miss Banner nodded, straight-faced. 'You'll know what's right.' She moved her chair back a fraction. 'I'll not keep you any longer, then . . .'

'There's just one thing,' Frank murmured.

'Oh aye?'

'Your weekly column.'

Miss Banner's jaw hardened. 'What about it?'

'Well . . .' Frank scratched the side of his nose, trying for a little diffidence in his approach. Miss Banner didn't invite straight attack. 'From what I've been hearing lately, it seems you might have been sailing a bit close to the wind with some of your stories.'

'How's that, then?'

'Apparently they've been touching a few raw nerves. Indirectly anyway.'

Miss Banner clasped her hands slowly. 'Have folk complained?'

Frank shook his head firmly. 'No.' It was important that she realized he wasn't over-reacting. 'Not so far. And the pieces have always seemed harmless enough to me. Just very amusing and highly entertaining.' He paused. 'But then I'm a stranger to Wrathdale. Obviously there's some, at least, who've been reading the stories in an entirely different way.'

'The past is the past,' Miss Banner said. 'And I write what I write. How folk read it is up to them. And if there's any that have a guilty conscience about summat or other and see themselves in what I've given you – well, there's nowt I can do about it.'

'No, I suppose not,' Frank said, frowning. 'Still . . .'

'You want to stop printing it,' Miss Banner said sharply. 'Is that what you're saying?'

'No. No way. It's proving far too popular. But I just thought I'd mention it.' Frank stood up and moved to the door. 'And bear it in mind, will you? The last thing we want is anyone sticking us with a libel suit.'

Miss Banner sniffed derisively. 'No one's likely to, are they? Not for summat that's just in their mind. Leastways, not without bringing whatever it was into the open for judgement.' She tapped the table with one stiffened finger. 'There's nobody with summat hidden who'd want that.'

Frank stared at her. The chilly calculation in her thinking was impressive, in an unpleasant way, even though it wasn't particularly convincing.

The garden party was held on the lawns between Aynsgill Castle and the Lodge. A colourful marquee had been set up for tea, and entertainment was being provided by a section of the CorVol silver band.

The number of guests had been strictly limited and most of them arrived on time. In front of the marquee a small group of guests quickly clustered around Lewis, Beattie and Lillian, who was resplendent in a bright trouser suit and carried a large tapestry handbag. Beattie beckoned forward and elderly clergyman and introduced him to Lillian.

'This is the Reverend Summers,' Beattie said, smiling nervously. Not even close relatives could be sure what Lillian would say to people.

'A great pleasure, Lady Wrathdale,' the old man said, extending his hand.

Lillian shook it firmly. 'How do you do, Father.'

Summers looked a little embarrassed.

'Mother,' Lewis said, smiling as grimly as his wife, 'Mr Summers is a Baptist minister.'

'Oh!' Lillian looked highly amused. 'I do beg your pardon. In Italy one gets so used to thinking of it all as Roman.' She patted the minister's hand before releasing it. 'Still, I imagine you were somewhere cheering the Pope with the rest of them when he came over here.' She watched the old man's eyes waver before she added, 'In the cause of ecumenism.'

'We all worship the same God,' Summers said lamely.

'That's true.' Lillian flashed her wickedest smile. 'Although sometimes you'd never think so, would you?'

A few yards away Donald and Sylvia Harper were standing among the other guests. Donald was smiling and nodding to everyone who caught his eye, but Sylvia had maintained the same bored expression since she arrived.

'Do try to look as if you're enjoying yourself,' Donald murmured from the side of his mouth.

'I am,' Sylvia snapped. 'Isn't it showing?'

At that moment, Fiona Neave's car was coming up the drive towards the Lodge. Sitting beside Fiona in the neat little MGB was Frank Scully. They had both received invitations to the garden party, and after a brief discussion of pros and cons, they had decided to accept – and to attend together.

Fiona parked the car among the others lined up in front of the Lodge and she and Frank got out. They stood for a moment and watched the mingling throng of guests over on the lawn.

'Right,' Frank said, slinging his camera on to his shoulder. 'Here we go again.' He took Fiona's hand and they started walking.

'Different this time,' Fiona murmured.

Frank nodded. 'I hope so.'

A hundred yards away Lewis was talking to three of the male guests, all of them businessmen. 'I couldn't agree more,' he was saying, adopting a tone and approach that was practically automatic by now. The subject under discussion was hikers, their damaging effect on the Wrathdale countryside, and the Rural District Council's laxity in dealing with them. The view Lewis had chosen to express was conservative and squarely on the side of the local Traders' Association. 'What's needed is some kind of direct action,' he went on. 'Like raising the matter with the Department of the Environment over their heads.'

'Aye, you're right there,' one of the men said. 'If we just let it drift on, then come next year we'll be overrun with them.'

Suddenly Lewis wasn't listening. He had seen Fiona and Frank approaching from the far side of the lawn.

'Not that I've anything against folk enjoying the countryside,' the man rambled on. 'None of us has. So long as they behave themselves. But it they open up this other footpath, you'll not see this dale for hairy great walkers with packs on their backs.'

Lewis nodded, feigning close attention while his eyes stayed fixed on Fiona in her bright, floral dress. He narrowed his eyes a fraction and noticed with a small jolt that the couple were holding hands. As he went on watching, he saw them move towards the Harpers.

'It isn't as if they bring much money with them,' the man was saying. 'They're not your hotel trade, are they? A cup of coffee here and there and a few pints maybe. But by and large they don't benefit local trade . . .'

Lewis continued to nod, his face solemn as he reluctantly forced his attention back to the trio in front of him.

Donald Harper had brightened immensely at the sight of Frank and Fiona. 'I've been looking for you two,' he said. 'Felt sure you'd be here.'

Frank nodded to Donald and Sylvia as Fiona stood just a pace behind him.

'Nice to see you again, Mrs Neave,' Donald said, eyeing her admiringly. 'You're looking very lovely, if I may say so.'

Sylvia, ignoring what her husband was saying, gave Frank a hard look. 'You're quite the stranger these days,' she said.

Frank shrugged. 'Been a bit pushed for time recently, what with one thing and another.'

'Yes,' Sylvia drawled, her teeth barely separating, 'I'm sure you have.'

Frank looked at Donald. 'So what happens now?'

'We mingle, I imagine,' Donald said. 'And wait to be introduced, of course.' He sighed. 'Garden parties aren't really my style. Still, when duty calls . . .' He caught Frank's enquiring look and lowered his voice confidentially. 'Lord Wrathdale's one of the UK directors of CorVol's parent company, Freedman Chemicals.' He jerked his thumb at the marquee. 'Hence the silver band. I'm just here to make sure no one pinches their instruments.'

Sylvia had finally forced herself to acknowledge there was another woman present. She smiled tightly at her, then scanned her slowly up and down. 'What an attractive dress, Mrs Neave,' she said. 'Did you make it yourself?'

To avoid the irksome game of exchanging veiled insults

189

with Sylvia, Fiona smiled, excused herself, then turned and wandered over towards a couple she had recognized. She spoke to them for a minute and was about to move on to another group of acquaintances when Lewis moved up alongside her. To maintain appearances he was smiling, but his eyes were grave.

'Hello,' he said.

Fiona nodded, issuing her own smokescreen smile.

'I miss you,' Lewis said. 'Desperately. I have to see you. Can I come to the Gatehouse tomorrow?'

Fiona looked about her, just managing to hold the smile. 'I'd rather you didn't.'

'But we can't leave things the way they are. At least let's talk about it.'

Fiona stared at him. 'We have. And there's nothing more to say. It's over, Lewis.' She moved past him. 'Excuse me.'

Beattie had brought Lillian across and introduced her to Donald, Sylvia and Frank. There was an immediate impromptu conspiracy between Lillian and Sylvia as they pretended to be encountering each other for the first time.

'I can't tell you how I've been looking forward to meeting you, Lady Wrathdale,' Sylvia said, suppressing a mischievous smile.

'How very kind,' Lillian replied grandly, shaking Sylvia's hand. 'Thank you.' She turned and looked at Donald. 'What a charming wife you have,' she told him. 'I hope you treasure her.'

'Oh, I know her full worth,' Donald beamed. 'Believe me.'

Lillian shot a glance at Sylvia, who was having to clamp her mouth shut. 'I'm glad to hear it,' Lillian went on. 'And what do you do, Mr Harper?'

'I handle PR for the Freedman Chemical Corporation.'

'Really!' Lillian looked fascinated. 'How interesting. I imagine that's very absorbing work, isn't it?'

Sylvia had to turn away, choking back her mirth.

Lillian went on cross-questioning Donald for another five minutes, until she got tired of the game and turned her attention instead to Frank Scully, who had been deep in conversation with Beattie.

They talked vaguely for a time about Frank's work, then Lillian said, 'John Wesley Banner's dead, I understand.'

'Yes,' Frank nodded. 'He died a couple of months ago.'

'And you've taken over *The Messenger*, have you?'

'Only as editor. His sister owns it now.'

Lillian's interest intensified a shade. 'She's still around, is she?'

Frank grinned. 'Very much so. And talking of *The Messenger*, Lady Wrathdale, I'd like to have a picture of you for next week's issue. Do you mind?'

'Not at all.'

'The three of you together, perhaps,' Frank said. He glanced at Beattie. 'If that's all right.'

'Of course.' Beattie looked around, frowning. 'Lewis seems to have got waylaid again, I'm afraid.'

'That's all right,' Frank asssured her. 'We can do it later.'

He turned and saw Fiona standing a few feet away. He called to her and she joined them. Lillian's polite boredom seemed to evaporate at once. She stared closely at Fiona as they were being introduced. She looked even more interested when Beattie used Fiona's full name – Mrs Lytton Neave.

'Mrs Neave owns the printing works now,' Beattie explained. 'She's made a great success of it.'

Lillian was now studying Fiona's face intently. 'I remember Albert Neave,' she murmured. 'He was the printer in Micklethorpe in my day. So you must be . . .'

'I married his nephew,' Fiona said. 'Geoffrey.'

'I see,' Lillian nodded. 'And is your husband here with you?'

'We're divorced.'

'Ah!' Lillian gave a slow, sympathetic nod. She turned to

Beattie and murmured, '*Lytton* Neave, you said?'

Fiona glanced sideways at Frank Scully, letting him see how awkward she was feeling under the Dowager's scrutiny. As Lillian began staring again, Fiona explained. 'My family name is Lytton,' she said. 'I wanted to hold on to it. Not that many people remember. Mostly it's just plain Mrs Neave around here.'

'You must be strict about it,' Lillian told her firmly. 'How long have you been in Wrathdale?'

'Ten years now.'

Lillian nodded, her stare undiminished. 'And where are you from originally?'

'I was born in Darlington.' The interrogation was beginning to annoy Fiona. Lillian hadn't asked anything impertinent or particularly searching, but her manner was unnerving.

'Were you indeed!' Lillian clapped her hands together. 'How very interesting. I used to know some people in Darlington called Lytton. A delightful couple. He was a doctor. They had a daughter as far as I remember.'

Fiona shook her head. 'My father was a bookseller.'

'Oh.' Lillian scowled delicately. 'Not the same Lyttons, then.' She rolled her eyes as if she were trying to look directly into her head, then she said, 'Now I come to think of it, I'm not sure it was Darlington they lived in, anyway.' She made a show of remembering suddenly. 'No, of course it wasn't. How stupid of me. I remember now. It was Doncaster.'

'I think it's time for tea,' Beattie said, and she led her mother-in-law, Fiona and Frank into the marquee.

At the first opportunity Frank and Fiona moved away from the long table with their cups and immersed themselves in their own conversation. They spoke about nothing of any importance. It was simply a device to get Fiona away from the old woman's uncomfortable scrutiny.

Lewis had come into the tent and was standing by the

192

serving table with his wife and mother, chatting with desperate brightness and trying not to stare at Fiona. Lillian was sipping her tea and ignoring what her son was saying. She was still watching Fiona, but now her expression was different; she was smiling, almost secretively.

Sergio came into the tent and Lillian was suddenly distracted. She put down her cup and saucer so quickly she nearly dropped them. 'I want a word with that young man,' she muttered. She hurried across to where Sergio was standing. He grinned amiably at her. 'At last!' Lillian hissed. 'Where have you been?'

Sergio's grin widened.

'Did you get it?' Lillian demanded.

Sergio opened his jacket just wide enough to let her see the half bottle of whisky tucked into the waistband of his trousers. Lillian glanced around cautiously. She opened her handbag discreetly then moved in close to Sergio, so that he was momentarily screened from Lewis and Beattie. Swiftly, Sergio slipped the bottle into the handbag and stepped back.

Lillian put out her free hand. 'And the change?'

Sergio looked at the hand, still grinning, then turned away and reached for a sandwich from a tray being carried across the marquee by a waitress.

Lillian sighed and shook her head, the way a mother would when a young child has exasperated her. She went back to the table and rejoined Lewis and Beattie.

'Is he enjoying himself?' Beattie asked.

Lillian shrugged. 'He seems to be.'

'And how about you, mother?' Lewis enquired. 'Are you enjoying the party?'

'It's been an absolutely fascinating afternoon,' Lillian said, glancing across at Fiona again.

Lewis was about to say something else when he spotted someone he wanted to speak to, standing further along the table. He excused himself and went off.

Lillian moved closer to Beattie. 'What a striking woman Mrs Lytton Neave is,' she murmured. 'Do tell me more about her.'

Beattie looked at Fiona and smiled distantly. 'Well, she recently came into money,' she said softly, and watched Lillian's cunning old eyes grow wider.

Chapter Twenty-four

The party was entering its second hour when Lillian led Sylvia through the French windows and into the drawing room of Aynsgill Lodge. Each woman was suppressing giggly laughter, and each carried an empty teacup.

'Here we are,' Lillian said, going to the table in the centre of the room and opening her handbag. She took out the half bottle of whisky, unscrewed the cap and poured stiff measures into the two cups.

Sylvia laughed. 'It won't be long before they come looking for you, you know.'

Lillian sniffed the scotch and moistened her lips. 'Time enough,' she grunted. She put the bottle back in her bag and then raised her cup in salute. 'Cheers.'

'Cheers.'

They drank and Lillian emitted a long, peaceful sigh. 'Ah, that's better. I needed that. I don't think I've ever been so bored before in my life.'

Sylvia pulled a face. 'I know what you mean.'

'I did predict it, didn't I?' Lillian was standing with one hand on her hip, the cup at the ready a few inches from her mouth. 'God, but I'll be glad to get home.'

'When are you leaving?' Sylvia asked her.

'Tomorrow.'

Sylvia looked surprised. 'So soon?'

Lillian nodded. 'I was supposed to stay another week but I told them Sergio was pining. And I'm quite sure they won't be sorry to see the back of us.'

'I will be,' Sylvia said. 'I was going to ask you both to dinner.'

'Oh, how nice.' Lillian looked genuinely touched. 'I'd

195

have liked that. Still, you must come and visit me in Venice.' Her eye made the shadow of a wink. 'On your own, if you can.'

'I think that could be arranged,' Sylvia said archly.

Lillian took another swallow from her teacup. 'Good. And I'll give a dinner party for you and invite all kinds of interesting people.' She wandered over to the fireplace and gazed up at the oil portrait of the previous Lord Wrathdale. Sylvia crossed and stood beside her.

'Your husband?' she asked.

Lillian nodded. 'And that's another thing about this place,' she said. 'It's full of ghosts. And memories. Few of them happy ones.'

Sylvia turned and looked at Lillian. 'You really haven't enjoyed your stay at all, have you?'

Lillian smiled at her. 'Oh, it's had its moments,' she said. 'Meeting you, for instance. And this dreadful garden party has been quite amusing in its own strange way.' She jerked her head towards the open windows. 'It's not often you come face to face socially with one of your husband's bastards, is it?'

'What?' Sylvia stared at her, astounded. 'You're not serious!'

'It was something of a surprise to me too,' Lillian said wryly. 'And I imagine *she'd* be quite taken aback if she knew.'

Sylvia blinked at her. 'Someone *here*? This afternoon?'

'Yes.'

'Who?'

Lillian gave her a warning look. 'Strictly between us,' she murmured.

'Of course.'

'She could be a friend of yours . . .'

Sylvia shook her head. 'I doubt it very much. Who is it?'

'Mrs Lytton Neave,' Lillian said quietly.

All Sylvia could do, for the moment, was stare at the old woman.

'Frankly, I'm surprised that no one around here has spotted it.' Lillian gazed up at the portrait again. 'It struck me the moment I first saw her.' She smiled. 'She's the image of Bernard when he was about the same age. I knew of her existence, of course. But I must say I never expected to meet her. And certainly not here.'

In little more than a whisper, Sylvia said, 'Your husband told you about the child?'

Lillian turned to her. 'No. At least not when it all happened. But I used to go through his desk from time to time. Just checking. Seeing what he was up to. There were these regular monthly payments listed on his personal bank statements which didn't make any sense.' Lillian sipped her drink and sighed. 'Went on for years, they did. Getting larger all the time. That made me suspicious. And then, when he was dying, Bernard told me everything.' For a moment her eyes were distant with the recollection. 'God knows why. He never had much of a conscience. A final act of spite, I think. Anyway, apparently the baby had been given to a couple in Darlington named Lytton, who couldn't have any children. They registered her as their own. The money was to help them raise her. There wasn't much profit in bookselling in those days. I don't suppose there is now.' Lillian drained her cup and took the bottle out of her handbag again. 'Another one?'

Sylvia nodded. 'Why not?' She held out her cup and Lillian poured another stiff measure. 'And Mrs Neave doesn't know?' she said.

Lillian poured her own drink and put the bottle back in her handbag. 'I'm sure she doesn't,' she said.

Sylvia could scarcely believe that. 'She settled here . . .'

'Yes,' Lillian said, 'but that was obviously just a fluke. She married Albert Neave's nephew and Albert died and left him the printing business in Micklethorpe. If he hadn't, she'd have probably never set foot in the place.' Lillian shrugged at the portrait. 'Life's odd, isn't it? The tricks it plays on all of us.' She raised her cup and turned to Sylvia again. 'Cheers.'

'So who's Fiona Neave's mother?' Sylvia asked.

Lillian's smile spread slowly above the rim of the cup, hinting at a rich fund of secrets, to be imparted only as she saw fit.

At mid-afternoon in the sitting room at Ravensfell House Miss Banner sat down, as she now did at the same time every week, to write her piece for *The Messenger*. In front of her was the lined pad of writing paper, a pen, and the group photograph she had mutilated several weeks before. She glanced at the picture as she took up her pen and slid the pad towards her; the whorls of ink around Fiona Neave's smiling head were like a black nimbus.

Miss Banner held the pen close to the blank paper and collected her thoughts. After a minute she wrote the first line; 'Wrathdale Remembered'. Under that, in her careful longhand, she added the sub-heading; 'The Miller's Wife'.

The band had just finished its last piece, a medley from *Iolanthe*, and the men were starting to pack away their instruments. Most of the guests had already gone. Donald Harper had finally managed to get away from a small man who had lectured him for ten minutes on the possibly harmful effects of one of CorVol's products; now Donald had wandered round to the rear of the Lodge, looking for Sylvia.

Just as he was about to turn around and try elsewhere, he saw her up ahead emerging from the French windows. He stood and waited for her to come to him. Sylvia was looking very pleased with herself.

'Time we were going,' Donald said as she came up to him. 'What were you doing in the house?'

'Having a chat with Lady Wrathdale senior.' She smiled

in a way that struck Donald as secretive. 'And a very interesting chat it was, too.'

They went round to the drive at the front of the house where the Volvo was parked. Lord and Lady Wrathdale were standing nearby and they approached as Donald was taking the car keys from his pocket.

'Ah, Harper,' Lewis called. 'Off, are you?'

'Just collecting up his belongings,' Sylvia said.

Donald went forward and shook hands with Lewis and Beattie. 'Thank you both for a very pleasant afternoon.'

'I wouldn't have missed it for anything,' Sylvia added.

Beattie nodded and smiled. 'We're glad you could come.'

Lewis was looking around him anxiously. 'We've been looking for my mother,' he said. 'Heaven only knows where she's got to.'

'Lillian's in the drawing room,' Sylvia told him. 'I've just left her there.'

Beattie immediately looked anxious. 'Is she all right?'

'Oh, yes,' Sylvia assured her. 'She's in great form. We were talking about the good old days. And the local goings on. She's a mine of information. Sorry to hear she's leaving so soon. Tomorrow, she tells me.'

Lewis nodded. 'It's a pity. We were planning on having her with us a bit longer. Still, there we are.' He spread his hands in resignation. 'She feels she must get back.'

As the Harpers were walking to their car Lewis stood gazing after them. 'You know,' he said to Beattie, 'they're probably the only people here today that mother hasn't managed to offend in one way or another.'

'On the contrary,' Beattie murmured, 'she seems to have made a friend there.' She smiled at Lewis and slipped her arm through his. 'Hold on, my dear. Less than twenty-four hours to go now. And I don't imagine she's done much real harm.'

Donald Harper hadn't quite reached the car when

199

Sylvia's murmured bombshell of information made him draw up sharp, staring at her. 'You're not serious!' he gasped.

Sylvia nodded, looking wonderfully pleased.

'Fiona Neave,' Donald breathed, shaking his head. 'She's Miss Banner's daughter?'

'And sired by the late Lord Wrathdale, what's more.'

'I don't believe it.'

Sylvia shrugged. 'It's true, according to Lillian. And it all fits. She gave me chapter and verse on it.'

Donald was still looking as if someone had struck him. 'Her husband and Miss Banner were lovers!'

'Nothing so romantic.' Sylvia stood and waited for Donald to unlock the car. 'But he tumbled her more than once. Apparently she was quite something when she was young. And it seems that old man Wrathdale harvested one or two of the local peasant girls in his time. A touch of the *droit de seigneur*. Only with Miss B his sins bore fruit, as they say.'

They got into the car. Sylvia eased herself down in the seat beside Donald and folded her arms. 'It explains why John Wesley Banner left Fiona all that money, doesn't it?' she said. 'Now we know. She wasn't his mistress. She was his niece.'

'Yes,' Donald said, starting the engine. 'Well I did say there wasn't any truth in that charming piece of gossip.'

'This isn't gossip. It's fact.'

'Maybe,' Donald grunted.

'Lillian's one hundred percent certain.'

Donald eased the car slowly down the drive. 'So who else knows?' he asked Sylvia.

'No one. Not even her son.'

'But she told you. Why?'

Sylvia had her half-lidded, secretive look again. 'It was an exchange of confidences.' Donald glanced at her and she smiled. 'Woman talk. We were comparing husbands. Oh, don't worry. You came out of it very well. Almost the ideal

– for both of us. We have a lot in common, Lillian and me.'

'So it would seem,' Donald said dryly.

'And she's relying on my discretion.'

'Well, I hope she can. It's not the kind of story to broadcast. It could cause a hell of a lot of embarrassment.'

'Could it?' Sylvia said, sounding sweetly innocent.

'Around here?' Donald glanced sharply at her. 'Of course it could. And not just up at the Lodge, either. For one thing, I doubt if Fiona would want it known that she's a Wrathdale bastard.'

Sylvia looked suddenly amused. 'Might do her a lot of good,' she said. 'Bring in some extra business. She could even have her own coat of arms on her letter-heading.' She laughed. 'With a bar sinister, of course.'

'That's not funny,' Donald warned her. 'True or not, keep the story to yourself. Don't go spreading it about.'

'As if I would,' Sylvia said, smiling softly.

That evening, Frank entertained Fiona to dinner at Half Mile Cottage. When they had finished and had done the washing up, they stood facing each other in the small living room.

'Thanks for the help with the dishes,' Frank said.

'Thanks for the meal.'

He nodded to the bottles on the table by the fireplace. 'Nightcap?'

Fiona shook her head. 'I must go.'

'Do you have to?' Frank drew her towards him and they kissed.

'Things to do tomorrow,' Fiona murmured.

'It's Sunday tomorrow.'

'Just the same.' She moved away from him. 'And I'm rather tired. This afternoon was a bit of a strain. Even more than I thought it would be.'

Frank was watching her eyes. 'Did you speak to him?'

'We said hello.'

'Nothing more?'

'He asked if he could come and see me,' Fiona sighed. 'I said I'd rather he didn't.'

'And did you mean it?'

She stiffened. 'Of course. It's over. There was never any future in it, I know that now. And there's no going back to the way things were.'

Frank made a little smile. 'Are you absolutely certain of that?'

'I've proved it, haven't I?' She was staring at him, though not quite resentfully. Frank's regular insistence that she examine her feelings was something Fiona valued; it was harder for her to deceive herself nowadays. 'I've proved it to you at least, surely,' she murmured.

'How about to yourself?'

'To me too.' She held his steady gaze. 'And in the same way.'

'I'm glad,' Frank said. He took her in his arms again. 'Are you really going?'

'It's best that I do.' She kissed him briefly. 'I mustn't make too much of a habit of you. It's not fair.'

'No complaints about that. I promise.'

Fiona stepped back, looking at him squarely. 'Not now, perhaps. But for how long, I wonder?' She kissed him on the cheek and moved away, picking up her handbag from the sideboard and going to the door. 'Goodnight.'

Frank followed her. 'Fiona, I . . .'

She sealed his lips with her finger. 'Better not,' she said.

'You don't know what I was going to say.'

'I think I do.'

'Oh?' He raised his eyebrows. 'And you don't want to hear it?'

'No.' She pulled the door open a fraction. 'Please, Frank. I know it's selfish of me, but it would only complicate things between us – make it all impossible, even. And I wouldn't want that.'

'Well.' He shrugged. 'That has to be a good sign. A start, anyway.'

'Maybe. But don't expect too much. I'd hate you to be disappointed.' She kissed his cheek again. 'Goodnight.' She went out, closing the door after her.

Frank remained where he was, staring at the door, missing her already.

Chapter Twenty-five

At ten o'clock on Monday morning Lord Wrathdale went into the printing works through the side entrance by the alley. He stopped just inside the door and looked around. Reuben Flaxman was setting up one of the presses and Tom Holliday was trimming some leaflets on the guillotine. The door to Fiona's office was closed.

Tom Holliday nodded respectfully. 'Morning, sir.'

'Good morning, Tom,' Lewis said brightly, coming across to the guillotine. 'Mrs Neave in, is she?'

'Yes sir. You've just caught her. I'll tell her you're here.'

'No,' Lewis said hastily, detaining Tom. 'That's all right, thanks. Don't bother. I'll just put my head round the door.'

He strode across to the office and tapped the door. After a moment he heard Fiona's voice telling him to come in. He slipped into the office quietly, closing the door behind him.

Fiona was at the desk, putting a file into her briefcase. She looked up, startled at the sight of him. 'Lewis, I told you on Saturday . . .'

He reached into his inside pocket and took out an account with a cheque attached to it. 'I've come to settle up with you for those garden party invitations you printed.'

'In person!'

Dropping the feeble pretence, Lewis went across to her. 'Fiona,' he said balefully, 'I've got to talk to you.'

'There's nothing else to say.' She snapped shut her briefcase and glared at him. 'We said it all the last time you were at my house.'

'But I've had time to think things over since then.' His eyes were pleading with her. 'You were right. Everything you accused me of, I had it all coming to me. I treated you very shabbily. So I'm asking you to forgive me. And if you can, I want you to know that . . .'

'No, Lewis,' Fiona cut in. 'No more promises. It's too late anyway. And please, I'd rather not discuss it any more.'

'Dear God!' Pain crossed his face, the deepest hurt he had ever shown her. 'You can't just toss away two years of what we had together – not just like that!'

'No, that's right,' Fiona said coldly. 'I wish I could. And believe me, I'm going to make damn sure I never go through it again.'

She picked up her briefcase and handbag and walked smartly to the door, pulling it open. With Lewis behind her she walked out across the works and stopped beside the big guillotine.

'I'm off then, Tom. See you tomorrow.'

'Righto, Mrs Neave.'

She turned to Lewis. 'Goodbye again,' she said. 'And do remember me to Lady Wrathdale, won't you?' She hurried on across the works and went out, leaving Lewis staring after her.

Upstairs in his office, Frank Scully was just preparing to start work. Twenty minutes earlier he had picked up Miss Banner's weekly copy; he took it from his jacket pocket now and put it on the desk, then he took off the jacket and hung it on the back of the chair.

He sat down and opened a paper bag he had brought in with him. He took out a sandwich and bit into it. While he was chewing, he removed a carton of milk from the bag and opened it. He drank some, then leaned back in the chair with the carton in one hand and Miss Banner's manuscript in the other, reading it slowly.

After a minute, disbelief began to spread over Frank's face. After another minute he looked alarmed. As he read on, faster now, turning the pages so sharply he almost tore them, the alarm gave way to anger. He glared at the final page and slammed the milk carton down on the desk. He shot to his feet, kicking back the chair and stamping out of the office and down the stairs.

Reuben Flaxman was alone in the works, standing at a bench sorting some old type. He looked up sharply as Frank came striding in through the door.

'Tell me about "Wrathdale Remembered", Mr Flaxman,' Frank said, coming straight over to the bench and standing in front of Reuben.

Reuben looked at him suspiciously. 'What's there to tell?'

'Well, if there is anything, you'll know it,' Frank snapped. 'You've lived here all your life.'

'*Now* you're asking,' Reuben said flatly. 'You've been publishing them stories for the past five weeks or more.'

'And I didn't see any harm in them.'

'Oh aye,' Reuben grunted.

'And no one's complained.'

Reuben examined his fingernails. 'Maybe they couldn't,' he said. 'Not without showing themselves up. Or others.'

Frank stared at him. 'Why didn't you say anything?'

'It were none of my business,' Reuben said solemnly. 'You're the editor.'

'Even so . . .' Frank looked as if he was resisting a strong urge to grab Reuben and shake him. 'I'm not local. You could have had a quiet word with me when the first one was set up.'

Reuben stared at him defiantly. 'Aye, I could.'

'I see. Well thanks a lot.' Frank strode away from the bench, heading for the door to the shop.

'You'd be best off talking to Jack Jefford's widow about "Wrathdale Remembered",' Reuben called after him.

Frank stopped and spun to face Reuben. He was frowning. 'You mean the farmer who hanged himself?'

'Aye,' Reuben said. 'Though I doubt she'd admit it were the story in the paper that caused it. She'll not want him at rest without the benefit of the doubt.'

Frank stared at Reuben, horrified. 'And if this story in

the paper *was* the reason for his suicide? What does that make both of us then, Mr Flaxman? If only by default?' He watched the sanctimony slipping from Reuben's face. 'Now there's a thought for you,' he said slowly, then turned and walked out.

It took him less than fifteen minutes to gun the old Marina out to Ravensfell House. When Miss Banner opened the door to him Frank stepped inside immediately, without being asked.

'I want to talk to you,' he told the old woman.

Without a word, she led him to the sitting room where she stood facing him placidly, waiting to hear what he had to say.

Frank held up the manuscript of her latest piece for *The Messenger*. 'This isn't going in the paper,' he said.

'Why not?' she asked coolly. 'Something wrong about it, is there?'

He blinked at her. 'Something wrong? It's a hatchet job on Mrs Neave, that's what's wrong with it!'

'It could be you're reading things into it.'

'Yes. Like you intended everyone around here should. That's the idea, isn't it? That's been the idea all along with each of these little stories of yours.' He brandished the crumpled paper under her nose. 'Hasn't it? Only I was an outsider and too bloody stupid to see it. Until now.'

Miss Banner looked at the copy. 'That's the tale of a woman who married a miller hereabouts.'

Frank nodded, barely in control of his temper. 'And she drove him out of the house so that she could get control of the business. Then later she took up with a preacher, a man twice her age, and seduced him into leaving her a small fortune.'

'And are you saying,' Miss Banner enquired calmly, 'that Mrs Neave's done those things, then?'

'I know damn well she hasn't!'

'So where's the harm in it for her?'

Frank took a deep breath. 'By association,' he said. 'With local gossip. Like all the others. Only in her case the gossip was started by something I printed in all innocence in *The Messenger*. Thanks to you. And in the fact that whatever Chronicler writes now is an allegory, a veiled revelation of something previously only whispered about.'

Miss Banner turned away sharply and went to the window. She stood there, looking out at the garden.

'And it's believed,' Frank went on. 'Every word of it. As the definitive account. That's what you've been doing since "Wrathdale Remembered" started.'

'You've said nothing before,' Miss Banner murmured.

'Because I didn't realize it. It wasn't until last week that I even got a clue about what you were up to. And even then I was prepared to give you the benefit of the doubt.' Frank crushed the paper in his hand. 'But not with this, I'm not.'

Still keeping her back to him, Miss Banner said, 'There's truth in everything I've written.'

'Enough,' Frank agreed. 'In the others, perhaps. Enough in one of them for a man maybe to have killed himself because of what you wrote, for God's sake! But there's no truth at all in this.'

'Are you sure of that?' she asked him. 'Certain sure?'

Frank hesitated for a moment, and the hesitation seemed to provide Miss Banner with vindication.

'No, of course you're not,' she hissed. 'You can't be, can you?'

Frank stared across at her, appalled by the pernicious logic. 'What harm has Mrs Neave ever done you? What harm had any of them done to you personally, for that matter? You're sick. You have to be.'

Miss Banner swung round to face him. Years of bitterness and resentment were on the surface now, contorting her features, making her grotesque. 'You think so, do you?' she shouted at him. 'It's sick to see folk breaking every one of the ten commandments and to want to show them up for it? To call folk no better than any to account?' She strode two steps towards him, her voice cracking. 'Folk that thought they were safe from scorn, but were always quick with it themselves and ready to judge others harshly for their mistakes! That's sick, is it?'

'You admit that's what you've been doing, then?'

'Aye.' The old woman's eyes were glittering with wild righteousness. 'But there's none can touch me for it. And I waited a long time to see them shamed.'

'Through *The Messenger*,' Frank said, nodding. 'Right from the moment it was yours. As soon as you found the right person to edit it for you. Someone vain enough and stupid enough. Someone you could use.'

'Someone with nowhere else to go,' Miss Banner said flatly.

'And Mrs Neave's sin?' Frank asked her. 'What was that?'

The old woman was in command of herself again. 'She corrupted my brother,' she grated.

Frank shook his head. 'I've told you. That's not true.'

'Aye, I heard you. But you can't prove it to me, can you?'

Frank's exasperation with her was making him restless. He walked over to the table and came back again. 'In any case,' he pointed out, 'from what I've heard, you hated John Wesley.'

'With cause, maybe,' Miss Banner said. 'But that's not to say there's any less justice in my holding that woman up to the light so folk can see her for what she is.'

'That's not going to happen,' Frank said. '*The Messenger*'s done her enough harm already.'

'Is that the reason?' Miss Banner took another step nearer him, her face a mask of condemnation. 'Or is it because she's warming your bed now that you've moved out of Rawden End and done with Mrs Harper?'

The shock was like a blow to Frank's stomach. He gaped at Miss Banner, seeing nothing but solid, malignant certainty in her. But as he stared it was a wave of sadness for her that began to surface in him, not hatred. Her wisdom was all blackness, there wasn't one shaft of light left in the embittered old woman's spirit.

'So where would it all have stopped?' Frank asked her. 'Who was next on your list, eh?'

'Any that call for it,' she grunted.

'Well, it's over,' he told her.

Miss Banner made a sour, humourless smile.

'Yes,' Frank said, 'I'm discontinuing the series. As of now.'

'On whose say-so?'

'Mine,' he said, stabbing a finger at his chest. 'As editor.'

'It's my paper,' Miss Banner reminded him.

Frank held up the wrinkled copy. 'It'll not publish any more of this.'

'Well!' Miss Banner clasped her hands in front of her and looked at him squarely. 'If you've found somewhere else to go, there's others that'll take your place. But I want to be fair. So I'll give you till Thursday to let me know.'

Chapter Twenty-six

Donald Harper poured Frank another drink and handed it to him. They were in the Harpers' sitting room area. Sylvia, acting bright and brittle, was moving to and from the kitchen and dining area, preparing the evening meal.

'You'll stay and have something to eat, won't you?' Donald said, sitting down opposite Frank.

'Of course he will,' Sylvia said airily. 'I've already laid another place. And dinner's almost ready.'

Frank made an apologetic face. 'That wasn't the idea. I just looked in for a minute.'

'Glad you did,' Donald said warmly.

Frank sighed. 'I . . .'

'Had nothing better to do,' Sylvia cut in.

'Actually,' Frank said, 'I wanted a word with Donald.'

Sylvia paused in the doorway to the kitchen, smiling tautly. 'A man-to-man, no doubt. And what better choice? Well, I'll leave you to it. I know my place.'

Donald laughed. 'Neither of us would deny that, would we, Frank?'

Sylvia moved off into the kitchen. 'Only a couple of minutes, though,' she called. 'Otherwise the food'll be ruined.'

Donald glanced at Frank, who was looking depressed in spite of his effort to appear no more than concerned about something. 'You've got a problem?'

Frank nodded. 'One or two.'

'Personal or professional?'

'Just things in general,' Frank said. 'So I'm thinking of moving on.'

'But you can't make up your mind.'

Frank was silent for a few seconds, then he said, 'I'm not sure I have a choice.' He saw the questioning look on Donald's face. 'I really ought to get started on that book of mine.'

'It's that important to you?'

'It's been nagging me lately,' Frank said. 'And it's what I started out to do when I stopped off here. Only you diverted me on to the newspaper.'

Donald grinned. 'You didn't put up much of a fight.'

'No,' Frank admitted, 'that's true enough. Been better if I had.'

'Nonsense. You stepped in where you were needed and you're fulfilling a very useful function. What's more you did me a favour, and I'm grateful.'

Frank took a long, slow taste of his drink, then eyed Donald levelly. 'I've become very involved.'

'You were bound to,' Donald said briskly. The PR man in him insisted that he make everything logical and concrete. 'You're the type. Anyway, I was counting on that. Seemed like a good idea to me.'

'Not just with the paper, though. Emotionally.'

'I see.' Donald shifted in his chair. 'Serious?'

'It's got that way.'

Now Donald was looking intrigued. 'Anyone I know?'

Frank nodded. 'Fiona Neave. But that's not why I'm thinking of leaving. Hopefully that'll work out.'

'But there are obstacles.'

'Aren't there always?'

Donald was gazing intently at Frank. 'Someone giving you trouble?' he said.

Frank began to feel uncomfortable. 'What made you say that?'

'It was just a thought,' Donald told him. 'It's always a possibility.'

'The obstacles,' Frank said, 'are memories and past commitments.'

'Hers or yours?'

'Hers,' Frank said, smiling faintly. 'I don't have any.'

Donald lowered an eyebrow sceptically. 'You have memories, surely?'

'But no commitments.'

Donald still looked sceptical. 'Not to anyone?'

'I've never had that kind of relationship,' Frank said patiently.

Now Donald was nodding, accepting. 'All very casual. Anything that was offered.'

'Well, not quite . . .'

'Pretty indiscriminate, though.'

'When tempted, yes . . .'

Donald leaned forward. 'And to hell with the husband, where there was one.'

'Their fault mostly,' Frank said, feeling his colour rise. 'One way or another.' It struck him how he had been led into this. He looked at Donald warily, but the faint smile was as ingenuous as ever.

'You're probably right,' Donald mused. 'Neglect. Other drives. It can happen, believe me. And you're left feeling guilty and distracted. He pointed a finger momentarily at Frank. 'So it could be you were doing them a favour, couldn't it? While it lasted.' He sat back, an enigma, either totally duped or as disarmingly cunning as a Machiavelli. 'Now there's a thought, eh? Mind you, I doubt if there are many men who are that generous.'

'Unless they didn't really care,' Frank said cautiously.

'Or cared enough.'

For one flashing instant Frank was sure Donald knew about him and Sylvia. A simple remark about emotional involvement had been skilfully manipulated to bring Frank, within seconds, to a point where he confessed fully to being an unprincipled wife-taker. Or it seemed that way. But the certainty began to recede as Frank looked again at the placid, innocent-faced man sitting opposite him.

213

Donald stood up and took Frank's glass from him and crossed with it to the drinks trolley.

Frank shot a look into the kitchen. Sylvia was still busy in there. And she was out of earshot. He got up and joined Donald at the trolley.

'So why the sudden urge to pull out?' Donald asked, handing Frank a fresh drink.

'Oh, you know me. Itchy feet. And if I let the book slide too long I'll never get around to it.'

'And you can't write your book and edit *The Messenger*?'

Frank shook his head. 'Not really. That way I wouldn't have enough incentive. I think I need to be hungry. And tackling both jobs, I'm not sure I'd do enough justice to either.'

'Well, if that's how you feel,' Donald sighed. 'You'll be missed. You've made quite an impression on the district since you took over the paper.'

'Yes, so I've discovered.'

'Yet you're still thinking of moving on.' Donald sipped his drink, then looked squarely at Frank. 'If you want my opinion, I think you're making a big mistake.'

'Didn't you know?' Frank said. 'That's a habit of mine.'

'OK, you two!' Sylvia called from the kitchen. 'Time's up. First course is on the table.'

Donald and Frank took their glasses with them into the dining area. Sylvia had set out small plates of pâté. She came through with freshly-made toast wrapped in a napkin and put it in the centre of the table. Donald went to the kitchen and came back with a bottle of wine.

Sylvia pointed to the chair opposite her own. 'Your usual place, Frank.' As they all sat down, she smiled at Frank and said, 'I hope your little huddle in there was productive. Sorted it all out for you, has he?'

'It was business, Syl,' Donald said, opening the wine. 'To do with *The Messenger*. Don't worry, you didn't miss out on anything.'

214

'Good heavens!' Sylvia put on an overdone look of shock. 'Did I sound as if I was prying?' She helped herself to some toast as Donald poured the wine. 'All on your own tonight then, Frank?' she asked.

'It's not unusual,' he said.

'Oh, really. You surprise me. I thought your social life was pretty hectic these days.'

Frank shook his head. 'Spasmodic.'

Sylvia picked up her knife then paused with it in mid-air. 'So how's Fiona?'

'Very well.'

'Good,' she said. 'Are you going to tell her?'

Frank gave her a puzzled look. 'Tell her what?'

Sylvia turned to Donald. 'You didn't say anything?' Her face was all innocent bewilderment.

'No,' Donald said sternly. 'And I told you not to. Not to anyone.'

'But Frank's not just anyone,' Sylvia protested. 'Besides, I think he ought to know. Especially if . . . Well, with the way things are.'

Frank looked from one to the other. 'I ought to know what?'

'About Lillian's bombshell,' Sylvia said.

Frank stared at her, mystified. 'Lillian?'

'The Dowager Lady W.'

'That's enough, Sylvia,' Donald warned her sharply.

She pouted at him. 'But I can't leave it there. Not now.'

'Drop it!' Donald snapped.

'I just thought that since Frank and Fiona . . .'

Donald's face was stiffening with anger. 'Drop it, I said . . .'

'No,' Frank said, realizing there was some fresh malice afoot. 'Sylvia's right.' He glanced at her coldly. 'I'm sure she's only got my best interests at heart. So tell me. What bombshell?'

'Well,' Sylvia said with feigned reluctance, 'it's just

that . . . Well, according to what Lillian told me, in the strictest confidence, of course – and I wouldn't have believed it if she hadn't been able to support just about every detail – apparently our Fiona's illegitimate.' She paused for effect, twiddling with her knife. 'And she's got blue blood in her veins. She's Wrathdale's half sister.'

Stricken, Frank sat in silence as Sylvia outlined the story Lillian had told her. Donald sat sullenly staring at the tablecloth. Food was forgotten.

When Sylvia had finished and Frank felt able to speak, he cleared his throat and said, 'When was Miss Banner supposed to have had this child?'

'Nineteen forty-seven,' Sylvia said chirpily. She was clearly enjoying herself. 'In her late twenties. How old's Fiona?'

Frank shrugged. 'Thirty-fivish, I'd say.'

'Well that tallies, doesn't it?'

'It's hardly conclusive.'

Sylvia switched on her innocent face again. 'I'm not looking to prove anything.'

'You might have to,' Frank said. 'If this story ever got out and it was traced back to you. You could find yourself facing an action for slander.'

Donald, who still looked angry, gave a sharp nod. 'Yes. Frank's right. You could, easily.'

Sylvia shook her head, dismissing the notion. 'It's between these four walls,' she said. 'I've not told another living soul. In any case, it's verifiable. Certainly while Lillian's alive and well. And John Wesley Banner's will, that's a pretty good clincher, isn't it?'

Frank recalled the snapshots again, hidden away in John Wesley's old safe. Fiona aged four. Fiona on her eleventh birthday.

'He was keeping his money in the family,' Sylvia said.

Frank was drumming his fingers on the table, looking puzzled again. 'If Miss Banner had had a baby, a juicy bit of scandal like that would have been all round the Dale in minutes. And it would still be talked about. So why isn't it?'

Sylvia was ready with the answer. 'His Lordship and her brother saw to that,' she said. 'She was whipped away smartish and ended up in a nursing home in Edinburgh. By the time the baby was born, John Wesley had found a good Methodist couple named Lytton who were only too happy to register it as their own. Then, in due course, Miss B returned to the happy family and no one else hereabouts was ever any the wiser.'

'Until now,' Frank grunted.

'Just the three of us,' Sylvia reminded him. 'That's all. Not even the present Lord and Lady Wrathdale know.'

'And twenty years or so later,' Donald said, 'Fiona ends up living no more than five miles away from her true mother.' He looked at Frank. 'That's ironic, isn't it?'

'And quite a coincidence,' Frank said.

'That's all it was,' Sylvia insisted. 'Pure chance. She just happened to marry the nephew of the man who owned the local printing works. And her husband inherited the business.'

Donald glanced at her. 'She hasn't a clue, you mean.'

'Of course she hasn't,' Frank sighed. 'As far as Fiona's concerned she's a Lytton. She even calls herself Lytton Neave.'

Sylvia put her elbows on the table and rested her chin lightly on her hands. She looked like a schoolgirl enjoying gossip about another girl in the dorm. 'Her turning up here must have been a hell of a shock for John Wesley,' she said. 'It's a wonder his heart didn't give out then and there.'

'Presumably,' Donald said, 'Miss Banner didn't know who she was.'

'Lillian thinks it's very unlikely. And going by what she told me, there's no way she could've done.'

'And she's still none the wiser,' Donald said, looking astonished at the thought.

Frank was entering a little reverie of his own. 'No,' he said, recalling his interview earlier with Miss Banner. 'That's for sure.'

On and off during the following hour, when dinner was over and they had retired to the sitting room area, Frank's imagination and his memory kept playing sombre little games with each other. His contribution to the conversation was fragmentary. For a time he stood by the record player, pretending to be wrapped up in the music while Donald and Sylvia talked to each other. He was becoming helplessly preoccupied with something grim and irreversible, but there was a parallel sense of something growing, a tiny light of justice kindling; his thoughts ran back and forward, providing the sparks.

'More coffee?'

Frank turned with a start, seeing Sylvia beside him. 'Sorry?'

'Would you like some more coffee?'

'No thanks.'

Donald was at the drinks trolley. 'Another brandy?' he called.

Frank shook his head. 'Not for me.' He looked at his watch. 'I must go.'

Donald looked disappointed. 'You don't really have to dash off, do you? It's early.'

'Busy day tomorrow.'

'Yes of course.' Donald understood. He had seen Frank on enough evenings when his work at the paper had left him drained. 'Which reminds me. I've got a copy of CorVol's annual report and accounts for you. It's embargoed until Friday, but I thought you might like to go through it in advance so that you can pick up anything of local interest for next week's paper.' He went towards the door. 'I'll get it. It's in the study.'

The instant he was gone Sylvia stood up and went to the table. Frank took his cup across to her.

'Sylvia, this story about Fiona . . .'

'You're not convinced?' she asked brightly.

'That's beside the point. If it was put about, it could be very damaging for her. And I wasn't kidding, you know. You might well end up in court, broadcasting something like that.'

'Oh, for heaven's sake! It's quite the in-thing to be a bastard these days. And to have one.'

'Not in Wrathdale.'

'Anywhere,' Sylvia insisted. 'Among sophisticated people.'

'And how many of those do you know around here?'

Sylvia rattled the cups and saucers into a pile. 'Your new lady friend isn't?'

'In some ways,' Frank said. 'But certainly not up to your standards. And by the way – that's exactly what she is. A friend.'

Sylvia glared at him. 'Really? You could have fooled me.' More softly she said, 'What happened to us, then?'

'Nothing's changed,' Frank told her, and immediately wondered at himself saying it.

'I can give you an argument about that,' Sylvia hissed. 'And a pretty good one.'

Donald came back, brandishing the report. 'Here we are.' He handed it to Frank. 'The usual boring stuff, but maybe you'll mine a paragraph or two out of it.'

Frank promised he would do what he could. He said goodnight to Sylvia and Donald saw him to the door.

'I'm sorry about tonight,' Donald apologized softly as they stepped into the open air. 'Syl should have kept her mouth shut. I think she will, from now on.'

'I hope so.'

Donald put a detaining hand on Frank's sleeve. 'About those problems of yours . . .'

Frank shrugged. 'You lose one, gain two,' he said. 'That's how it goes, isn't it?' He smiled. 'Goodnight, Donald.'

Chapter Twenty-seven

Late on Thursday night, a few minutes after Miss Banner had put the final stitches in her sampler, there was a loud knock at the front door.

Miss Banner sat still for a moment, staring in the direction of the hall. There was another knock, as loud as the first. She stood up and walked out slowly into the hall. She opened the door and saw Frank Scully.

'Can I come in?' he asked her.

'It's late.' Miss Banner stood back and let him step into the hall. She closed the door and led the way to the sitting room. 'What do you want?'

Frank handed her a copy of *The Messenger*. 'I've brought you your copy of the paper.'

Miss Banner snatched it out of his hand. 'It couldn't wait?' she snapped. 'Till the morning, like always?' Sullenly, she went to the table and put the paper down.

'And this,' Frank said. He took a folded sheet of paper from his pocket and brought it to her. 'It's a proof of next week's "Wrathdale Remembered".'

There was an immediate, triumphant glint in Miss Banner's eyes. 'Oh, I see.' She looked down at the paper and back at Frank again. 'Changed your mind, have you? You're not moving on after all, then?'

'No,' Frank said. 'Not till I choose to, anyway.'

'Well, we'll have to see about that, won't we?' Miss Banner drew back her chair and sat down at the table with the folded proof in front of her. 'You had a lot to say the last time you were here. And none of it easily forgotten.'

'Read it,' Frank said curtly.

Miss Banner frowned, surprised at his firmness.

'I've done a rewrite on your original,' Frank told her. 'An editorial decision. It's a totally different story now. I've not used real names, of course – like you never have. But it's all there and I don't think anyone'll have any difficulty in recognizing who it's about.' His mouth twitched in what was almost a smile. 'And you'll find it particularly interesting.'

Miss Banner was looking wary. Frank's unflinching gaze and his stance before the table betrayed an aggressive self-confidence she hadn't encountered in him before. She unfolded the proof and began to read it.

Frank moved away from the table and went to stand by the window. He watched Miss Banner's stooped head, as he often had. He waited.

It took her three minutes to read the proof. It was five minutes before she looked up. Her face was contorted with pain and dismay.

'Yes,' Frank said coldly, 'it hurts, doesn't it? But our readers'll love it. Just like they did the previous ones.'

'You can't,' Miss Banner said hoarsely.

'What's to stop me? It's as much in the public interest as the others were. And it's very revealing.' He put his hands in his pockets and stood looking at her with his head on one side. 'Because that's why you started out on "Wrathdale Remembered", isn't it?' He shook his head with more disdain than sadness. 'My guess is that when he found out you were pregnant, John Wesley didn't give you any option. He bullied you into leaving the district and having the baby miles away. Terrorized you even, with the wrath of God. Worse, with stories about how the local people would talk if they ever found out.'

'You've no right . . .'

'I've as much right as you had,' Frank snapped, his voice rising. 'And no less of a reason. The way you saw it, it wasn't just your brother who robbed you of your child. It was everyone around here. And all these years you've hated them and him for it.' He came back to the table and looked down at her. 'And lately you've been getting your revenge. By pillorying them as you were told they would pillory you.'

Miss Banner's eyes were off-focus, blurred by tears. 'I weren't allowed to hold it,' she croaked. 'Not even for a minute. They just told me it were a girl. And my brother got down on his knees and made me pray for forgiveness.' She drew a long, shuddering breath. 'And then all I were left with were him and his God, under his roof and on his charity.'

'Yes, I don't doubt that John Wesley always treated you badly,' Frank said. 'But there are some things to his credit.' He leaned down, putting his hands on the table and talking directly into Miss Banner's face. 'Bigot he may have been, and cruel and unfeeling towards you. But he kept an eye on your child. He made sure that its father provided for it and that it was brought up decently. With love and care. And in the end he left his niece a tidy sum, as I think he'd always intended to. So don't spit on his grave too often.' Frank straightened, still holding Miss Banner's gaze. 'And now you know what happened to your daughter. For the past ten years she's been living in Wrathdale – and you were about to crucify her.'

Miss Banner's lips moved but no sound came out. She looked down at her trembling hands, clasped on the table.

'It's not quite in the Chronicler style, of course,' Frank said briskly, picking up the proof and folding it again. 'But it'll do, I think. And it should sell a good few extra copies of *The Messenger*.'

Miss Banner looked up at him, moistening her lips, fighting to control her breathing. She tried, but she was able to say nothing. Instead, she sat and watched in silence as Frank turned and walked out of the room, leaving her alone with her memories and the growing, crushing weight of despair.

Chapter Twenty-eight

Tom Holliday was sitting at the linotype machine. He was reading a piece of copy, looking puzzled by it. 'What's this, then?' he murmured.

Frank Scully, who was standing alongside, leaned across and had a look. 'It's the first article in the new series I'm going to be running on page four,' he said. '"Hints for the Handyman". It should go down quite well, I think.'

Tom looked at him. 'We're done with "Wrathdale Remembered" then, are we?'

'Yes,' Frank nodded. '"Wrathdale Remembered" is finished. This is taking its place.'

'Well,' Tom said, looking dubiously at the copy, 'there's some that'll not be sorry – but there's a lot more that'll not take to this.' He looked up at Frank again. 'Wouldn't surprise me if sales came down a fair bit, Mr Scully.'

'Probably.' Frank looked unconcerned. 'But it can't be helped. The source has dried up. Chronicler's got no more tales to tell.'

'There's others that have, I don't doubt,' Tom murmured. 'And they'd be happy to, given the chance.'

Frank turned, heading for the door to the shop. 'That's for sure,' he said. He went out, waving a farewell to Tom.

Thirty minutes later, the Marina drew up outside the Harpers' garage. Frank got out and gazed thoughtfully at the house for a while, then he walked around to the rear.

It was still early. The back door was open, and through it Frank could see Sylvia in a bright kaftan, standing at the kitchen table arranging some flowers in a vase.

Frank moved forward and stood in the doorway. 'Nice,' he said.

Sylvia turned to him, startled. 'Well, well!' she said acidly. 'Leave something behind the other night, did you?'

Frank smiled placatingly. 'Maybe this is the wrong time, eh?'

'Depends what you had in mind.'

'I want to talk to you,' Frank said quietly.

'Great!' Sylvia snatched up the vase and started walking towards the sitting room area with it. 'Good conversation – nothing I like better.'

Frank closed the back door and followed her.

Sylvia put the vase on a side table and turned sharply to face him. 'But if you're thinking of taking up where we left off . . .'

'I didn't know we had,' Frank said. 'Not altogether. That's not what I wanted.' He stepped closer to her. 'It's not what I want.'

'That's why you've been so eager these past weeks, is it?'

'I told you . . .'

'Yes, you just haven't had the time.' Sylvia was almost sneering. 'Charming. You've got a lousy set of priorities, Frank.'

'I thought you'd understand.' His expression was open, conciliatory. 'What with the move and the pressure of work lately, it's been difficult.'

Sylvia narrowed her eyes at him. 'You didn't even have to come to me. I had a key cut for your front door, remember? But you made me give it back.'

'I didn't have much alternative, did I?' There was a trace of pleading in Frank's voice. 'Anyway, that wouldn't have made much difference. I just haven't been available.'

'So you put me into cold storage. Until today.' Sylvia put her hands on her hips and glared at him. 'Well you made a bad mistake, darling. You misread the use-by date.'

'I honestly thought . . .

'What did you think, Frank? That abstinence makes the heart grow fonder?'

'I didn't think you were keeping a log,' Frank said. He turned and started walking back towards the kitchen.

'Where are you going?' Sylvia demanded sharply.

He stopped. 'That's the end of the conversation, isn't it?'

'No.' She came towards him. 'We'll change the subject, shall we? Talk about something else.' She looked mock-thoughtful for a moment. 'I know,' she said brightly. 'Let's talk about bird-watching. I'm sure that's a fascinating subject. And you're into it in a really big way now, aren't you?'

Frank shook his head. 'You've got that all wrong, too.'

'Oh? Tiring of it already, are you?'

'It was only a passing interest, never anything more.'

'Really?' Sylvia's voice was heavy with sarcasm now. 'And you seemed so absorbed, too. No more nesting with Fiona Neave, then.'

'For God's sake!' Frank said helplessly. 'It wasn't like that.'

'Oh, no, of course not. I forgot.' Sylvia smiled and folded her arms. 'She's just a friend, isn't she?'

'And someone I work with,' Frank said, nodding. 'A business colleague.'

'A pretty intimate friend though, wouldn't you say?' Sylvia came closer still, lowering her voice. 'Or are you in the habit of sleeping with all your business colleagues?'

Frank opened his mouth to issue a denial, but the knowing, informed look on Sylvia's face stopped him.

'That night I came to your cottage and you were out, I waited bloody hours,' she said. 'I finally fell asleep. In the morning when I drove past the Gatehouse your car was parked outside the front door.' She pushed her face close to Frank's. 'What were you doing there at that time of day? Blowing eggs?'

Frank managed to hold her look for a few seconds, then he sighed.

'You're not going to deny it then?'

'No,' he said.

'You were in bed with her?'

'Yes.'

'And how many times before then? And since?' Sylvia's vengeful edge was tightening her lips. 'Don't lie to me, Frank. Try any other stroke you like, but don't lie to me.'

'Never before,' he said quietly, looking straight at her.

'But since, of course. It's such an easy habit to get into, isn't it?'

'It's all over now,' Frank assured her. 'Has been for a while. It was . . .'

Sylvia smiled tightly. 'Just one of those things?'

He nodded. 'Something like that.'

The interrogation wasn't over. Sylvia stood searching Frank's face, revelling in what was happening. 'And does she feel the same way about it?'

'I'm not her type, really . . .'

'No, I wouldn't have thought so. But a reasonable substitute, obviously.' Sylvia was silent for a moment, then she offered an interim summary. 'You were both just amusing yourselves.'

'Apparently,' Frank said.

'And did she ring down the curtain, or did you?'

Frank made a vague gesture with his hands. 'Neither of us needed to. It was no big thing. After a while it just wasn't happening any more.'

'Oh, shame!' The sarcasm was back. 'I feel for you. So now you've both lost interest, I get defrosted. Is that the idea?'

'I told you,' Frank said, and his voice was openly pleading now; 'nothing's changed. It's the same way it's always been with us. As far as I'm concerned, anyway.'

'You just got sidetracked.'

'Briefly.'

'Seems longer to me,' Sylvia spat. 'And of course, if I hadn't known already that you'd been screwing her, you were going to tell me. Bring it all out into the open.'

226

'Hardly,' Frank said. He saw the small change in Sylvia's expression. 'You're surprised? What did you expect me to say?'

'Well, nothing as honest as that, anyway,' she admitted.

'You once said,' Frank reminded her, 'that you wouldn't mind that much.'

She looked amused. 'And you believed me?'

'The way it was, neither of us had exclusive rights, did we? Or any great claim on the other.'

'Not exactly an ideal relationship,' Sylvia murmured.

'We settled for it,' Frank said, moving closer.

'And it meant something to you?' she asked, looking up at him.

'Why else am I here?'

'I'm the best lay you've ever had,' Sylvia said flatly.

He smiled. 'No argument.'

'But more than that, eh?' she coaxed.

'Of course.' He moved closer still. 'Sylvia, I need . . .'

'To hell with what you need, Frank Scully!' Her hand shot out suddenly and she slapped him viciously on the face, forehand and backhand. She watched him blink back the stinging pain and saw the angry red patches growing on his cheeks. 'Welcome back,' she said, stepping close and putting her arms around him. She kissed him and he drew her to him, enclosing her tightly. Sylvia groaned deep in her throat as Frank's mouth covered her own, symbolically devouring her.

After a minute she pulled back her head, keeping her body in firm contact with Frank's. 'Now ask me to forgive you,' she demanded. 'And say it won't happen again.'

Later that morning, as Fiona Neave was locking her car in the market space opposite the printing works, she saw Lord Wrathdale coming across from the saddler's shop towards his Range Rover, which was parked a few spaces away from Fiona's car. There was no way they could avoid meeting.

There was a brief moment of embarrassment, then Lewis smiled politely. 'Good morning,' he said. 'How are you today?'

'Very well, thanks,' Fiona replied. 'How are you?'

'Fine.'

'And Lady Wrathdale?'

'Never better,' Lewis assured her. 'Looking forward to getting away. We thought we'd have two or three lazy weeks in Barbados. We could both do with a break.'

'I envy you,' Fiona said. 'Enjoy it.'

'I'm sure we will.' Lewis cleared his throat. 'Well I mustn't keep you. Goodbye, Mrs Neave.'

'Goodbye.' Fiona watched for a moment as he went towards his vehicle. In the front passenger seat she caught sight of Beattie, smiling at her husband. Fiona felt a small pang in her stomach – much smaller, she reflected, than it would have been a week before.

There was a busy schedule that morning. Fiona had been preparing the new town guide for several weeks, and now the proofs had to be made ready for approval by the council. She worked on them for over an hour, then telephoned to say she would be bringing them across personally.

As she was leaving the works by the shop entrance, she met Frank on his way in.

'Good morning,' Fiona said brightly. 'Just starting, are you?'

'Do you mind!' Frank said indignantly. 'I was here at half-eight, I'll have you know.'

Fiona frowned at him. 'You weren't here when I looked into your office about an hour ago.'

'I've been out on a story,' Frank told her. 'Something you wanted, was there?'

'No, it was just a social call. Thought we might have coffee together.'

Frank smiled broadly. 'Good idea. Let's go.'

She shook her head. 'It's a bit late. Anyway I can't now.

I've got a call to make.' She moved towards the door, then paused. 'You're looking a bit more cheerful today,' she observed.

'I'm looking on the bright side,' Frank said. 'Help me keep it up. What are you doing for lunch?'

They met in the hotel restaurant at 12.30. The place was busy and there were no empty tables. It was the kind of atmosphere that suited Fiona at certain times. The people around her were involved in their own business, chatting and eating, leaving her free of scrutiny.

During the first course Frank let her tell him all about her haggling over the town guide. When she had finished and the waiter was clearing away the plates, Frank poured two glasses of wine, then sat back and gave Fiona his own news.

She stared at him. '*Managing* editor! That sounds very impressive.'

'Miss Banner's idea,' Frank said modestly. 'She seemed to think it was a good one.'

'What would it mean, exactly.'

Frank tasted his wine. 'I'd have total control of the paper,' he said. 'No outside interference at all.'

'Miss Banner doesn't interfere now, does she?'

'Not really. But while I'm just the editor, that option's always open to her. She could tell me what to print, or what not to. If I were managing editor she'd no longer have that right. At least that's how it would be in this instance. I'd have the last word on everything.'

'If it was Miss Banner's idea,' Sylvia said, 'then it's obviously the way she wants it.'

Smiling, Frank said, 'I must admit that I manoeuvred her into it.'

'Even so.' Fiona leaned forward, thinking at a new tangent. 'What if the paper changed hands?'

'I'd have to re-negotiate my position with the new owner.'

'I'd keep you on,' Fiona said loftily. 'Promote you again, even. Executive managing director.'

Frank laughed. 'Thanks. You're as keen as ever on buying the paper, then?'

Fiona nodded. 'I'd like to. I've always thought it would be a good investment. And at one time . . . But I told you, Miss Banner would never sell it to me. As far as she's concerned, I'm a scarlet woman.'

'Oh, I don't know,' Frank said. 'You might find her more receptive than you think. In any case, I said I'd act for you, didn't I? The paper could be bought in my name and then transferred over to you.'

Fiona was frowning. 'That was the idea originally when Lewis . . .' She shook herself. 'Sorry. Thinking about it now, though, I don't really think I'd want to do it that way any more. If I bought it, I'd like it to be out in the open from the start. Nothing underhand.'

Frank shrugged and spread his hands. 'So put in a bid. Off your own bat. As I said, you might be pleasantly surprised.'

Fiona pulled a long mouth. 'Frankly,' she said, 'I doubt it. But it's possible I suppose.' She clapped her hands together softly, deciding. 'All right then! Why not? I will – but I think I'll give the dust a little longer to settle. Meanwhile, are you going to take her up on the offer?'

Frank drank some more wine before he replied. 'I'm not sure,' he said.

Fiona looked mystified. 'Have you had a better one?'

'No. But I still haven't convinced myself that staying on with *The Messenger* is right for me. In any capacity.'

'I see.' Fiona made no attempt to conceal her disappointment. 'Is there something else you want to do?'

'My book. I'd like to get that written.'

'Oh yes, of course.' Fiona toyed with her wine glass, staring at it, making the pale liquid swirl. Her face had become a little sad. 'Shut away from everything,' she murmured. 'In a cottage in Scotland.'

'Possibly,' Frank sighed. 'If it's still available. Anywhere.'

Fiona looked up at him. 'Wrathdale?'

'Given peace and quiet,' Frank said, nodding.

'That'd be up to you.'

He shook his head. 'Not entirely.'

In a small voice, Fiona said, 'I wouldn't disturb you.'

He smiled, wanting to reach across and touch her hand. 'I hope you would. From time to time, at least.'

Fiona drank some wine, looking very thoughtful. 'What's your book going to be about?' she asked.

Frank hesitated, then he said, 'It's a love story, of a sort. More a psychological study of a woman who discovers that she's deeply involved in an incestuous relationship.'

'Oh, my God,' Fiona groaned softly.

While Frank was outlining the plot Sylvia Harper entered the restaurant. She was looking very attractive, but deeply bored. She ran her gaze around the tables for a minute, then suddenly she saw Frank and Fiona, blissfully unaware of her presence. Her instant displeasure was visible. She turned as if to leave, then changed her mind. Instead, she began making her way across to their table.

'And how does the story end?' Fiona was asking.

Frank shrugged. 'I don't know yet.'

'I couldn't live with a situation like that,' Fiona said, shuddering. 'It would destroy me.'

Frank nodded, perhaps more gravely than he had intended. 'Yes,' he murmured. 'My character's very much like you.'

'Well! Surprise, surprise!' Sylvia yelped, coming up to the table. 'Familiar faces. And the last thing I expected.' Frank was staring at her, startled and alarmed; Fiona looked vaguely irritated. Sylvia beamed a bright, malicious smile at both of them. 'I do hope I'm not butting in or anything.'

'No, of course not,' Fiona said smoothly. 'Hello, Mrs Harper.'

Sylvia's agitation was causing her attention to twitch between the two of them. 'This is a business lunch, is it?'

'No,' Fiona said, 'just lunch.'

'How nice. May I join you for a minute?'

Fiona glanced quickly at Frank, then nodded. 'Please do.'

Sylvia sat down, clasping her hands to keep them steady. 'Donald's eating here with one of his Belgian cronies,' she explained. 'He wants me to meet him, but they haven't arrived yet.'

Frank offered her a glass of wine.

'No, I'll wait, thanks.' She watched him as he topped up Fiona's glass and his own. 'You're looking quite drawn, Frank. Not overdoing things, I hope. And getting to bed on time, are you?'

He mumbled that he was fine.

'Well I wouldn't have thought so,' Sylvia went on spikily. She turned to Fiona. 'What do you think?'

'He looks all right to me.'

'Definitely off colour,' Sylvia insisted. 'But then perhaps I know him better than you do. Still, that's enough about Frank. How are you, Mrs Neave? I haven't seen you since that dreadful garden party.' She shifted in her chair as if it were burning her. 'Wasn't that the most boring afternoon since Adam ate the apple? Still, as I was saying to Frank the other night, old Lady Wrathdale's good value. Well worth talking to. And such a gossip. She knows where all the bodies are buried.'

Frank's anxiety was climbing. He was clutching the stem of his glass tightly, and as Sylvia began to say more it snapped suddenly. His wine spilled over the tablecloth.

'Oh, I'm sorry. That was stupid of me . . .' He mopped at the puddle with his napkin.

Fiona was halfway out of her chair, startled. 'What happened?'

'Yes,' Sylvia said, letting her bitter amusement show;

'what happened, Frank?'

'No idea, but it's made a bit of a mess, I'm afraid . . .'

A waiter hurried across and took over the mopping-up operation. Donald Harper came over to the table behind him, shaking his head and grinning.

'What a waste!' He nodded to Fiona and Frank and touched Sylvia's shoulder. 'I've been looking for you in the bar,' he told her.

'You're late,' she snapped.

'Yes, sorry about that.' He glanced across the table again. 'You're a mucky devil, Frank.'

'The stem of his glass broke,' Fiona said. She was still looking concerned. Frank was sitting glumly by, watching the waiter.

'I think our table's ready,' Donald said. 'I hope you don't mind me dragging Sylvia away like this.'

'If you must,' Fiona said with measured charm.

Sylvia stood up. 'I enjoyed our chat,' she said to Fiona. 'We must have a real heart-to-heart some time.' She wrinkled her nose impishly. 'Just the two of us. We've got a great deal in common, you know. More than you realize, perhaps.' She shot a penetrating glance at the other side of the table. 'See you, Frank.'

'Yes, see you,' Donald said, grinning again. 'And thanks for looking after Syl for me.'

As the Harpers left the waiter laid a linen napkin over the wine stain and re-set Frank's place. He put a fresh glass on the table and filled it as a second waiter brought the main course on a trolley.

Fiona was still watching Sylvia. 'You know,' she said, 'I get the distinct impression that Mrs Harper doesn't like me.' She smiled pensively. 'I wonder why?' She looked across at Frank. He was pale. 'Are you sure you're feeling all right?'

He nodded, looking far from all right; certainly, he looked a lot more shaken and disturbed than a man normally would over the simple breaking of a wine glass.

Chapter Twenty-nine

The afternoon sun was gilding the water where it rushed and divided over the weir, dropping to sparkling, rumbling foam. The green stillness of the surrounding fields and hills was perfect counterpoint; Wrathdale had an elemental, breathtaking beauty that owed nothing to the intervention of people.

The impulse to come out here had been irresistible. Frank had needed the curious sanctuary of the open space, and now that he was here the place seemed to absorb him, making him quiet.

Fiona had been standing on the bank for several minutes, looking across the weir at the rising ground opposite. She turned and looked at Frank, standing a few feet away. He was staring into the river, apparently seeing nothing.

'This was a nice idea of yours,' she said, walking slowly towards him. 'I haven't been out here for ages.' She looked at her watch. 'We mustn't stay too long, though. There's a pile of work waiting for me at the office.'

Frank turned to her. He still looked as pale as he had in the restaurant earlier. 'Fiona, if I did decide to leave Wrathdale, would you come with me?'

She stared at him. 'You're not serious, Frank . . .'

'Very.' He took a few steps towards her. 'You see I'm in love with you, believe it or not.'

After a moment she nodded. 'Yes, I believe it. I think you are. In your way. But I warned you against that, didn't I? The other night.'

'It was too late then,' he sighed.

'Before that, even,' Fiona insisted gently.

'Yes,' he said, nodding, 'you warned me. But it's not

something you can control that easily, is it?'

'No, of course not. It's just that I thought . . . Oh, I'm sorry, Frank. I really am.'

He shrugged. 'Well, that's that, then.' He turned and glanced across at the narrow road where the Marina was parked. 'We'd best be getting back. I've got a busy afternoon ahead of me, too.'

He turned and began moving up the bank, but Fiona put a hand on his arm, detaining him. 'Don't leave,' she said. 'Not unless you feel you really must.' She hesitated. 'I'd miss you.'

Frank looked at her. 'Would you?'

'Very much.' Her expression was unveiled, open and sincere. 'Stay. And be patient. Give me time. I'm not promising anything, I told you weeks ago. I don't want to fall in love again. I'm doing my damnedest not to. But you *are* special to me. And things don't always work out the way you plan, do they?'

They stood looking at each other for a long time, until Frank took Fiona in his arms and kissed her tenderly, closing his arms around her as if he would be prepared to protect her from the whole world, if need be.

At four o'clock Reuben Flaxman, Tom Holliday and Frank were working on the type layout for one of the centre pages of the next issue of *The Messenger*. As usual there was dissent, and as usual it was being generated by Reuben. Fiona was working in her office with the door wide open.

'Yes,' Frank was saying patiently to Reuben, 'but this way we don't have to make a new block, do we?'

Reuben was pulling a sour face. 'What about the caption?'

'Soon have that off,' Frank muttered. 'And then I'll . . .' He looked up and broke off, staring.

Reuben and Tom were staring, too. Miss Banner, dressed in her Sunday best, had come in through the door from the alley. Ignoring the trio completely, she crossed to the open office door.

Fiona looked up from her desk and saw Miss Banner in the doorway. She was gazing at Fiona as if she was seeing her for the first time.

Recovering rapidly from her surprise, Fiona immediately adopted her pleasant, professional manner. 'Good afternoon, Miss Banner. Is there something I can do for you?'

Miss Banner didn't reply. She stared at Fiona for a few seconds longer. Then, looking as if she had satisfied some special curiosity, she turned and walked back out across the works. By the bench she paused for a moment and gave Frank a long, hard look. He returned the stare, his face expressionless, until Miss Banner turned and left the works the way she had entered.

Reuben and Tom were gaping at each other, mystified.

Fiona came and stood in the office doorway. 'What the hell was that all about?' she asked, looking bemused.

Frank looked at her and shrugged. 'Who knows?' he murmured. He cast one quick glance at the door and then, as casually as he could, returned his attention to the job in hand.

A little after eight o'clock, Sylvia Harper drove up to Half Mile Cottage and parked her mini in the road behind Frank's car. She got out and stood looking at the house for a minute, then walked up the path and knocked on the door.

Frank opened it a moment later. He had a large whisky in his hand. He made no move to admit Sylvia, whose anger was only just covered by her air of quiet resolution, which she had been gathering about her for the last half hour.

'You have to be on your own,' she said. 'I'm sure you were expecting me.'

Reluctantly, Frank stepped aside and let her come in. He closed the door and watched as she walked to the middle of the floor and then turned, looking pointedly at his glass. 'Yes I'd love a drink,' she snapped. 'Scotch, thanks.'

Frank went to the sideboard and poured a whisky, adding

236

a little water. He took it across to Sylvia.

'Cheers.' She went over to the fireplace and stood with her back to him. 'Oh, and I hear that congratulations are in order.'

Frank looked mystified. 'What are you talking about?'

'I understand from Donald that you're thinking of getting married.'

'He's putting you on. Or getting even.'

Sylvia spun round to face him. 'What's that supposed to mean?'

'Forget it,' Frank murmured.

'Maybe that's not exactly what you said, but it's the inference he drew from the little chat you had with him.'

'People shouldn't jump to conclusions,' Frank told her. 'You included.'

'I never do,' she said icily. 'I think things through.'

Frank took a slow, deep breath. 'About today, then. You've only got to . . .'

'Did you enjoy your lunch?' Sylvia cut in. She was trembling, no longer able to contain the pent-up rage. 'You bloody bastard!' she screeched, hurling her glass at Frank. It narrowly missed him and smashed against the wall.

'The sheets hadn't cooled off before you were cosying up to your "friend" again!' she howled at him. 'And when you were ordering your meal I bet you didn't tell her you'd already had an hors d'oeuvre!'

Frank watched the hysteria churning in her, twitching her head and neck, clenching and unclenching her fingers. 'If you'll calm down,' he said, 'I'll explain everything.'

'What's there to explain?' Sylvia demanded. 'You were buttering me up, keeping me sweet. You came round this morning for that express purpose. To humour me, to distract me in bed . . .'

'Oh come on! For what possible reason, for God's sake?'

'Exactly.' Sylvia was getting herself under control again, fixing him with a hard, analytical stare. 'I couldn't work that

237

out, not at first. But then it came to me, and it's the only explanation that makes any kind of sense.'

Frank sipped his drink, working hard to keep his anxiety below the surface.

'First of all,' Sylvia went on, her voice low, 'I tell you what I've found out about your beloved and you get all uptight and po-faced about it. You try to warn me off with talk of slander actions. Then, when you're afraid that maybe you're overplaying your hand, you switch to the "nothing's changed" bit. And first thing this morning you're round to prove it. That way, you think that if I should be tempted to spread the news for any reason, you'll be in the best possible position to see that I don't.' She stepped closer to Frank. 'And anyway, with you servicing me again from time to time, I'll have other things on my mind,' She glared up at him. 'You wanted to shut me up. It was as simple as that.'

'Shut you up about what?'

'Fiona Neave's background.'

Frank was standing his ground. 'I was prepared to go to those lengths to do it? Don't be so stupid! Why on earth should I?'

'Good question,' Sylvia murmured. 'Why should keeping her in the dark about the fact that she was born on the wrong side of the blanket be *so* important to you?' She searched Frank's face, pursing her lips as she did. 'I don't know the answer to that one,' she said finally. 'But it is important to you . . .'

'That's crazy!'

'Really?' Sylvia was in total control of herself again. Her slow-growing smile was confidently malevolent. 'Well in that case, you won't mind much if I drop in on her on my way home, just to enlighten her.' She walked smartly to the door and pulled it open.

'Don't, Sylvia,' Frank said quietly.

She turned to him. Her expression demanded more.

'Please,' Frank said.

Sylvia hesitated, then she closed the door again. 'On my terms, Frank,' she said, walking across to him. 'Pour me another drink, will you?'

He went to the sideboard and poured a fresh scotch, adding water as before. When he brought it to Sylvia she thanked him, almost politely, and began wandering idly around the room. She inspected the ornaments and the books in the bookcase as Frank stood by, watching her.

'I think we ought to regularize our relationship,' she said casually. 'Don't you? Put it on a definite footing. And get a few rules established – like territorial rights and exclusivity.' She paused in front of Fiona's picture of the short-eared owl, which was now hanging on the wall to one side of the fireplace. 'Of course,' she went on, 'that can't apply entirely as far as I'm concerned. Donald does have some claims on me. Not that he exercises them very often.'

Frank felt a jolt in his stomach as she carefully removed the photograph from the wall.

'And under the circumstances,' Sylvia continued, 'that's hardly being unfaithful to you, is it? But I'll not share you with anyone.' She tossed the picture into the waste basket.

Frank had to restrain himself from grabbing her. 'I've no feeling whatever for you, Sylvia,' he hissed. 'I've never loved you.'

Sylvia turned to face him. 'Of course not,' she said. 'You're quite incapable of it. The only thing you know about love is how to spell it. So I'll have lost nothing, will I?'

Frank turned aside, gulping down his whisky.

'Besides, what's love got to do with it?' Her voice was light, assured. 'Animal satisfaction, that's all we've ever shared, Frank. And I'm content to go along with that. At least until I find something better. And then,' she said, her tone getting harder, 'you can do what you damn well like. And with anyone you choose. Who knows, Fiona Neave might even still be around. And available.'

Frank looked at her, appalled. 'So suddenly I'm avoiding

her. What do I tell her?'

'That's up to you. You'll think of something effective.'

He was slowly accommodating a new sensation, the onset of hatred. 'And who do you think is going to end up more humiliated by this?' he asked her. 'Me or you?'

'That's a risk I'll accept.'

Frank shook his head. 'It won't work.'

Sylvia pouted at him. 'We'll see,' she said. 'And if it doesn't, it had better not be for want of trying on your part. And another thing. That spare front door key of yours. The one I gave back to you. Well that was stupid. Be a good idea if I had one, wouldn't it?' She looked at him challengingly. 'Well, wouldn't it? It's up to you, Frank.'

They stared at each other for a long moment, then Frank slowly took his bunch of keys from his pocket, detached the spare for the front door and laid it on the table.

Sylvia smiled.

Frank stood motionless, looking at the key, willing the emptiness to swell and cancel his pain.

As the darkness gathered over Ravensfell House, Miss Banner sat in her favourite chair, rocking back and forth with her hands clasped over her mouth. Tears ran along her cheeks as she stared at the sampler in front of her.

BURNING FOR BURNING,
WOUND FOR WOUND,
STRIPE FOR STRIPE.

The only sound beyond the ticking of the clock was the old lady's muffled crooning, a sound like the rhythmic whine of a lonely, frightened child.